LOVE & RETALIATION

LOVE & RUIN SERIES BOOK NINE

J.A. OWENBY

EXCLUSIVE LOVE & RUIN BONUS SCENES

Enjoy exclusive Love & Ruin bonus scenes, giveaways, and new release updates! Sign up today at https://www. authorjaowenby.com/newsletter

1

Four days. It had been four days since my wedding had turned into a bloodbath. Four days since Dad had been kidnapped. Four soul-obliterating days. What should have been the happiest day of my life had left me struggling, searching for answers and finding none.

The days had passed in agonizing slowness, ripping my heart out with each second that ticked by. Gemma was the only reason I was still partially sane, and at times, I even questioned that assumption.

I'd worn a hole in the floor from pacing the hall outside of Dad and Janice's bedroom, but I didn't want to leave Janice alone. A soft snore reached my ears through the crack in the door, and I slipped into Dad's room, then stared at the lump beneath the blankets. Janice had finally agreed to take the medication the doctor had prescribed to help her sleep. Her exhaustion and grief had left her on the brink of delirium. It was only five o'clock in the evening, but grief and stress didn't have a sleep schedule.

I folded my arms, a sharp pang stabbing me. I was wired differently from Janice. If anything had happened to Gemma, the devil himself wouldn't have been able stop me from hunting the motherfucker down. Janice and Dad had just found each other again, and I couldn't imagine what she was going through. As her son, it had been my responsibility to take care of her until Dad came home. Then it was up to me to find and finish off the bastards who'd taken him.

I leaned against the wall and listened to her soft breathing. Out of respect, I now referred to her as Mom when I spoke to her, but in my mind, she was always Janice. The M-word was attached to a careless, heartless woman I didn't even know. It probably shouldn't have bothered me anymore, but on occasion, it did. Although the word carried a sting, I realized that Janice wasn't any of those things my biological mother was. Janice had raised me and helped me through some fucked-up days after I lost Kendra.

At that time, Dad had been buried in a bottle. He might have been physically alive, but he was dead to me. Dead to the world. A screwed-up tango between him and the alcohol numbed him into oblivion. If it hadn't been for Janice and Mac, I might have ended up like Dad. Drunk. A slob. Most days, Dad had been passed out by ten in the morning. I had no idea until one day I came home early from school because I felt sick. There he was in his pajamas, stinking up a VIG Chesterfield sofa in the living room. On days like that, anyone could have walked right through the front door and robbed him blind. Thank God he'd left that all behind and started attending Alcoholics Anonymous meetings.

My phone vibrated in my hand and I stepped into the hallway. I tapped the answer button. "Hey, man."

"We've got a lead on Franklin," Pierce said.

I froze in my tracks. Judging by Pierce's tone, it didn't sound like good news. I rolled my shoulders, attempting to relieve the tension and knotted muscles. "Is … is my dad alive?" My heart rate skyrocketed as my attention landed on Dad's empty office chair. I wondered if he would ever sit in it again.

"We think so, but you need to come over so we can talk," Pierce said.

Hope kicked my ass into gear, and I took off running down the hall, then up the stairs. "On my way." I hung up on him before he could say another word.

My sock-covered feet slid on the floor, and I grabbed the doorway of the game room in order to stop myself from busting my ass. "Mac, Cade. I gotta go." I flipped my hair out of my face.

Mac flashed me a huge grin. "Does Gemma need you for a quick smash and dash?"

My expression must have tipped her off because her smile faltered.

"Dude." Cade tossed his gaming control on the floor and stood. "Did they find Franklin?" He straightened his navy polo shirt and approached me.

Mac got to her feet, then nearly cleared the back of the black over-sized couch, her big brown eyes wide. "Is it about Dad?" She tugged at the oversized teal-and-white T-shirt that hung to her knees, covering her small baby bump. She'd opted for yoga pants that day, and I suspected comfort would be more important to her than wearing designer clothes sooner rather than later.

"Pierce said he has a lead. I'm on my way over now." I kissed my sister on the forehead, then hurried down the stairs. "Keep an eye on … Mom, but don't tell her anything. I don't want to get her hopes up."

I checked my pocket for my wallet as I made my way through the house, then picked up the keys from the kitchen counter and located my tennis shoes. In record time, I was behind the wheel of my Lexus.

"Hey, Siri. Call Gemma."

Although Gemma was with Sutton, having some much-needed girl time, I had to interrupt her. Gemma's phone rang twice, then sent me to voicemail. *Dammit.* Maybe she'd set her cell down for a minute. When she was with her friends, she often forgot to keep it near her. An eerie feeling swept over me, but I shook it off. Of course, I would feel off. My dad had just been kidnapped.

"Hey, Siri. Text Gemma."

"What do you want to say?"

"Gem, meet me at Pierce's. He thinks he has a lead. Love you."

Siri finished confirming the text, then sent the message.

I gripped the steering wheel as my mind tossed up a million different scenarios about Dad. His years as an attorney had left him with a lot of enemies. At one time, I'd wondered if he'd gotten mixed up with some illegal activity, but I never found any information to validate my suspicions. That had been a lifetime ago, but I was well aware that criminals never dropped a grudge.

Gemma and I suspected Brandon was behind kidnapping Dad and shooting up our wedding, but we didn't have any proof yet. Fury burned beneath my calm exterior. If that bastard had organized it, I would end him. He had nearly killed my future wife ... my jaw clenched so hard that pain shot through the right side of my face. I should have been on my honeymoon with the love of my life. We should have been fucking like bunnies and making love on every available surface of the beach rental. I should have been bringing her strawberries, pancakes and whipped cream in bed, then licking off the creamy goodness from her porcelain stomach. Gemma should have already been Mrs. Harrington. She should have been in my arms every night and every morning.

I clamped down on the emotions before they swallowed me whole. After losing Kendra, I'd had to work hard to contain my temper. What I needed was an intense sparring or boxing session to blow off some steam. *Hitting someone sounds really good right now.*

Twenty minutes later, I rolled up to Pierce's gated log home and waited for the state-of-the-art security system to scan my face. Sutton had created some badass technology. She had a brain that could outthink anyone else I knew. The girl was off-the-charts smart.

I parked my car between two identical black Mercedes, which belonged to Pierce and the Westbrook Security company. I wasn't sure who they belonged to, though. Zayne was following me, Vaughn was at Dad's, and Sutton was with Gemma.

A soft breeze blew through the maple and aspen leaves. Soon everything would be covered in white, and the holidays would arrive. The previous year, we'd had Friendsgiving at Pierce and Sutton's. Claire had barely recovered from surgery, and we'd all been holding our breath concerning Dillon Montgomery.

I rang the doorbell, and my toe tapped the sidewalk impatiently while I waited for someone to let me in. Whenever I was in Pierce and Sutton's place, I took note of the details that I would love to have when Gemma and I built our house—for starters, Pierce's open living room with the twelve-foot-tall stone fireplace. The exposed log beams in the ceiling were stunning too. I would want to expand the outdoor area and have a larger kitchen than the Westbrooks, though. I loved to cook and grill when I wasn't touring. What I liked the most was that it was a huge-ass home but still managed to feel comfortable and cozy. The gorgeous features weren't why, though. The amazing people who lived inside it made it feel that way.

I heaved a sigh. Whatever was going on, it was big, or Pierce would have told me over the phone. He was a straight-up guy. It was one reason I liked him so much. There was never a question about where you stood with him. He would tell you flat-out.

When Pierce first began to work for Dad, it had taken me a little while to get to know him, but once he toured with my band, August Clover, I saw his more personal side. And lucky for him, I liked it. So did Gemma, which caused a few arguments between us. Gemma was a bit naïve about relationships and dating, but I knew when another dude had feelings for my girlfriend. I could smell his interest a mile away, but he never crossed a line. Not once. He was always professional, and I had mad respect for him.

The mahogany door swung open and my heart skittered to a stop. Sutton. Her red-rimmed eyes were swollen, and her pink nose matched her top. I wasn't sure I'd ever seen her cry. *Shit. What is going on? I thought she was with Gemma.*

"Are you all right?" I stepped inside the house and gave her a brief hug. "Is Gemma here with you?"

She closed the door and slid the deadbolt into place. "No." She bit her bottom lip and folded her arms across her chest. "Pierce is in the gym."

"Oh, okay. I didn't realize she was with Zayne again." I wasn't sure I really wanted to hear Sutton's answer, but I asked anyway. "Is the reason you're upset because of what Pierce found out about Dad?"

She peered up at me. "We'll know more soon. I hope. For now, Pierce wants to explain what we've learned."

Sutton quietly led me through the living room and into the gym, where Pierce was beating the shit out of the bag. Sweat dripped down his bare back, and his arm muscles flexed with each swing. There was no doubt he was a powerhouse. Pierce looked pissed as hell, but there was a flicker of something else in his expression that I couldn't get a read on. He hammered the bag one more time, then dropped his hands to his sides and adjusted his dark-gray sweatpants. He grabbed the black hand towel off the floor and wiped off his face.

"Hendrix." Pierce tilted his chin up, then his gaze landed on his wife. The tension that radiated off of them was intense. I would have been happy to walk right out of the room, but I needed to know what he'd learned about Dad.

"What's going on?" I put my hands on my hips, wishing I'd thought to change out of my worn-out Patrick Droney T-shirt into something a little more appropriate for outside the house.

Sutton gave me a small wave, then she left, clicking the door closed behind her.

"You need to check your email."

"Why?" That was an odd request, even for Pierce.

"Just do it."

My brows furrowed, but I removed my phone from my pocket. I tapped the app on the screen and waited as it refreshed. Two hundred four new emails appeared. "What am I looking for?" I scrolled through the messages.

"There should be one from Gemma."

"From Gemma? What—why?" I eyed Pierce, who was pacing on the mat.

"Just open it." He wiped the sweat off his forehead with his arm and blew out a big breath.

Puzzled with what this had to do with Dad, I opened it, then downloaded a video.

"Hi, baby," Gemma started. She glanced away, tears in her blue eyes. "I'm not sure where to start, but I love you. No matter what happens, please know that my heart will always find its way back to you." She paused and tucked her hair behind her ear. She was nervous, but I had no clue why.

"Pierce, what is this?" I demanded.

Gemma's voice pulled me to the video again. "Brandon contacted me and offered an exchange for Franklin. I accepted. I don't have any idea when Franklin will return, but he needs medical care from what I saw. He's alive, though." She briefly looked at the floor.

My throat tightened as a twisted mixture of relief and despair lodged itself in my chest. Dad was alive, but Gemma ... no, I wasn't hearing her right. There was no way that she would agree to those terms with Brandon.

"I couldn't take a chance that you would stop me." She shook her head. "You and your family have loved me and taken me in, baby. I had to do everything possible to bring Franklin home. Please know that I did this because I love you more than my own life."

Terror pulsed through my veins. *Oh, God. No. No. No.*

"I can't say anything else, but you need to reach out to Sutton immediately. She should be able to help you track me down." Her chin trembled. "Baby, if this fails, just know that you gave me wings to fly. I love you so much. Please ..." She kissed her fingertips, then touched the screen. "Come find me."

The video stopped. The phone dimmed, then went completely black as it timed out and locked. Everything around me was eerily quiet in the absence of Gemma's voice.

"She's gone?" I looked at Pierce. His mouth moved, but I couldn't hear him. *Gone.* Gemma was gone.

My pulse pounded loudly in my ears, and the sound of the HVAC unit kicked on. A raging fire licked through my veins. This couldn't be happening. Brandon Montgomery had my fiancée. Gemma had traded herself for my dad. *God dammit. How did I not see this coming?*

"What the actual fuck, dude? You were supposed to take care of her! That's literally your entire goddamn job!" My tone grew louder as I found myself aggressively moving toward him.

"I know. Dammit, I know. Sutton ..." A pained expression twisted his features.

A maniacal laugh escaped me. I was losing it. I was officially plunging off the cliff into darkness. "Sutton." Her tears made more sense now. "Sutton helped Gemma leave and turn herself over to a psychopath? What is wrong with you people?" Before I realized it, I closed the gap between us, balled my hands into fists, and punched Pierce square in the face with a satisfying crunch. His head popped backward.

He grimaced and wiped the blood from his nose with his hand. "Let's go, Harrington. You're seeing red right now, so let's do this." He growled and raised his hands to protect himself.

He was right. My anger was so intense that I was dangerously close to blacking out. My future wife might be lying on the floor beneath a sick son of a bitch who had made it clear he'd rape her. Not to mention that two of my best friends had let it happen. *Motherfucker.*

I spotted an opening and hit Pierce in the gut with a left, then right. Before he could tag me, I'd moved away and dodged his blow.

"I didn't know about the trade until Sutton told me an hour ago. We got into a big fight, then I immediately called you." He swung, clipping me in the side, but I shook it off.

"Maybe you should learn to control your wife, then, huh?" I took a shot at his chin. Pain exploded through my knuckles, and I welcomed it—fed on it. I craved the distraction from the darkness that loomed in the corner of my mind.

"I should control *my* wife? That's rich coming out of your mouth when you have a strong-willed one yourself. Gemma does what she wants to, and anyone who knows her is well aware of that fact."

My mind buzzed with his words. He was right, but no way in hell would I admit it. I delivered three more jabs. The moment he let his arms drop a little, I nailed him in the jaw.

"God dammit. You're fast as hell." Pierce shifted to the left, then landed a solid punch to my gut, and I doubled over.

I grunted and backed away while I attempted to identify another opening. Pierce dropped his hands, and his eyes narrowed. He wiped his nose again, then clocked me in the kidney. Pain shot through me, breaking through my craze-driven anger.

Before I could recover, Pierce swept his leg to the side and knocked my feet out from beneath me. I landed on the mat with a thud. Pierce grabbed my arm, forced me to roll over, and pinned me facedown. "I know you're pissed right now, but Gemma would have done this without telling anyone. If Sutton hadn't helped her, we wouldn't be able to track her at all."

Little pieces of the truth began to penetrate my muddled and furious thoughts. Pierce stood, and I hopped up and went full throttle. Punch after punch landed on his stomach. He held his arms in front of him as I forced him off the mat. I placed my foot behind his knee with a quick move, driving him to the floor. Before I realized it, Pierce snatched my ankle and jerked it from under me, and I toppled down next to him. Air whooshed out of my lungs, and I lay on my back and stared at the ceiling. I glanced at Pierce, who still had blood dripping from his nose. He would most likely need to reset it.

"She's gone," I whispered.

Agony ripped through me, leaving me broken and devastated in its wake. Cradling my head in my hands, I struggled to keep my heart from shattering. *How could Gemma think I could live without her? That her trade would make my life better?* I loved my dad, but I loved Gemma more. I didn't want to choose, but if I had to, there was no contest. I would choose Gemma *every single time*. Knowing that she was with that sick son of a bitch … it fucking wrecked me.

I pulled my phone out of my pocket and called her. "Please pick up," I pleaded.

The call went straight to voicemail. My fingers flew across the screen as I texted her, begging her not to do this. Maybe I wasn't too late and she would turn around. I scolded myself for losing my temper instead of trying to reach her first. I waited for the three dots to pop up, indicating her reply. They never showed.

I sat up and looked at Pierce while my anger dwindled, and a thick silence filled the room. "I was a dick. I shouldn't have said that shit to you about Sutton."

"I get it. I would have done the same and probably said even worse." He stood and held his hand out to me. I took it. "Are you at a point where you can listen, and we can explain what happened?"

I nodded. "Do we know where Gemma is? Do we have a plan to

get her back? Have we heard anything about Dad? If she traded herself, then where's Dad? How did this shit even happen?" If the situation hadn't been so messed up, I would have laughed at myself. I sounded exactly like my sister.

Pierce held up his hand to halt my rapid-fire questions. "Sutton was with her, and if you haven't noticed, she's torn up about it."

"I did notice. I've never seen her cry before."

Pierce picked up his plain black T-shirt from the weight bench and pulled it on. He patted me on my back. "Come on. Let's talk to Sutton and figure out how to bring Gemma home."

My thoughts were spinning faster than a weathervane during a tornado by the time we reached Pierce's office. *Why is my father paying Westbrook Security to keep us safe if they can't take care of my fiancée? How did Gemma slip through their fingers and turn herself over to a rapist who's been obsessed with her since she arrived in Washington?*

I shook my head, wondering what had come over me. I'd never gone off on Pierce like that before, but after that video Gemma had left me, I lost my shit.

Pierce's earlier words echoed inside my brain. *Gemma does what she wants to.* Internally, I grimaced. I was upset and looking for someone to point the finger at.

I followed Pierce out of the gym and through the house. Sutton was sitting at the desk, peering at a laptop, when we joined her in the office. Stacks of files and papers were scattered near her computer. It was apparent that she was working hard on something. Hopefully, it was locating my father and future wife.

"Hey, guys." She brushed the moisture from her face, then stood eyeing both of us. "I see you two worked out your differences."

Pierce grabbed a tissue from the box on the bookshelf and wiped the remaining blood from his nose. "Hendrix is fast. I didn't realize it since we've never fought before. We've sparred and trained, but not this. I had no idea he could box that well. But yes, we're fine now."

"Guess that's why he was the state boxing champ year after year." Sutton offered me a weak smile.

I ran my fingers through my hair and sat down in the black leather chair, my attention bouncing between Pierce and Sutton. A wave of nausea rolled over me as I fisted my hands together in an attempt to keep a level head. "What happened, Sutton?"

She heaved a sigh as she stood, walked around to the front of the desk, and leaned on the edge, crossing her ankles. From her expression and rigid body language, I knew her heart was crushed as well. She probably held herself responsible. I would. If I were in her shoes, I would totally blame myself for Gemma's decision.

"Hendrix, I'm so sorry. Gemma was with me when I picked up a prototype for Pierce. We came here to eat lunch." She visibly swallowed and ran her palm along her jeaned leg. "It's a tracking injection that Pierce and his friend have been working on for undercover agents, military, and other professionals that are in dangerous situations. The idea is that the serum is injected into someone's neck, it enters the bloodstream, and twenty-four hours later, we can track them. This is new, Hendrix. It's not on the market, and it's still in the development phase. There is no surefire way to know if it will work or not." Sutton shoved off the desk and walked to the window.

"I had a phone call and left Gemma in the kitchen so that I could talk privately. When I returned, she was holding the tracker gun in her hand. She'd administered the serum, and that's when I learned about her plans. Unfortunately, it was only a few hours before she was leaving. I was shocked to learn that Brandon had reached out to her, but I shouldn't have been. Maybe we should have monitored her devices, but she's our friend and family, and I trusted that she would have come to me instead of taking this on all by herself. I was obviously wrong."

Sutton gazed at the floor and crossed her arms over her chest before she continued. "At that point, Gemma had already made up her mind, and there was no talking her out of it. I figured the best thing for me to do was to help her. If I did, the odds of her returning to us would be significantly greater than if she'd gone into this situation alone. When I realized that, my brain kicked into solving the problem."

My knuckles turned white as I gripped the arms of the chair and listened to everything Sutton was telling me. All I could think of was how to get Gemma. "Does this mean that we can track her whereabouts and go get her? Is that what this serum does?" If that was the case, she wouldn't be gone long.

"Yes, but it takes twenty-four hours to activate in someone's system, and there are glitches we're still ironing out. Mountains and hills can affect the signal, making it more difficult to get a read on her. As I said, it's new and not on the market, so I'm not sure what we're working with yet. Hendrix, I'm not sure if it will do the job that we need it to." Her voice trailed off, and she glanced at her husband. Pierce nodded, and I assumed he was giving her some encouragement to continue. "If she is able to have her phone on her for a little while, it will help us find her."

"What happens if we don't get Dad and Gemma back alive?" I breathed my fear into the room.

"We can't afford to think that way," Pierce said. "Keep your mind from going dark, and when it does, rein it in."

I wondered if that was how he dealt with these situations. This wasn't the first time Pierce had a friend or family member in grave danger. Sutton's sister had been kidnapped almost two years before. If I hoped to stay sane, I would have to try it his way.

"What's the next step, and what can I do to help?" I needed to work out my feelings about this shit show and why Sutton hadn't called me immediately. But for the moment, I had to table my frustration and focus on getting Gemma and Dad home safely.

"Before Gemma left, she rented a car, and I placed three trackers in it so I could see where she was meeting Brandon and his men. Right now, I'm waiting to see when the vehicle begins to move in our direction. When that happens, I can assume that Franklin is driving, and I will dispatch the police and medical teams."

I jumped out of my chair. "Are you tracking her on your laptop?" I pointed at the computer as I hurried around to the other side of the desk, not waiting for permission.

"Yeah." She leaned around me, and I moved out of the way and allowed her access to the screen again. "I think her car has stopped."

We all huddled together and waited in silence.

"I do know that they're in Montana," Sutton said. "If the vehicle begins to move toward Washington, I'll wait a few minutes, then call for help. I hope like hell Franklin won't be followed."

"Not to mention, we hope he's actually the person driving." Pierce placed his hands on his hips and paced the room. "Brandon is capable of anything, and I don't trust that little shit not to put a decoy in the car and blow it up."

I turned my head so fast it nearly gave me whiplash. Pierce wasn't helping me stay calm.

"Babe, maybe we should keep those comments to ourselves while Hendrix is with us," Sutton said. "I know we're all on edge, not only about Franklin's return but Gemma's too. Let's try to stay as positive as we can. Gemma is smart. She knows some of Brandon's weaknesses, which will be to her advantage if she remains calm. Her intentions were to bring Franklin home and to learn everything she could to stop Brandon once and for all."

"How did I not see this coming?" Shame clung to my words.

"You can't do that, Hendrix. Every one of us could say the same, but we're wasting time and valuable energy. We need to stay focused," Sutton said.

She was right. Playing the *woulda, coulda, shoulda* game would only fuck me up, and I needed to be as clearheaded as possible.

Sutton nervously drummed her fingers on top of the desk. "I haven't seen any movement for the last five minutes. I think the trade is occurring right now."

Gemma, don't. Please. I attempted to call her one last time as I mentally begged and pleaded for her not to make the exchange. I wasn't expecting her to answer, and my heart plummeted to my toes as a small red dot began to move on the map. "Sutton, is that …?" I pointed at the laptop.

Sutton flipped her hair behind her shoulder and stared at the screen. "We have movement."

2

Conflicted feelings churned inside my gut. Dad might have been on his way home, but Gemma wasn't. She had just entered the gates of hell with Brandon.

Rubbing my face with my hands, I slowly inhaled while I attempted not to let the dam break and allow my turbulent emotions to reach the surface. I'd already gone a round with Pierce, and I couldn't do any more stupid things. If anyone would be able to bring her home, it was Pierce and his team, and deep inside, I knew it.

"What does this mean exactly?" I shoved my hands in my front pockets, trying not to fidget.

"I don't know yet. We have to wait and see." Sutton enlarged the map and remained quiet.

I released a frustrated sigh and ran my fingers through my hair, praying to a God that I no longer believed in that Gemma would return to me safely.

"The car is moving in the opposite direction and fast." Sutton glanced up at me. "We'll know if it's Franklin in a few more minutes." She squeezed my hand, a glint of hope in her eyes.

Pierce pulled his cell out of his jeans pocket and tapped the screen. I hadn't ever seen him this wired before, but I shouldn't have been surprised. Everyone loved Gemma. No longer hearing her laugh, seeing her smile, or watching the sunshine glint off her red hair … those ideas threatened to paralyze me, and I shook my mind free of them.

"He's six miles away now." Sutton looked at Pierce, and he nodded.

He tapped his phone screen and stared at us. "Brian, it's Pierce Westbrook. I need your help."

I listened as Pierce lined up a rescue team across the state lines and filled Brian in on Dad and Gemma's details.

Pierce hung up. "He'll call me in a few minutes with confirmation that Franklin is safe. Additional men will search the site of the exchange for any clues too."

There was nothing else I could do except wait. With each passing second, the air thickened and closed in, condensing the room's small space. I distracted myself by imagining that I was singing. Music had saved my life more than once, and I needed the protection of it now more than ever.

Tick. Tock. Tick. Tock. The clock in the office was the only sound. I found myself holding my breath, willing Pierce's phone to ring again. When it did, I nearly cleared the desk and answered it myself.

"Yeah." Pierce closed his eyes while he listened, not indicating who was speaking to him or what he was hearing. "Thank God." Pierce's intense gaze landed on his wife and me. "So, you're going to airlift Franklin to the Sacred Heart in Spokane?" He paused. "Thank you for your help. I'll let you know what we find out next." Pierce disconnected the call and peeked at his watch. "They have Franklin. He needs medical attention. I don't know how bad his injuries are, but he managed to drive, which is a good sign."

Air whooshed out of my lungs, and I doubled over. Placing my hands on my knees, I leaned my butt against the wall for support.

"I'll reach out to Janice," Sutton offered. "I suspect everyone will want to be at the hospital when Franklin arrives."

"Sutton?" I straightened. "How much longer before the serum kicks in and we can locate Gemma?" My voice cracked with fear.

She pursed her lips, her eyes flitting to the clock on the wall. "Eleven o'clock … tomorrow morning."

Tears threatened my vision. "Tomorrow morning?" I whispered. *Jesus, she could be raped or dead by then.*

"I'm so sorry." Sutton jumped out of her chair and threw her arms around me. "I'm sorry I didn't handle the situation as well as I should have."

I hugged her as our hearts broke even more. "Just bring her home."

Sutton pulled away and wiped the moisture from her cheeks. "On second thought, I'll let you call Janice. I'll be back in a minute." She patted my arm, then left the room.

I glanced at Pierce, who had remained quiet. "What is it? What aren't you telling me?"

He cleared his throat. "Brian's men searched the area where the exchange was made. They found a phone on the side of the road."

"Gemma's?" I knew the answer before the question had left my mouth.

Pierce confirmed my suspicions with a gentle nod.

"Shit! Now we can't track her from her cell." The realization punched me in the stomach. Brandon had her. *Oh, God.* I silently swore that I would dismantle that motherfucker, then burn him alive, if he hurt her. I nearly laughed out loud. "If *he hurt her.*" *Who am I kidding?*

"It was a slim chance, man. Brandon would know her phone would be tracked, and although I hoped she would be able to keep her phone on her for a while, I was well-aware it was a long shot."

An unbearable ache spread through me. "I know." *That didn't stop me from holding onto a tiny thread of optimism, though.* "I need to call Janice."

"Before you do …" Pierce crossed his arms over his chest. "Are we good, man?"

I eyed Pierce. In my heart, I knew that he cared deeply for Gemma, and he would never allow her to get hurt, but he was also human. He made mistakes. Shit, we all did. At the same time, he was the owner and boss of a security company. He was responsible for his employees' actions. I also understood that Sutton had no control over Gemma's choices. It still stung a little that she hadn't called me, but they were my friends, and Sutton had been thrown into a suck-ass situation. She'd had to make the best decision she could in a short amount of time.

I strolled across the room and looked him in the eye. "We're good." I meant it. One thing about most guys—they didn't hold grudges like girls did. We beat the hell out of each other, then it was over, and we moved on.

Pierce patted me on the back. "Excellent. I'll let you make your call, then you can meet us downstairs. I need to change clothes too."

I sank into the chair again and pulled up Janice's number in my favorites. Hopefully, she would answer. After the third ring, she picked up.

"Hendrix?" Fear laced her tone.

"Dad's on his way home, Mom."

"What? He is? How? Oh my God, I hope he's okay." Her pitch escalated with each question.

I could hear rustling in the background, and I assumed she was hopping out of bed and scrambling to find her clothes.

"He's on his way to Sacred Heart from Montana. Pierce contacted his buddy from the FBI, and they located Dad. I don't know how bad his injuries are, but they're airlifting him to the hospital."

"Oh God. Okay. I'm getting dressed. I'll grab Mac and Cade—wait, where are you? How did they find Franklin?"

Anger bubbled inside of me. "I'm at Pierce's house. I'll meet you at the hospital." My knee bounced with anxiety. "Gemma traded herself for Dad." I nearly choked on my words.

"What? Hendrix, I didn't hear you right."

I could imagine Janice furrowing her brows as she shook her head, too afraid to admit she'd understood what I said.

"Gemma's with Brandon." I shoved down the gut-wrenching yell that wanted to burst from my throat. "We're going to get her back. Dammit, we're going to get her back." My voice sounded haunted, vacant, and unrecognizable to my ears.

Janice gave a quiet sob, then she sniffled. "Okay, I'll do anything I can to help. We all love her so much, Hendrix."

"I know. Are you able to … you know what? Don't tell Mac and Cade about Gemma yet. Let's get to the hospital, then I'll talk to them. That way, I'll be there to help when Mac falls apart."

"Mac will need you, Hendrix." More shuffling filled the line. "We'll be out the door in a few minutes. I'll have Jaxon drive us to meet you. I'm too groggy and worried."

"See you there." I disconnected the call, then made my way downstairs to meet Pierce and Sutton.

FORTY MINUTES LATER, Zayne pulled the Mercedes into the hospital parking garage. Pierce and Sutton had insisted that he drive since I was a mess. The wail of the ambulance siren reached my ears, and my breath caught in my chest. My dark thoughts expanded, and I was thrown into my past.

"Kendra!" I bolted across the front yard. Her little body lay still on the cruel pavement as the black Chevrolet Cavalier sped down the road. I dropped to my knees, fear seizing me.

"Kendra, it's Hendrix. Wake up. Kendra, wake up for me." Tears streamed down my face as I touched her tiny wrist and checked for a pulse, but I already knew the result. Her neck was twisted at the wrong angle. Nothing. She was gone. My shoulders shook with sobs as I continued to speak to her, begging her to come back to me.

My baby sister would never peer up at me and call me "Hendwix" again. She would never crawl into my lap for a bedtime story or slip into my bed when she had a nightmare. In seconds, her life had been snatched away from her, leaving a gaping hole in my heart that would never heal. I would never recover from seeing her tossed into the air like a rag doll.

An anguished roar burst from my throat as I gently scooped her fragile body into my arms and carried her into the house to call 911. In shock, I refused to let her go until the paramedics pried her away from me. I'd failed her. I'd failed to keep Kendra safe.

A soft knock on the passenger-side window pulled me out of my head.

"Are you all right?" Pierce waited for me to respond, but there was nothing to say. He ran a hand over his slightly damp hair. He must have been in a hurry to get dressed because he wore a gray Westbrook Security polo shirt and left it untucked over his jeans.

I climbed out of my car. "I'm fine." My phone chimed. I took it out of my jacket pocket and read the text. "Janice, Mac, and Cade are here. Hopefully, Dad is too."

Tension snaked through my neck and shoulders as Pierce, Sutton, Zayne, and I walked to the elevator.

"After you spend time with your family, I would like to see what Franklin remembers. Maybe there's some information he can share that will help us find Gemma," Pierce said.

"I hope so." My upper lip felt sweaty. Between the stress and the additional clothing, I was suddenly hot. I shrugged out of my jacket.

The elevator doors whooshed open and we strolled onto the main floor. After I'd checked in at the front desk, I was provided with Dad's room number. Sutton and Pierce patiently waited as I called Janice. She answered on the first ring.

"Hey, where are you guys at?" I asked.

"We're almost at Franklin's room." Excitement and dread threaded her words.

I understood completely. "Okay, we're on our way up." I tapped the red button on the phone and kept it in my hand. I needed something to tap my fingers against, since I wasn't sure what to expect when I saw Dad.

The slap of my feet against the cold tile floor of the hospital rang in my ears as we grew closer and closer to Dad's room. I immediately spotted Mac pacing, anxiously waiting. She pulled her maroon hoodie tighter around her, then seconds later, she shrugged out of it and fanned her face. She tied the sleeves around her slender waist, allowing it to hang over her jeans. I suspected her hormones were messing with her.

Cade was rigid with tension and had one of his hands shoved into his jeans pocket. His attention moved everywhere Mac did. Mac placed her hands on Cade's chest and smoothed his wrinkled dark-green shirt.

I rolled my shoulders and cracked my neck as Mac glanced up at me, our eyes locking. Hers were swollen, and tears stained her cheeks. She bolted toward me. I braced myself for her hug—otherwise, we would have both landed on our asses in the middle of the hall.

"Hendrix, how could she do this without telling us?" She sniffled against my shoulder while I held her.

My attention settled on Janice, who pursed her lips. Although she looked more put together than she had a few days earlier, she still seemed wrung out. Somehow, she'd had the clarity of mind to put on a nice black top and jeans. I'd been so worked up when Pierce called me that I'd run out of the house in clothes I usually wouldn't have worn in public.

"They had too many questions. It wasn't fair to keep her in the dark," Janice said.

"Mac." I couldn't find the words to reply to her because I didn't know the answer myself. Although Gemma had explained that she wanted to return Dad to us, I still couldn't grasp why she'd thought this was the only way. At the same time, my logical side remembered how Brandon had destroyed my family and how he'd ripped us apart. When I thought about that, I loved Gemma even more for risking her own life to send my father back to me—to us. I would never recover if she didn't come home to me. I wasn't even sure how I would piece myself together again, much less help her heal and live a full life if Brandon hurt her, but I would never give up trying. Never.

"I know, Mac." We remained silent as we held each other. I kissed the top of her head, comforting her to the best of my ability. Mac was my ultimate focus. She and the baby would get me through while we searched for Gemma.

After I released Mac, Janice approached me and threw her arms around me. "He's back. Let's go see him."

An eerie silence hung over us as we all stared at each other, waiting to see who would go in first. No one had verbalized it, but we were afraid of what we might see. *Who has returned to us—Franklin or a man we no longer recognize?*

I glanced at Pierce and Sutton. Although we hadn't discussed it, the family would be allowed in first, then Pierce and Sutton would join us while Zayne remained on duty in the hall. If Dad was holding it together mentally and physically, we had questions for him. I knew my father, and he would want to do everything in his power to help us find Gemma.

A little voice whispered inside my mind that he didn't know any details that could help with Gemma. He might be so torn up he couldn't remember. A lump lodged itself in my throat, and my chest tightened as an ache spread through my entire body. Gemma should be by my side. At the same time, if it weren't for her, my father wouldn't be in the room, waiting for his family to join him.

I sucked up my anxiety and attempted to rein in my nerves while holding Mac's hand. She gave Cade a quick peck on the cheek and inhaled deeply. Janice grabbed my arm, then she opened the door, and the three of us entered Dad's hospital room.

3

Mac gave a small gasp. Although I attempted to stop my
mouth from hitting the floor, I failed. Dad was a fucking
wreck. He was propped up against the pillow in the bed.
His face was ashen, and the white hospital gown wasn't helping any.
He appeared to be asleep, but it was evident that he'd been beaten. His
lip was busted, he sported two black eyes, and his nose was broken. I
wasn't sure how he'd driven away from the exchange in the condition
he was in, but I realized that adrenaline could make someone do
extraordinary things.

A quiet fury bubbled below the surface, and I struggled to contain
my temper. This wasn't the time to lose my shit, but once again, I
swore that I would take Brandon Montgomery down if it was the last
thing I did.

My hands shook, and a brutal realization dawned on me. *If that
sick son of a bitch did this to my father, what unnatural horrors is he
inflicting on my fiancée?*

Janice gingerly stepped toward Dad while I remained in the back
of the room, waiting to see if he would wake up. To be honest, I
needed time to process what I was staring at. There was no way that
he would walk away from this experience the same man he was the

day of my wedding. If I allowed myself to sink into the darkness, it would eat me alive, and I would never reemerge sane. No matter how difficult it would be, I had to stay positive. Dad would need me.

Mac practically ran to Dad, then grabbed his hand and kissed his knuckles. I inhaled deeply and approached the foot of Dad's bed. His eyes fluttered open, and he peered at us.

He bolted upright, his expression wild with fear. He frantically looked around the room, trembling. "Wh-Where am I?"

"Dad, it's Mac. You're safe. You're in the hospital."

"Janice? Mac?" Dad blinked furiously, trying to focus. I wasn't sure how much pain he was in, but I assumed the doctor had given him some medication to help him manage.

"We're right here, honey. We're right here." Tears streamed down Janice's face as she pulled a chair up next to Dad. She gently took his hand in hers, then leaned over and kissed him on the forehead.

His attention landed on Janice, Mac, then me. After a few moments, the tension left his body and he began to relax. "I'm home? With my family?"

Mac sank into a plastic seat, her brown-eyed gaze never leaving Dad as she gripped the side rail until her knuckles turned white. "We're right here with you, Dad. You're in the hospital."

Finally, I gently sank onto the mattress near his feet. "Welcome back." I wanted to touch him, but I was afraid to. I wasn't sure if his legs were hurt.

The color began to return to his cheeks as we spoke to him. "I'm glad to be here." Dad's voice was gruff, and he winced.

"Are you in a lot of pain?" Mac asked.

"Not as much as I was. I'm exhausted, and I have a few broken ribs."

Dad's attention swept over us, and his eyes connected with mine. What little color he had in his checks faded away. "I'm sorry, son. I'm so goddamned sorry, Hendrix. I tried to bring her with me, but there were too many armed men. We would never have made it to the car alive." He choked on his words as tears welled in his eyes. "I can't tell you how awful it was to leave her. I hope you can forgive me."

As his words broke through my thoughts, I realized there was no way to convince myself that Gemma would get through this unscathed. Guns. Armed men. She would be surrounded twenty-four seven.

"It's not your fault, Dad. I know you did everything you could. I don't blame you, so let's move forward." I hoped Dad heard me because I meant every word. He loved Gemma. I couldn't even begin to imagine how he'd felt as he walked away from her.

"Do you remember how many there were?" I ran my hand through my hair, hoping he could give us any information that we could use to track her down.

"It was dark when I saw her. The other times, I had three men guarding me. I would assume she has that many or more. Son—" He swallowed, his Adam's apple bobbing up and down. "Brandon's no longer … after he spent time in prison, he walked out of there hardened. He's smarter and more dangerous."

I cringed. If Dad hadn't been pumped full of pain meds, I'm not sure that he would have shared that information with me. All it did was twist my gut into a million knots.

"I'm so sorry, son." Regret and guilt hinged on Dad's words.

"Gemma is a fighter." I spoke the words before they'd fully formed in my mind. "She's strong and smart. Before she left, she injected herself with a serum that will activate inside of her body within twenty-four hours. Gemma will lead us straight to Brandon and his men."

Dad's brows knitted together. "We can find her?"

"Yeah, that's the plan." I couldn't bring myself to tell him that it might not work or that the kinks weren't ironed out yet.

"Oh my gosh. I didn't know!" Mac's eyes widened, and hope flickered to life in them.

"The shitty part is that it won't activate until eleven tomorrow morning." I glanced at my phone. Fourteen more hours before we *might* have a lead on where Gemma was. Fourteen fucking hours was a lifetime away.

Mac slumped in her chair and covered her hands with her face.

She gave a soft whimper. I rounded the bed, then knelt beside her and took her hand. "Mac, at least she gave us something to work with. Once Sutton can track her, we're going to get her. Not only do we have hope of bringing her home, but we can also finally take down Brandon once and for all. Stay positive. Don't give in to the fear right now. You have a little one to protect. Maybe you can get a baby book and scrapbook, then you and Gemma can put it together when she's with us again."

The more time passed, the more I understood why Gemma had made the sacrifice. She'd selflessly risked herself to save Dad and end Brandon. I wanted the same, but not at the risk of losing the love of my life forever.

Mac dropped her hands to her lap and peered at me. "You think she would like that? She hadn't said a word, but I know my pregnancy has been hard on her. Ya know, because of Jordan and everything." She chewed on her thumbnail, which was already down to the quick.

I gently removed her thumb from her mouth and held her hand. "Yeah, she's mentioned it, but she's working through all of it. Don't worry. I think you're helping her more than you realize. Gem loves you and already loves her niece or nephew because they're a part of you."

Mac bit her bottom lip and nodded. "Okay. I'll think of some easy projects we can do together when she's back."

I stood, my attention landing on Janice. She gave me a weak smile. I might have managed to calm Mac for a little while, but I suspected that Janice had picked up on what I wasn't telling her daughter. Janice probably understood that the serum might not work. Instead of sitting down again, I paced the small room and laced my fingers behind my head.

"I can tell you what I know," Dad offered.

"Honey, are you sure that's a good idea right now? Maybe you should rest first." Janice rubbed his arm.

My nostrils flared. I had no clue why Janice would object, unless she was too stressed to think straight. Gemma was out there with a psycho, and Dad needed to share any helpful information as soon as he could. The quicker we had leads, the faster I could get Gemma the hell away from Brandon and into the safety of my arms.

"Pierce and Sutton are waiting in the hallway. I'll bring them in, then you can share anything you remember."

"Can you tell Cade to come in too?" Mac asked.

"Of course." Before Janice could object, I hurried to the door and into the hall. Seconds later, I followed Pierce, Sutton, and Cade back into the room. I remained in the back corner while the three of them hugged and fussed over Dad.

"Can you tell us what happened?" Pierce asked, not wasting any time.

He had no idea how much I appreciated the fact that he got right to the point. I assumed he wanted any helpful information while it was still fresh in Dad's mind. Sutton stood near Mac and Cade, but she remained quiet, remorse flickering in her eyes.

"I heard one of the men mention Montana. I'm not sure that's where I was being held, but it sounded like there was a house there. Brandon wanted to stay off the radar after Gemma showed up." Dad gulped as guilt clouded his features. "Brandon only stayed the first day I was taken. After that, three of his men guarded me. I was in the room when Brandon contacted Gemma and suggested that if anyone wanted to see me alive again, she needed to meet him. If she did, then he would release me." Franklin hung his head. "I tried to tell her not to, but she refused to listen to me. If I had any say about it, there was no way Brandon would be allowed to get his hands on her." His teary gaze traveled across the room and searched me out. "It's my job to protect this family, and I let you all down."

I stared at Dad. Although I expected his emotions to be all over the place, he was oddly calm and had offered more details than I'd hoped for. With all his years as an attorney, he could flip his brain into legal and informative mode, but there was something else. I just didn't know what it was yet.

I crossed the small space until I stood near his feet. "Gemma's a grown woman, Dad. She did what she felt was right. Hopefully, by tomorrow morning, the tracker will activate and we can locate her."

"Sutton is constantly keeping an eye on her phone in case the serum works sooner." Pierce glanced at Sutton, and she nodded.

"What serum?" Franklin attempted to sit up in his bed and grimaced.

Shit. He'd already forgotten about our conversation. Dad definitely wasn't thinking clearly yet, which made me wonder how accurate the information he was providing really was. Maybe that was what Janice was concerned about. We had to try, though.

"The tracker Gemma used was in the form of a serum. She used it before she met you," Sutton said patiently.

Janice helped Dad get into a more comfortable position while Sutton explained how Gemma had injected herself.

"That's what she was trying to tell me when the exchange was taking place. She was talking so quietly I couldn't make out half of what she was saying." Dad grabbed his side and took several shallow breaths, his cheeks burning bright red from the pain.

"Honey, are you okay?" Janice smoothed the hair.

"Yeah." Dad sighed. He looked like he was trying to relax.

"I never thought I would see you again." Dad kissed Janice's fingers and tears pooled in his eyes. "The only thing that kept me going was … all of you. When I couldn't take anymore, I could hear your voices in my mind or see you laugh, Mac. I imagined you singing, Hendrix. I love you all so much."

A messy lump of emotions engulfed me, and I repeatedly swallowed, forcing them down. I didn't want to alarm Dad by having a meltdown. "I'm just glad you're here."

Mac stood and kissed Dad's forehead. *How will I even begin to process this?* In my heart, I knew we were one of the lucky families. Most victims never made it home, or if they did, it was in a body bag.

"I'm sorry. What were you saying?" Dad pretended to inspect the ceiling for a moment.

"If it all goes well, Gemma will be with us tomorrow." I wanted to believe what I'd said, but something in my gut wouldn't allow me to. When Gemma was safely in my arms again, I would feel like I could breathe. Not until then.

"Do you know why Brandon took you?" Pierce asked.

Franklin inhaled slowly, then his attention landed on Pierce. "When Brandon was younger, his father came to me for financial help. I'd heard rumors that Dillon was involved with some illegal activity, and there was no way I wanted my name or money to be tied to him. I said no."

"I didn't know that," I said softly.

"I never discussed it with anyone. The further I stayed away from Dillon, the better. Shortly after that, I learned that Dillon and the boys were homeless. Apparently, it didn't take him long to bounce back, though. I didn't wish that life on anyone, but I couldn't take the risk. I assumed Dillon had family that he could send the boys to live with while he got on his feet. Brandon brought it all up when I was with him. Plus, he wanted Gemma. He knew if he took one of us that she would be open to making the trade."

"Dammit." I scrubbed my face with my hands. "He probably planned all of this when he was in prison and waited for the right opportunity."

Franklin leaned against his pillow. "He has help. He's well-connected and cunning."

The questions were draining Dad. A wave of guilt surged through me for needing any details before he felt better. The clock was ticking, though.

Dad raised his hand, then looked at Pierce. "I did overhear Brandon talking on the phone. He's taking over the Dark Circle Society. He was discussing specifics of several new headquarters. One of them was nearly finished. I didn't hear everything he said, but he mentioned Oregon. If he's smuggling women, then somewhere near ports is the perfect location. There was another on the East Coast, but I don't think it was ready."

I shook my head at Pierce. Oregon was too close to us. Brandon would only be an hour away by plane, and with the money that flowed in from the society, Dillon probably owned at least one. Gemma and I would never stop living in fear, and neither would Mac and the rest of the family. I ground my molars and wondered if Dad might be remembering incorrectly, but my instincts told me he wasn't. It would be just like Brandon to live right under our noses.

"Claire was smuggled through the Shanghai Tunnels in Portland. The coastal states are prime locations for trafficking," Pierce said, frowning.

"That breaks my heart," Mac whispered. "It's awful that such evil shit goes down in some of the prettiest cities I've ever seen."

Cade leaned against the wall and rubbed Mac's back. Other than welcoming Dad home, he'd been really quiet. After we all left, I would catch up with him to see how he was holding up. I nearly barked out a laugh. I was beyond messed up. If Mac were with Brandon, Cade would be out of his mind with worry just like I was. It was a different ball game when a significant other was in danger.

I tuned toward Dad's voice again. Apparently, I'd missed Pierce's question directed at Dad. Sutton was busy typing on her phone, then she held it up. "Pierce. I located a blip. I think the serum might be working sooner than we'd hoped."

I rushed over to Sutton as Mac stood and peeked over Sutton's shoulder.

"What are you looking for?" Mac asked.

I listened intently as Sutton explained how the software picked up the signal. I witnessed another green flash of light on the map, and hope skyrocketed in my chest.

"Yes! That was it!" Sutton glanced at her husband, excitement filling her face. "I'm going outside to see if the reception is better."

Sutton practically ran out of Dad's room, and I was hot on her heels. *Come on, Gem. You've got this, babe.*

Once Sutton and I were outside, we found a bench to sit on, and she zipped up her purple Nike windbreaker. We waited in silence while our attention was trained on her phone screen.

"This gives me hope that the serum will work, Hendrix."

Afraid to verbalize the spark of enthusiasm I was feeling, I nodded. After a few more minutes, I stood and walked down the sidewalk. The crisp night air might help me clear my thoughts. A part of me was relieved that Dad would make a full physical recovery. As for his mental health, I wasn't as sure. Those types of scars had the ability to last a lifetime.

"How are you holding up?" Sutton asked from behind me.

I offered her a half shrug. "I'm happy Dad is back, but at the same time, I'm angry Gemma made the exchange."

"Me too. I'm also pissed at myself for not bringing Pierce into the situation and calling you. She was so adamant about going through with it. I figured I had two choices—make phone calls and risk her running off without my assistance or help her prepare. I would be way angrier at myself if she'd given me the slip and met Brandon all on her own. In my opinion, those were the only options I had."

A heavy weight crushed my chest, knocking the air out of my lungs. I was upset that Gemma hadn't included me, but Sutton was right. Gemma would have ditched her and met the son of a bitch all on her own to save Dad. Once Gem had made up her mind, there was no changing it.

"I'm grateful you were there with her. I can't even begin to wrap my head around the thought of her being in this alone. And for the record, I would have made the same choice. I just—I wish you'd called me the second she left. I could have followed her."

"She was too far ahead of you, Hendrix. You wouldn't have caught up to her. Besides, you would have been in danger as well."

I kicked the cement wall with the toe of my tennis shoe.

"I hope you can forgive me," Sutton said, her voice cracking.

I faced her, the sound of my heart ripping in two filling my ears. For the second time in the two years that I'd known Sutton, tears streamed down her cheeks.

"I do." I swallowed the lump in my throat. "I know you love Gemma too."

"Thank you." She wiped the moisture from her face with her fingers and pursed her lips. "So, you know, Pierce reamed me pretty good over letting her go. We don't argue very often, but we did this time."

"Did you hold your ground?" The corner of my lip lifted in a lopsided grin.

"I did." Sutton laughed. "I explained my decision to him the same way I did to you."

"Not that I'm happy that you two argued, but I'm glad you didn't budge. Pierce is a good man, but every once in a while, he needs a reminder of who really runs the business and home."

Sutton gave a soft chuckle.

Although the situation was fucked-up, I no longer wanted her to shoulder the blame. One of the things I loved most about Gemma was her determination, but it had nearly destroyed me this time. All I could do was hope that the same drive for justice inside of her would bring her home.

I leaned down and gave Sutton a quick hug. "What's next?"

"The tracking software will alert me with either a beep or a vibration. Right now, I have them both turned on. My volume is up as well. I don't want to doze off and miss anything. I suspect Pierce and I will sleep in shifts so one of us is near the phone at all times."

I liked that idea. It was too much for one person to stay awake all the time when everyone was exhausted.

"Do you want to hang out at our place? We have plenty of guest rooms."

"I need to have some privacy for a bit, but I might take you up on it later." Hopefully, Gemma would be back in my bed by the next day, and my words would mean nothing.

"I'll have Zayne bring your car and meet us here. He'll follow you back to your house and stay with you." She flipped her hair behind her shoulder and stared at her cell again.

"If Brandon has what he wants, why do I need a bodyguard?" I wanted time on my own to think and process.

"You haven't seen the news yet, huh?"

I frowned and held up my phone. Swiping right, I gaped at the screen. "Shit, what was I thinking. Of course Dad and the entire shit show made the news. The cops and FBI were involved." My shoulders sagged. "I'm surprised they haven't found us here."

"They will, but hopefully not until after Franklin is discharged. At least he was checked in under an alias for security purposes. There will be two guards posted at his door when Pierce and I leave too." She squeezed my arm. "He'll be safe, but I need to make sure you are too."

After being tagged in multiple articles with the headline *August Clover's Lead Singer's Father Kidnapped*, I was shocked the media wasn't hunting me down.

"Let me see if the house is surrounded by news teams and paparazzi," I said. "If not, I'll go in and grab some clothes and belongings, then I'll stay with you and Pierce. That way, if we find Gemma, I'll be with you guys and ready to go."

"We have plenty of space, and you can work out. I'm sure one of the guys will spar with you too. I know sometimes it feels good to hit something. Maybe some rules of engagement should be in place next time, though."

I gave her a weak smile. "Yeah, I was a dick for clocking Pierce in the nose. I lost my shit."

"I understand. Plus, you both are grown men, and you can work your differences out however you want, but as the wife, I say his face is off-limits." She cocked a brow for emphasis.

"Understood."

Sutton called Zayne and filled him in on the plan. "Let's go back in so you can spend some time with Franklin before we have to leave."

4

It was close to midnight when Zayne and I arrived at my house. I eased my Lexus into Gemma's parking space, my pulse spiking. She wasn't there. I gripped the steering wheel, swearing under my breath. Zayne approached me, and I lowered my window enough to hear him.

"Stay put. I'm going to check the perimeter and inside the home. If I'm not back in three minutes, haul ass out of here and call the police."

Before I could agree, he hurried up the sidewalk. He held his weapon tightly, the moonlight glinting off the metal as he rounded the corner. I shook my head. *How did this happen?* One minute, I was getting married, and the next, my bodyguard was skulking around my property with a loaded gun in his hands.

My heart pounded in my ears while I waited, attempting to gather some courage to walk into an empty home. Whispers of Gemma would haunt me everywhere I turned. Her favorite cinnamon-and-vanilla-scented candle in the living room, her soft beige UGG blanket on the couch, and the closet full of clothes she wouldn't wear were all reminders that she wasn't there.

The night she'd left Spokane after her Mom died, I walked into this house torn up over her. She and Mac were supposed to move in that evening, but instead, Andrea Wallace had set hell into motion, and Gem rushed off to Louisiana because her mother had passed away in a car accident. Gem had been so broken she wasn't able to handle Andrea's rape accusation against me. Andrea's words had sent Gemma into a tailspin, but her mom's death on top of that had been more than she could manage.

But at least when she was in Louisiana, I'd known where she was and that she was alive. This time, I had no clue, and it was so much worse.

Zayne reappeared and used his code and fingerprint to open the door. He slipped inside. Not even a minute later, he waved at me to come in.

I climbed out of the car, locked it, and heaved a huge sigh. As I entered, the faint smell of Gemma's Coach perfume lingered in the air. She'd finally found a light floral scent that she loved. Her smile had lit up her beautiful face when she spritzed it on her wrist for me the first time. I'd loved it. My heaviness lightened briefly with the memory. Gem was so happy discovering new things in her life. They were small luxuries I'd taken for granted for years, but Gemma had never known because she'd been robbed of her teen experiences.

As much as her past screwed with me, I was one lucky son of a bitch to be next to her as she learned more about herself. My favorite moment was the first time she'd selected a hot little number from Victoria's Secret. She'd been so shy when she poked her head out of the bathroom that I'd had to muffle my chuckle. Once she'd stood in front of me with only a small slice of fabric in the shape of a triangle covering her nipples and a flimsy piece of lace over her pussy, I'd nearly came in my jeans.

The thought of the black lingerie against her porcelain skin, the curves of her breasts, and her slender hips made my cock twitch. The chilling thought that she wasn't here seized me. My body buzzed with my churning emotions as Brandon's sneer flitted across my mind. Within a matter of seconds, I'd flipped between Jekyll and Hyde. Ending Brandon once and for all was high on my list, but it would have to wait.

A deep longing came over me as I closed the door and made my way into the kitchen. I dropped my keys on the counter while loneliness cloaked me in its embrace.

"Do you want one?" I opened the cabinet, grabbing a glass along with the bottle of tequila.

"No, I don't drink when I'm on duty." Zayne quirked an eyebrow at me, but he didn't say a word as I poured a shot and drank it. He removed his black Westbrook Security coat and draped it over the back of the kitchen chair. He was wearing blue jeans and a navy button-down shirt. I wondered if his plans for the evening had been interrupted when Sutton had called him. He hadn't been on duty that I was aware of. Gemma was gone, and I'd been with Sutton and Pierce, which might have allowed him a little time off.

I grimaced as the alcohol burned my throat and esophagus. I filled the glass again and tipped it up, draining the amber liquid. "Fuck." I wiped my mouth with the back of my hand.

"You should probably slow down." Zayne tilted his head toward the Patron.

I narrowed my eyes at him, then I refilled the glass two more times and slammed it down. "You ever lost anyone?" I didn't wait for his response. "Then don't tell me what to do. It's not your job."

His expression remained stoic as he stared at me. "You're right, it's not my responsibility, but you and Gemma are my friends. Harrington, you're drinking like a spiritual man trying to talk to Jesus. I get that you're gutted right now, but what if Sutton called and said that she found Gemma, is this the way you're going to show up? Drunk? Man, don't go down that road. I know about Franklin's past, and it can run in the family. It's up to you to break that cycle for you and Gemma, not to mention any kids you two might have." A hint of sadness flickered in his eyes. "I've lost someone in my life as well, but that's another story for a different day. My point is, I've been in a similar situation, waiting and wondering about someone I cared about."

Although I knew he was talking to me, my alcohol muddled brain wasn't registering it. I grabbed the bottle and began to pour another shot. In one quick move, Zayne approached the bar and swiped the glass away from me.

"What the hell, man?" I reached for the shot glass but missed it. I was quick when sober, but after drinking shots, my equilibrium was already off, and I stumbled into the counter.

"Quit being a dick, Hendrix. Give yourself permission to be pissed at Gemma and stop taking it out on everyone else. And I'm going to say this: I've got mad respect for her in every way. I liked her before, but she took it to a whole new level. She saved your dad and brought your family together, and right now, she's paying attention to every detail of her surroundings. Her senses are alive no matter what's happening, and when we get her—and make no mistake, we will—Gemma will be the reason Brandon Montgomery and the organization will tumble to the ground. So yeah, be irritated at her because she left without telling you, then get over it. She's going to need you when she's back. *She* is the one person that can get inside Brandon's head like no one else can. So instead of seeing Gemma as the victim, remember how much she's grown. She took Brandon down once, and she'll do it again. Shit, Gemma's a hero in my eyes."

I wasn't sure how long it took me to realize I was gawking at Zayne. I had no idea what he'd lived through, but I wasn't so shitfaced that I didn't recognize the voice of experience and wisdom.

Holding my hands up in surrender, I backed away from the tequila bottle. "I think I'm losing my goddamned mind."

Zayne snatched up the lid and twisted it back onto the bottle. "I'm not your fucking babysitter, but I'm not interested in watching you destroy yourself either. I know what Franklin went through, and I've spent enough time with him and Pierce to see how it haunts him. Don't go there, man."

I staggered over to the dining room table and plunked down in the chair, trying to remember when I'd eaten last. It had probably been at least eight hours earlier, but my brain was too discombobulated to count very well.

"No one is expecting you to be Mary Poppins, Harrington. Just focus the anger on something constructive. Try to look at the situation differently. That, my man, will keep you from sinking into the black abyss. If you go there, it will suck you in, chew you up, and never spit you out."

I gulped. *What the hell am I doing?* "I know. I lived there so long I fucking decorated my dark corner after Kendra died."

"I can't imagine how bad that shit sucked." Zayne pulled out a chair and sat across from me.

An unbearable silence filled the room, and my thoughts drifted back to Gemma. "The first day I saw Gemma … I was behind the library, trying to write a song. It was quiet and peaceful, and I'd battled writer's block for a month. Out of nowhere, this girl darted around the corner and dropped to the ground facedown. I couldn't see her very well. Her clothes were huge, and she wore a floppy blue hat. From what I could tell, she had no idea I was there. After a minute, she stood, squared her shoulders, and walked away." I ran a hand along my jaw, lost deep in the memory. "She took my heart with her. What I witnessed wasn't a broken girl having a panic attack. I witnessed determination, strength, and courage. From that moment forward, I knew she was mine, and I've never loved anyone else the way I love her."

Zayne tapped the table with his pointer finger. "That's what I'm talking about. Gemma's strong. She gets back up over and over again, and when she gets tired of getting knocked down, she'll get up anyway."

He was right. I was so focused on the fact that she'd left without speaking to me about her decision that I'd let it screw me up and had lost sight of what was important. I dragged my hands across my face. "I'm not sure how to deal with everything. Dad is back, and Gemma is with a monster. What the hell do I even do with that?"

The corner of Zayne's mouth twitched, then he cracked a small grin. "We take that motherfucker down. Every minute we're awake, we plan and strategize. When we're asleep, we dream about closing in on him and ripping him apart limb from limb. That's how you get through it."

Zayne's green eyes glinted with a fierceness I'd never seen. I wondered what he'd been like while serving in the military. One thing I'd learned that night—I wasn't interested in being on the opposing side.

"I need some food and water." I stood, the legs of the chair scraping across the wood floor of the dining room. "As soon as I'm able to pull myself together, we'll go back over to Pierce's. I can't sleep in our bed without Gemma next to me."

"I get it. What do you have to eat? I'm starving."

We grabbed the ingredients for peanut-butter-and-jelly sandwiches since I wasn't in the mood to cook. Once the food was in my stomach, it began to absorb the alcohol, and I started to feel more like myself.

"When Gemma is home, we need to discuss whether or not to sell the house in Maine. I don't think I can ever go back there."

"No shit." Zayne downed a huge glass of milk after his three sandwiches, then rinsed his dishes and loaded them in the dishwasher. "It was gorgeous too."

"Gemma loved it there. The shock on her face when I told her we could buy it was priceless." I chuckled softly, recalling how excited she'd been when I handed her the paperwork. "She thought it was a Valentine's Day weekend at a bed and breakfast. It was, but the first time I walked through the front door, all I could see was her running through the house, laughing and happy. I saw a glimpse of what our lives might look like there." My throat tightened. I hoped like hell we still had a future.

As if my thoughts were written on my forehead, Zayne said, "You'll still have a future. Your fiancée just wants to ensure that Brandon won't be able to mess with you guys again."

There was a considerable risk associated with what Gem was doing, though. She could lose herself in the process. It wasn't worth it to me.

"Where do you want to get married now?" Zayne asked.

This was a question I'd asked myself since the day Dad was taken. "Somewhere safe."

"True that." Zayne crossed his arms across his chest and leaned against the kitchen counter.

"I don't know where that place is. I mean, if we're outside again, we're a target. If we're inside a building, we're a target. Brandon got to us in a bar and on an open ocean cliff, so what makes the most sense?"

"England," Zayne said without missing a beat.

"England?" Puzzled, I ran my hand through my hair.

"Yeah. I have a good friend over there—Vicki. She's a kick-ass wedding planner and knows the area really well. I can reach out to her if you want. I'm sure she has a few tricks up her sleeve since she specializes in celebrity weddings. And you, Hendrix Harrington, are a huge celebrity."

I groaned. "I love the band and touring, but some days I don't want to be recognized or need security everywhere I go. No offense." I shot him a glance.

"None taken, but you and Gemma have to face the facts. She's in the same space you are. She doesn't realize how famous she is."

I chewed on the England idea. If Vicki was as good as Zayne said she was, I would be willing to talk to her and see what she suggested.

"Do you think Vicki would shy away from working with us? I mean, the shooting and Dad being kidnapped is all over the media. For all I know, she saw the articles and shit." I drummed my fingers on the table. Maybe gathering some information would help me stay focused until Gemma was in my arms again. It might give me some hope, along with something to look forward to.

Zayne removed his phone from his back pocket and peered at the screen. "She's eight hours ahead of us. It's ten in the morning there." Before I realized it, he'd pulled up Facebook and called her.

"How's my favorite American?" a sultry female voice asked. Her accent was thick, and I wondered if she was from the northern part of England.

Zayne cracked a grin. "Hey, babe. How are you?"

Babe? Do they have a past?

"Much better now," she purred.

I wasn't sure what I was in the middle of, but I hoped the conversation didn't get steamy while I was sitting there.

"I've got Hendrix Harrington with me." Zayne looked at me and held his finger up. "Wait for it," he mouthed to me.

A loud clatter filled the line, and Zayne chuckled.

"Am I on speaker?" Vicki asked a few seconds later.

"That would be a yes," Zayne said, grinning.

I leaned closer to the cell. "Hi, Vicki. This is Hendrix."

Her squeal was muffled, then the she went silent.

"She muted the phone while she fangirled." For the first time since I'd met him, Zayne threw his head back and laughed. Hard.

"Hello?" Vicki asked, a little more composed.

"We're here," I said. "Zayne mentioned that you might be able to help with my wedding."

"Oh my gosh, I would love to! Is Gemma with you as well?"

I cringed, grateful that she couldn't see me.

My brows knitted together and stared at Zayne. He tapped the mute button. "For whatever reason, Gemma's exchange didn't make the news. Maybe the FBI shut it down, which is a good thing. Play it off."

I agreed, then he unmuted the call.

"She's out of town right now, but she'll be back in a few days. I thought I might surprise her with some ideas." I couldn't bring myself to tell her the truth.

"I hope this isn't out of line, but I'm so sorry about your wedding. I heard that your dad is home safely, though."

"Thanks. It wasn't the day I'd planned for. I'd like a quiet and secluded place to get married, and I'm open to suggestions."

"I can certainly help you with that. I could email some ideas over, then you can narrow down a few places you would like to see. When you fly over, I can schedule a few days to show you some the options."

Dammit. I had no idea when Gemma would be back. For the moment, I would plan on her being home by the next day.

"I would love that." I rattled off my email to her.

"Zayne, will you be coming with him? I mean, as his bodyguard," she said, a twinge of excitement in her tone.

"I'll see what I can do. It depends on where my boss needs me the most."

"I understand, but it would be nice to see you again," Vicki said softly. "Hendrix, I'll round up some possibilities and email them over by the end of the day."

"Thanks. I appreciate it."

"Have a good day, guys." She ended the call before we could respond.

"Did I detect some history between you two?" I lifted a brow at Zayne. I'd never known him to have any long-term relationships, so Vicki had my attention—at least part of it.

"I spent some time in England after I left the military. Let's just say we're really good friends."

I heard what he was saying, but I also listened to what he wasn't. At one point, this girl had been more to him than a friend. This wasn't the time to pry, though. I would let Gemma do that. She was great at getting people to talk about their personal lives. Probably because she never judged anyone unless they were causing others harm. Her heart was wide-open, and I loved her for it.

Zayne's phone vibrated across the table. He scooped it up. "Yeah?" He listened intently. "I'm with Hendrix at his place. I'll bring him to your house now." He hung up and turned to me. "Pack whatever you need. Sutton got another signal. You can shower and clean up at Pierce's."

I flew out of my chair and ran up the stairs to my room. In record time, I'd packed a backpack full of clothes and other items I would need and returned to the kitchen for my keys. I grabbed my jacket and followed Zayne outside.

"We're going to leave your car here to mislead the media." Zayne tucked his phone into his pocket, then we locked up the house and hurried to his company Mercedes.

I hoped like hell Sutton would have some good news by the time we arrived.

5

Suddenly exhausted and emotionally drained, I stifled a yawn as Zayne pulled up to the log house. The car's headlights pierced through the darkness and illuminated the black iron gate. I'd stayed up all night, and the sun would rise in a few more hours.

"When Gemma comes home, I want to design and build our next house together."

"I bet she'll love that idea. Do you want acreage?"

The gate opened slowly, and Zayne eased forward. I appreciated him hopping on the train of distraction with me. The best I could do was plan for our future. The rest was out of my control. At some point, I also had to put faith in Gemma. Zayne was right—she'd gone in willingly, which meant she was ready to do whatever was necessary to end Brandon. I clenched my hands into fists, the dark thoughts tugging at the corners of my mind.

I climbed out of the car, reminding myself of why I was here. Sutton had picked up Gemma's signal again. I stood and stretched my arms in the air, willing my knotted muscles to unwind. A wave of hope washed over me as I followed Zayne into the house.

My nose twitched as I caught the aroma of fresh coffee that greeted me. "Man, that smells good."

"Agreed. Let's get some, then head up to the office." Zayne secured the locks behind us.

"I'm taking a wild guess that the tracking signal isn't very strong, or Sutton would have called us back." I stuffed one hand into my jacket pocket.

"Yeah, not to mention the FBI. Since the last blip was detected in Montana, I'm guessing we would have been hauling ass to the airport instead of here."

My stomach plummeted to my toes. He was right. Apparently, I'd been too exhausted to realize that on the way over, but I highly doubted I could sleep.

Zayne and I located a few coffee cups and filled them with the steaming black liquid before climbing the stairs. He knocked on the door, and we entered the office.

"Hey, guys." Sutton leaned back in the leather executive chair and stretched. Even though she'd mentioned that she and Pierce would take shifts watching for the tracking signal, she looked like she hadn't slept since Gemma had left. I sure as hell hadn't.

"Is there anything new?" I dropped my backpack on the carpeted floor, sank into the comfortable seat, and took a drink.

"The signal is sporadic, but it's appearing more often." Sutton picked up a Westbrook Security thermos from the desk and refilled her hot pink mug. "This is my third pot of coffee." She cracked a smile. "Under normal circumstances, I would be wired for days."

"You and me both." I took another swallow, willing the caffeine to kick in. "This is good news, right? You said the tracker wouldn't start to work until twenty-four hours after it was injected, right?" I paused, glancing at the clock on the wall. It was almost four o'clock in the morning.

"Yeah, much faster than the last few times it was tested. I'm documenting information too. This is the first time the serum has been in the field, so to speak."

I flinched. Gemma wasn't some experiment. She was a human being.

"I'm sorry, that probably sounded callous. What I meant is that someone is using it in real life rather than one of the test subjects."

"I get it. If Gemma's experience can fine-tune the product for our military and FBI … well, I think she would be happy about being able to help."

Sutton stared at me, then her attention landed on Zayne. Maybe she thought I would jump down her throat for the comment about Gemma testing the serum, but I'd moved through the anger phase and was ready to take some action.

"Hendrix needs to shower," Zayne said, speaking for the first time.

"Ah." Sutton pushed away from the desk and stood. "Zayne, would you keep an eye on the laptop while I get him situated?"

Ah? Do I reek or something? I'd showered the previous day. *Crap. I probably smell like alcohol and desperation.*

"You can use the bathroom in one of the guest rooms. If you can sleep, I recommend it. Once I can pinpoint Gemma's location, we'll be off and running."

I massaged my forehead, sensing a headache creeping up on me. Then I slung my backpack over my shoulder and followed her.

"If you can't get any rest, feel free to use the gym. Just let me know where I can find you in case I have an update," Sutton said.

"I will." Following Sutton up another set of stairs on the opposite side of the house from her office, I imagined Gemma taking the same ones when she'd spent time with Claire. Maybe it was stupid, but it helped me feel closer to her.

"Here we go." Sutton waved her hand, and the light came on. "It's the same as your dad's, so flip the switch and turn off the sensor if you want to sleep."

I nodded, eyeing the huge room. A king-sized bed with a navy comforter and matching pillows beckoned to me. Maybe I was more tired than I realized. A large television was mounted to the wall over the tall dresser, but I wasn't sure I wanted to channel flip until I found a distraction. If all else failed, maybe I could watch the next episode of

Sons of Anarchy. It might give me some good ideas on how to torture Brandon once I got my hands on him.

"The bed is adjustable too." Sutton folded her arms and leaned against the wall.

"I'll see how I feel after a shower. If I can, I'll try to sleep."

"Unless I hear otherwise, I'll assume you're getting some rest. I'll let you know as soon as we hear something." Sutton closed the door, leaving me standing in the middle of the room with my thoughts.

Most of the time, I enjoyed being alone. I was a musician, and my creativity depended on solitude. Now it was my worst enemy. There was no one to throw me a life preserver if I lost my way. I slid the bag off my shoulder and unzipped it. An unbearable quiet filled the large space while I unloaded my clean clothes and headphones and placed them on the bed.

I strolled over to what I assumed was the bathroom and peeked inside. The light came on, and my mind wandered to Gemma. I wondered if this had been her guest room when she'd stayed the night. My attention swept across the details. The deep jetted tub that could easily fit two and the white-and-black marble counters, which were clean of any items other than a soap dispenser. I toed off my shoes and began to walk toward the shower, but my reflection in the large mirror halted me. I turned slowly and peered at the man looking back at me. Haunted, sad eyes returned my gaze.

After I'd lost Kendra, there were so many mornings I would stare at myself and wonder who I was. My little sister had been such a big part of my life. I felt like my heart had been cut out and I'd been squeezed until the life had drained out of me. I directed my attention to the task ahead, which was to smell better and feel more human. Once I'd turned on the water and the steam billowed over the glass, I removed my clothes, then stepped under the spray. I leaned my palms against the walls and hung my head, allowing the heat to soak into my tense muscles. My neck ached like a son of a bitch, and I longed for Gemma's nimble fingers to work out the knots.

I flipped my soaked hair back and lifted my face. The last shower Gemma and I had taken together was after Dad had been kidnapped in Maine. We'd made love and whispered our vows to each other. Our tears mixed with the water, then swirled down the drain.

My cock hardened as I remembered how slick her walls had been when I entered her. It was the first time I'd cried since I lost Kendra and the first time I'd admitted that I wasn't okay. I closed my eyes as the memory cloaked me in its false security.

"God dammit. We were being so fucking careful." I ran my hand through my wet hair. "How are we going to win this war? How am I going to protect you?" I leaned my forehead against hers, then a silent cry shook my shoulders. Gemma wrapped her arms around me, and I sank into the warmth of her.

"I love you, Hendrix. I'm here. We're here together."

Her soft voice was the healing balm I needed so desperately. I hid my face in her neck and clung to her as I broke down. "I failed Kendra and now Dad. I almost failed you." My words sounded as broken as I felt.

I sucked in the steamy air and grabbed the shampoo while the memory of that night continued to roll in on a wave of grief and desperation.

"Oh, baby, no." Her forgiveness easily slipped from her lips. If I could only capture it and allow it to permeate my being, maybe I could forgive myself. "Those men were trained and came out of nowhere. No one is to blame," she said softly.

My body finally stilled, then I looked down at her. My erection pressed against her flat belly, and I swallowed hard. I wanted her. I wanted to feel something other than the pain that was shredding me to pieces. Being inside of her was more than just sex. It was the closeness and the emotional connection. Even when we fucked, it was the deepest connection I'd ever had with anyone. And at the moment, I was desperate.

I lathered my hair, ignoring my painful hard-on.

"I need you. I need to touch you and make sure you're all right. I need to lose myself in you. I'm not okay, Gem. For the first time since Kendra, I'm not okay."

"Baby, I'm here." She kissed me gently.

I placed my lips on hers, dominating her mouth. "I love you." I said softly in her ear. "You're my world. My heart." My desperate kisses interrupted her response. I bent my knees, then lifted her. She wrapped her legs around my waist as I gently eased inside of her, and she slid her arms around my neck. I stilled, losing myself inside her. Her touch. She was my everything. If I'd lost her that day, it would have destroyed me. But I hadn't. Thank God I hadn't.

I rinsed my hair, hoping it would wash away the crushing agony of losing her now.

Her beautiful blue eyes penetrated mine, and her breath hitched. She kissed me, then whispered her vows.

"No matter what happens, my soul is forever tethered to yours. Hendrix, no matter how lost I might feel, your love continues to be the light in the darkness. Your love set me free, and you taught me how to live. You're the air I breathe, the song I sing. You're the reason I found my voice again. It's you that I dream of at night, you that I long for when you're not by my side. Nobody moves me like you, Hendrix Harrington. You're my heaven. You're my always." Tears spilled down her cheeks as I remained inside of her, connecting on every possible level. This woman owned my heart. She always had. From the second I'd laid eyes on her, my soul had recognized hers. She was born to be my wife, and I was born to be her husband.

I pressed my mouth against hers, then spoke quietly, searching her face as I shared my oath with her. "Until I found you behind the library that day, I was in this world alone. I'd faded into the background. You gathered the fragments of my heart and pieced them together. Your courage, your quiet strength touched a part of me I didn't even realize still existed. Gemma, you're not my other half—you're the fire that burns inside of me. My life has a purpose because of you. As long as you're by my side, I'm a whole man. Today and every day, I vow to protect you ..." I swallowed, tears streaming down my face. The world halted, and nothing else mattered except us. We were suspended in time, two souls seeking, surging, and becoming one.

She kissed me. "You protected me, Hendrix. You kept your promise."

My grief eased, and I had a flicker of hope that we would be all right.

I slapped the palm of my hand against the shower wall, welcoming the sting. I hadn't kept Gemma safe. I'd let my guard down when she'd needed me the most, and that son of a bitch had contacted her right under my nose. An agonized cry escaped my throat as I sank to my knees and surrendered to all of the emotions that were raging a war inside of me—anger, fear, desperation.

The water finally cooled, and I pulled myself together long enough to soap my body. If I thought I'd been emotionally drained earlier, it wasn't anything to how I felt now—empty and hollow. I turned off the shower and grabbed the navy towel that was hanging on the bar near me. I dried off, then stepped out on the plush black bathmat. I was exhausted. Maybe I could sleep for a little while. Sutton was right—once she had a good signal on Gemma, life would be a whirlwind.

Since I wasn't at home, I blow-dried my hair so the pillow wouldn't get wet. After I located my phone in my backpack's side pocket, I put on a fresh pair of jeans and a clean polo shirt. If Sutton located Gem in the middle of the night, I wanted to be ready to haul ass out the door. I didn't want to lose precious minutes stumbling around and searching for something to wear.

Stifling a yawn, I crawled into bed with my clothes on. I tapped my Photos app and opened my favorite picture of Gem. "I'll find you," I whispered. "I'll find you."

My eyelids grew heavy, then I slipped into a fitful sleep.

6

"Are you alive?" someone asked, gently kicking my foot.

"Huh?" I shot straight up, my groggy brain struggling to register my surroundings.

"You've been asleep all day. Sutton wanted me to check on you. Vaughn and Claire are here, and two pot roasts are in the oven. I realize you probably aren't—"

"I'm starving," I said, interrupting Zayne.

"That's a good sign. We're all hanging out in the kitchen, so come on down when you're ready. I'll let Sutton know you're still breathing."

I rubbed my eyes and flipped my hair out of my face. Glancing around for my phone, I finally located it on the bed next to me. I hadn't even remembered putting it there, but as stressed as I was, that didn't surprise me. I checked the time, my brows shooting up. *Holy shit.* It was almost six in the evening.

Once I relieved myself, brushed my hair and teeth, and applied deodorant, I felt a little more human. The first thing I needed to do was check on Dad. I collected my cell from the bed and called Mac.

She answered on the first ring. "Did you get some sleep?"

"Yeah. Did you?"

"Some. Sutton called and let me know where you were. The last I'd heard, you and Zayne were at your place. I wasn't sure it was a good idea for you to be there under the circumstances, but you're a grown man."

"You're right. It wasn't a good idea. For some stupid reason, I thought it would be smart to start slamming tequila shots."

Mac groaned, and I imagined her smacking her forehead with the palm of her hand.

"Yeah, not the best idea I've had, but you'll be happy to know that Zayne set me straight really quick."

"Wh-What? Did you say Zayne? I mean he actually had a conversation with you? Or are you still drunk?"

"Yup, I don't think I've ever heard him talk as much as he did last night."

"You've got to fill me in, but first, I need to tell you that Dad is coming home tomorrow. He's doing great."

"That's fantastic news." I massaged my temple, wondering if I should mention what I was really concerned with. "Mac?"

"Yeah?"

I sank onto the edge of the bed, my heart heavy with the question that was forming on my lips. "I realize that oxy isn't alcohol, but it triggers a relapse for some people. Not only that, but what he just lived through is traumatic. I'm worried he might slip."

"I know, Hendrix. The same thought crossed my mind when we saw him in the hospital." Her vulnerability bled through the phone. "But he's been sober for a while, and I have to believe that he has too much to lose to turn back now."

Mac was too young to have many memories of Dad's behavior when he and Janice were married the first time. I secretly wished I had her naivety concerning the situation. But for the moment, I had to squelch the fear and focus on Gemma.

"How's Mom holding up?" I asked, changing the topic.

"Tired, but she's so relieved Dad's coming home. We all are. And Hendrix?"

I pulled at a small thread on the comforter and sighed. "I'm listening."

"When Gemma gets back, I'm going to let her have it, but then I'm going to full-on ugly cry and thank her for bringing Dad back to us."

"Same, Mac. Same." *If she comes home.* My stomach churned, and I dismissed the thought as quickly as I could, but not before it had stabbed another hole in my soul. "Tell Cade to text me later. I suspect I'll be here until Sutton has a fix on Gemma."

"Hendrix, please, *please* tell me as soon as you do." Mac's voice softened as she pleaded with me.

"I will. Try to rest. You're taking care of my future niece or nephew as well. I know Cade is probably hovering over you too."

The line was silent for a minute. Then she whispered, "He's driving me crazy, so if you can call him soon, I would really appreciate it. I think he needs some dude time." she whisper-yelled into the phone.

I couldn't help but grin. My man loved Mac as much as I loved Gemma. With the pregnancy and the added stress of Gemma being gone, he was probably going out of his goddamned mind.

"I will. Until then, don't forget to breathe." I mentally scolded myself for not reaching out to Cade sooner, but my life had been consumed with Brandon ripping my family apart. Again.

"Right back atcha," she said, and we were both quiet for a moment. "I love you, Hendrix. I don't say it often enough. My world wouldn't be very good if you weren't in it."

My heart melted right out of my chest. "Love you, too, sis. There's no doubt you make my world a happier place." If I'd learned anything over the last several days, it was to tell the people in your life that they were special and loved because in a blink of an eye, they could be gone.

"I'll text you later," Mac said.

"I promise I'll keep you posted, and please keep me updated about Dad." I disconnected the call and sucked in a deep breath. My stomach growled, reminding me that food and my friends were waiting for me.

I hurried down the stairs and toward the heavenly aroma of the roast. Vaughn was a beast in the kitchen, and my mouth was already watering.

"I can smell dinner all the way to the guest room." I patted my belly as I joined Sutton, Pierce, Zayne, Vaughn, and Claire. "I guess I'm hungrier than I realized."

"We all are. We're not eating on a regular basis, and our sleep schedules are messed up." Pierce rounded the island and patted me on the back. "Glad you got some rest, though."

"Hey," Claire said, bounding over to me, then throwing her arms around my neck. "I don't know what to say." She released me and offered a sad smile. "Do I tell you I'm glad your dad is going to be okay, or that I'm sorry Gemma isn't with us?" Her face fell.

"Say whatever you need to, Claire. I think we all feel the same. I'm learning there's no right or wrong way to think in this screwed-up situation."

"No shit," Vaughn muttered while he used the hand mixer on what appeared to be homemade mashed potatoes.

"How are you so thin when he cooks like this all the time?" I asked Claire.

"A high metabolism runs in our family," Sutton chimed in as she reached into the cabinet and unloaded water and wineglasses from the shelf.

"Dancing helps too." Claire walked over to Sutton and began helping her.

"What can I do to help? I feel awkward just standing here." I kneaded the aching muscles in my neck.

"You can set the table with me," Zayne said, motioning for me to follow him.

I walked into the same dining room that we'd gathered in for Friendsgiving after Claire's surgery. It was one of the best days I'd ever had. There had been so much love-filled laughter and appreciation for everyone. It was what the holidays should be about. The only person who was missing this time—I slammed the door on the thoughts. If I allowed myself to even start thinking about Gemma and what she might be going through, I would be a mess in less than thirty seconds. I had to stay positive.

"Is there an update on Gemma?" I asked Zayne as I grabbed plates from the middle of the table and began to distribute them.

Zayne stopped setting the forks down and looked at me. "No. Sutton hasn't had a signal the entire time you were asleep."

I froze, unable to move. "How long was I out?"

"About fourteen hours." The corner of his eye twitched.

I sank into the nearest chair, anxiety and fear churning inside me. "Shit." Through a clenched jaw, I asked Zayne the question that terrified me the most. "If she's …" I stared up at the ceiling. "If Gemma is dead, will the tracking device still work?"

Zayne placed the last fork on the table and sighed. "No." His tone was thick with worry.

Bile crept up my throat, and I choked it down. *Is Gemma gone forever?* Dark thoughts overwhelmed me, and I stood. "I'm not hungry." I shoved my hands in my pockets and stormed out of the dining room and toward the gym.

"Harrington, wait up." Zayne jogged after me. "Let's box. I'll even let you get a few hits in."

I met his suggestion with silence, but he refused to take the hint and continued to walk beside me. I headed straight for the heavy bag. I pummeled my fists into it, my breathing becoming ragged as I beat the hell out of it.

Pieces of skin ripped off my knuckles, but I didn't care. Zayne stood near the entrance and allowed me to vent my aggression. Drops of blood landed on the mat. The muscles in my shoulders and arms burned, but I kept going. I was trying to stay positive and believe that Gemma would be able to do this and come home to me. *Who the hell am I kidding? Brandon is a rapist and a sex trafficker. There's no telling what else he is into after several years in prison.*

Tears blurred my vision. *Gemma, please be alive. Kendra, send her help. Please.* That was the closest thing to a prayer I had inside me. Gasping for air, I wrapped my arms around the bag and stilled. The creak of the door opening caught my attention, but I didn't turn around to see who it was. I didn't care. Soft voices exchanged words, then the sound of footsteps grew closer.

"Let's get your hands bandaged," Sutton said gently. "I came to find you. We picked up a weak signal again."

I spun around, afraid that I'd misunderstood. "You did?"

"Yeah. It didn't last long, but it was there. This isn't over, Hendrix. Not by a fucking long shot. Gemma's a fighter."

I slammed my eyes closed, holding the tears at bay. "Thank you for letting me know." I looked down at the mat. Blood had splattered all over the blue material. "I'll clean up, then I'll let you bandage my hands."

Sutton walked to a cabinet and pulled out a bottle of cleaner and a rag. "This isn't the first time we've had blood on the floor, and it won't be the last." She held the items out to me. "I know how difficult it is to hang on. We all do. You're not in this alone, though."

I accepted the cleaning products, then knelt and began to wipe off the mat. "Thanks."

A heavy silence descended the room while I finished taking care of my mess. Sutton held out a bag for the dirty towel. Zayne hadn't said a word, just watched as I collected my dignity. I had a niggling feeling that he understood what I was going through more than the others, but he'd never opened up about his past. Hell, I'd been shocked when he'd shared about Vicki with me.

"We have a bathroom across the hall for occasions like these." Sutton placed her palm on my back and led me out of the gym. "Sit." She motioned to the toilet, then located a first-aid kit out of the bottom cabinet. "I'm sorry."

I quirked a brow at her. "For what?" I held out my right hand for her to clean and bandage.

"That Zayne jumped the gun and told you there hadn't been a signal on Gemma. Maybe ask Pierce or me from now on. It's not that we'll withhold any information, but Pierce and I have more experience with the serum than Zayne does."

"Has this happened before? Not being able to detect the tracker for long periods at a time?"

Sutton dabbed my busted knuckles with antiseptic and I released hiss. Shaking my head to clear the pain, I focused on what Sutton was saying.

"Yeah, and the person was downstairs in a basement for several days. Abe, who is working with Pierce to perfect the product, made adjustments, but we weren't sure if it would work yet. Gemma could very well be belowground, and I don't mean as in buried. I would suspect that wherever she is, there are some types of barriers the signal can't get through. It would also explain the short periods that we do see activity."

A glimmer of hope spread through me. "Do you think she's ..." Fear hung on my every word.

Sutton stepped back and stared directly into my eyes. "There isn't a single doubt in my mind that's she's alive."

My shoulders slumped forward, and I inhaled a shaky breath before I looked at her again. "I don't know if I'll make it if she—"

"She'll make it," Sutton said with so much confidence it nearly convinced me that Gemma was invincible. "Other hand."

I held it up for her. "Thanks for your help." Suddenly, I was embarrassed about busting up my knuckles and bleeding all over her floor.

"It's what friends do for each other." She smiled gently. "I was a disaster when Claire was kidnapped. More than once, we thought the FBI had found her dead. The constant bombardment of dread, anxiety, and lack of sleep messed with me too. It's why I'm pushing you to take care of yourself, because when Gemma comes home, she's going to need you." Sutton finished bandaging my hand, then put the first-aid kit away. "On the hard days, when Gemma is struggling, be patient and love her. Also, it can be a sensitive issue, but I would recommend counseling for both of you. Under your layers of anger, there's a lot of fear and hurt. Gemma left without discussing a life-changing decision with you." Sutton paused and cleared her throat. "And I helped her. I know that we're all family and we love each other, but the trust issues and all of the emotions wrapped into her choice will pop back up unexpectedly if they're not dealt with in a positive manner. It will eat you alive. Trust me on this one."

I was suddenly grateful that Pierce, Sutton, and Zayne had so much life experience. Whether they realized it or not, it was helping me keep my shit together. "It happened with Kendra. The anger finally faded, and all I was left with was my pain. Music saved me from a destructive path." I glanced at my bandages. At least the sting of my wounds distracted me for the moment. I stood and sighed. "If you or Claire have someone you would recommend, I'll schedule us some appointments. I'm not angry at Gemma anymore. I know she made the best decision she could under the circumstances, but she also broke my trust."

Sutton patted my arm. "I did too. Hopefully, with a little time, we'll all heal. I'm still mad at myself, though."

I gave her shoulder a gentle squeeze. "I guess I have some work ahead of me. When she's home, I think I'll be able to process what happened. Right now, I'm out of my head with worry. It's hard to focus on anything else."

"We all feel that way." She tucked her hair behind her ear and gave me a sad smile. "Let's see if Claire and the guys left us any food."

"Sounds good."

There was no trace of Gemma for the rest of the evening, and I continually played Sutton's words over and over in my mind in order to stay sane. If Sutton believed Gemma was alive, I would too.

7

The next three days passed with no new information. Gemma's signal would appear, then disappear again. Each time that happened, it stole another piece of my heart. My hope was dwindling fast. We should have brought her home by now. Gemma should be in my arms with her leg tossed over mine and her hand on my chest. My mood was sinking faster than the Titanic, and I was spiraling out of control. There was only one person who might be able to provide some relief and help me not plunge over the mental cliff—my dad.

Late in the afternoon of the fifth day of waiting, I mentioned visiting Dad to Pierce. He recommended I not drive since I was so stressed out, so Zayne quickly became my chauffeur. We rode in silence, and I decided it would be a good time to check my email. I tapped the screen on my phone, and my pulse spiked. As I tried to focus on the list, my head swam, terrified that I would find another message from Gemma, but there wasn't one. Instead, there was one from Vicki that waited for my attention. I wasn't in the mood, though, so I sent her a quick reply that I'd received the information and would be in touch soon.

"Was Vicki the one that got away?" I asked Zayne, desperate to think about something other than Gemma.

He adjusted his sunglasses, then tapped his index finger against the steering wheel. Either we were becoming friends, or I was getting better at reading him. Until recently, I'd never noticed his tells. Vicki was definitely a difficult topic for him.

"I'm not sure what she is."

At least he was honest about it. "Did you two have a thing while you were in the England?"

Zayne gave me a half shrug. "I enjoy her company. She was there for me during some dark days after the military." He paused. "I'd just returned from Afghanistan, where I was recognized for the highest number of enemy kills."

"Shit." He had my attention now.

"Yeah, it was a fucked-up thing to do so well. It got inside my head. Bad. I was at the end of my military contract, and the day it was over, I went straight to England. I'm not sure why, other than I'd always wanted to spend some time backpacking around Europe, and it seemed like a good place to start."

"I want to take Gemma."

"There are some really beautiful places to get married over there." Zayne flipped on his turn signal as we approached Nine Mile Road. "Anyway, I thought if I spent time in nature, I would be able to get my shit together. It didn't work, though. Every damned night, I would wake up in a cold sweat, thinking there were dead bodies piled from floor to ceiling in the bedroom of the apartment I'd rented."

I was stunned that Zayne was confiding in me, and I didn't want to shut it down by saying the wrong thing, so I chose to remain silent.

"One evening, I found myself in the bar. I thought drinking myself into oblivion would block the PTSD, but it didn't."

"That's why you were so quick to stop me the other night?" I asked. It made sense now. He'd traveled down that shitty road himself.

"Yeah. It's a waste of time and energy. Anyway, it became a nightly ritual. I'd go to the bar, then stagger home until I passed out. Some nights, my dreams didn't haunt me. Others, I wasn't so lucky. So, like a dumbass, I thought if I started drinking earlier in the day, I wouldn't remember shit, and that would fix the situation." The corner of his mouth lifted in a slight grin. "I had barely sat down with a beer when she walked in. It'd been pouring rain for the last twenty-four hours, and she was soaked. Her thin blouse clung to her tits, and I wanted nothing more than to strip her down and towel her dry." Zayne chuckled. "She was … *is* fucking fine. Long brown hair, big brown eyes, and legs for days. I, being the gentleman that I am, offered her my jacket to cover herself with. Every man in that place was staring at her, and I didn't like it. For some reason, I felt immediately protective of her."

"Was that new?" I asked, shifting in my seat.

"Yeah. There was only one girl I'd ever felt that protective of before."

I waited for him to elaborate, but he didn't.

"Anyway, we spent the afternoon together at the bar. I bought her a few drinks and some food. She was easy to talk to, and before I realized it, I'd made it until midnight without getting drunk. Finally, I invited her to my apartment, and she accepted. We tore my place up. We fucked on the sofa, the kitchen counter, the floor, and the coffee table. I didn't even bother moving stuff—I just swept the magazines away and cleared the space we wanted. Eventually, we crawled into my bed and fell asleep. With her, sex was better than the booze, but it was still an escape."

He didn't have to say it. I knew what was coming.

"Then the dead-body shit started, and I woke up yelling. I know I scared the crap out of Vicki, but she never would admit it. She slipped out from beneath the covers and returned with some water. After I gulped it down, she straddled me and kissed me. She never asked what happened or how often. She just held me."

"She sounds like a really good person." I suspected Vicki had previous experience with someone who'd struggled with PTSD. It sounded like she knew what to do.

"We stayed together for a year. Some nights, she'd stay at her place, and others, mine. She never pressured me for more—no explanations were necessary. It was easy to be with her. Most people would have demanded answers about the night terrors, but she was consistent and helped ground me, bringing me back to the present moment. Although it took a while, my bad memories softened a little." Zayne turned onto Dad's winding driveway.

"Why didn't you settle down with her, then? I mean, in my opinion, it's always easy with the right person. No one has to prove anything. The relationship lines up. Gemma and I are like that."

Zayne remained quiet as he parked in front of the garage. "After all of those months, she finally told me she was in love with me. I realized that she was before she ever said anything, but I was too selfish to leave. She'd saved me, and she had no idea." Zayne stared out the driver's-side window. "I cared a lot about Vicki, and I still do. But it was nothing permanent on my end. It was great sex and a safe place to get my shit together. I had no intention of staying in England. Plus, Pierce and Vaughn had finished their service with the military. Pierce said his dad had a job for me when I was ready to come back to the States. It paid really well, and I could use the skills I'd learned as an Army Ranger."

"Damn. I had no idea you were a Ranger." I rubbed my chin, trying to digest all the shit he'd done. "You obviously came back and took the position." My focus drifted to Dad's house, then I spotted Jaxon and Tad walking the perimeter of the property.

"Yup. It's more than security, though. We get top-dollar gigs that are dangerous. You get used to the adrenaline after a while. Normal life looks boring as hell."

"I can't imagine. I've had more danger in the last several years than I care to have again. I'll take boring over this shit any day."

Zayne climbed out of the car. "I know you're hanging on by a thread, but don't let go, man. This whole shitstorm could turn in our favor at any second."

I hopped out of the Mercedes. "I hope you're right. I can't take much more of Brandon and his family. Every single day, it takes a chunk out of my soul."

Zayne slapped me on the back. "Maybe it's time we take matters into our own hands."

Before I could ask what he meant by that, Mac flung the door open and bombarded me with a hug. I staggered backward, attempting to keep us both upright. My heart swelled as I wrapped my arms around her. "Hey, sis."

"I've missed you." She cried against my shoulder. "Cade needs dude time before I drive him insane." She released me and wiped her tears with the sleeve of her plaid flannel shirt.

"I'll catch up with everyone while I'm here. How's Dad doing?"

Mac grabbed my hand and dragged me farther into the house. "I don't know." Worry lines creased her forehead.

"What do you mean?" I whispered as I slid my arm around her shoulders and led her into the kitchen, where I hoped we could talk in private.

She hopped up on the granite countertop and selected an orange from the stainless-steel bowl. Mac nervously tossed it in the air and caught it over and over.

"Mac, focus." I seized the piece of fruit and took it away from her.

She stared at the ceiling for a minute as her foot gently banged against the cabinet beneath her. *Shit. Mac is a mess.*

I took her hand in mine, hoping the warmth of my skin would help ground her. "Talk to me."

"I didn't want to say anything to you because you're already a wreck about Gemma and—" She waved her other hand in the air while she attempted to find the right words but said nothing more. I appreciated her not mentioning the devil's name anyway.

"Mac, I know you're trying to protect me, but it's not helping. Please, tell me what's going on with Dad."

"Nothing." Big tears streamed down my sister's cheeks.

"I don't understand."

She fidgeted with a string on the hem of her shirt and sucked in a shaky breath. "He won't talk to us. Not even Janice. He refuses to eat, shower, or leave his bedroom."

My heart hammered against my rib cage. Logically, I understood that he'd been through a traumatic experience, but it still scared the shit out of me. "How long has he been like this?"

"Ever since he came home."

I stepped back and ran my hand through my hair. "You should have told me. I would have been here sooner."

"Hendrix, you can't run around fixing everybody when you're trying to keep your own shit together. I don't think I realized how much we depend on you, though. When Dad was drinking, it all fell on your shoulders, and you're still trying to take care of everyone. Gemma, Mom, me, Cade."

"You're my family. That's what families do, Mac. We take care of each other. You and Mom saved me after Kendra's accident. I wasn't taking care of anyone back then. I couldn't. You guys need me now, and I'm here. That's how it works. We share the responsibility because we love each other."

Mac nodded and sniffled. "Dad is in his room. Mom left to run some errands, so you should have some time alone with him."

I squeezed her shoulder. "All right. I'll see if I can get him to talk."

"Thanks."

I left the kitchen and made my way to Dad's bedroom near his office. At one time, I wondered if I would ever see him sit in the chair at his desk again. Now that he was home, the same question swirled around in my brain.

I knocked on the door. "Dad, it's me, Hendrix."

There was no response, so I eased the door open and let myself in. I was immediately overwhelmed with the stench of days-old sweat and body odor clinging to the stagnant air. "Damn." I hurried over to the heavy drapes and carefully opened them, then cracked open the window.

"Shut the goddamn window," Dad growled.

I stiffened at his rudeness, but at least he'd spoken to me. Nowhere in his obnoxious tone could I find my father, though. He never spoke to me or anyone else like that—not since he'd been sober, anyway.

"When you shower and the room smells better, I'll shut it." I approached the bed, finally able to see him in better light.

He looked like absolute shit. It wasn't that I'd thought he would be clean-shaven, in button-down shirt and dress slacks, but I didn't expect this either. He had several days of stubble, and his hair was stuck to the side of his head. I was certain that his rumpled blue-and-white pajamas were begging to be washed. *Why didn't Janice call me to help?*

"Get up," I said, my voice sounding gruff and closed off even to me. My patience was definitely on the short side. His appearance and attitude brought back all the god-awful memories of his drunken days.

"You should leave, son." He leaned back on his pillow and shut his eyes.

"Are you on drugs or drinking again?" I put my hands on my hips so he couldn't see them trembling. "If you are—if you don't get help—I'm done. I'm not going through this with you again." I trailed off, hoping he would get the impact of my statement. My breath hitched in my chest. *Jesus. What is happening?* I couldn't handle losing Dad again. Not now. Not ever. We finally had a great relationship, and I trusted him. I trusted him to stay sober.

Dad stared straight through me. "I haven't relapsed." His words were thick and heavy, full of remorse and grief.

"You had lying down to a science when you were drinking, so forgive me if I don't believe you." My words held a frosty bite. It was odd how quickly my walls slammed back into place.

He mumbled something that I couldn't make out.

"Okay. If this is how it's going to be, then I'm out of here. I'm done." I tossed my hands up in surrender. "Don't call me. Don't visit. You also won't find an invitation to my wedding arriving at the door." I hated myself more and more with every word that left my mouth, but I hoped my anger would shock him out of his funk. For some reason, I'd thought a visit with Dad today would help me with Gemma, but this was pure hell. Instead, I found myself searching for the courage to put difficult boundaries in place, and it fucking sucked.

I spun on my heel and left. I wasn't interested in hanging around, watching him slip further and further away from our family and me. Not again.

From the hallway, my fingers wrapped around the doorknob as I silently pleaded with him to stop me, but he said nothing. Not one word. Not even a sound. I jerked the door open, then slammed it behind me. *Fuck him.* If Dad wanted to return to his old life, that was on him.

My feet grew heavier with each step I took down the hall, then my ears perked up. I hurried to his room and burst back in. My heart stuttered and cracked wide open with what I saw.

8

My badass attorney father was curled up in a fetal position, sobbing. His entire body shook with tormented cries.

"Dad," I whispered. Tears welled in my eyes at the broken man in front of me. "Dad, what is it? What's wrong?" I knelt next to the bed and continued to talk to him. I reached for his hand, and he gripped mine so hard that pain shot up my arm. "Talk to me." I kept my tone even and soothing, hoping to bring him back to me enough to explain what was happening.

"I can't. I can't." He covered his face with his fist and proceeded to break down.

"Dad, there's nothing you can't tell me. There's nothing we can't figure out together. We're Harringtons. I love you, Dad. Please." My voice cracked as I softly pleaded with him.

Minutes ticked by without another word, then he raised his head and peered at me through swollen eyes. "I can't talk about it."

I frowned. "I don't understand." Men didn't talk about a lot of things, so his clue wasn't helping me any. "It's obvious something else happened when Brandon took you."

Dad shuddered.

"Did he shoot you up with drugs? Are you struggling to stay clean?" I had to start somewhere. If he couldn't tell me, then it was up to me to ask the right questions.

"No."

"We know you were beaten, but did he threaten you or the family if you talked?"

"No."

I struggled with what to ask next, fearing I wouldn't figure it out in time to help him.

"Did you see him abuse young girls?" *Shit, that would fuck anyone up.* I held my breath until he answered.

"No."

His tone was different. I was getting closer. One thing you learned from having a successful attorney for a dad was to pay attention to someone's tone and body language.

Shit. I didn't want to ask the next question that popped into my mind. I swallowed hard. Perspiration dotted my upper lip as my anxiety kicked up a notch. "Dad ..." *Shit. How am I going to ask this?* "Were ... were you ...?" *Dammit, Hendrix, spit it out.* "Were you hurt?"

He hid his face from me again. *Shit. Shit. Shit.* This wasn't happening. My mind had just reached out for the worst scenario I could think of. That was all. He hadn't confirmed anything.

"Were you sexually assaulted?" I asked barely above a whisper.

The clock ticked loudly while I mentally pleaded that he would say no. He didn't shake his head. He didn't speak or move.

My heart skidded to a stop, and my stomach churned. His silence was confirmation enough. Every nerve ending inside me stood on high alert. Those words sat in my gut like sour milk as I scrambled to digest the situation. Dad remained still, but his breathing was ragged. I'd heard once that an alarming number of men were raped, but it wasn't something that was ever talked about. Tears streamed down my face. No wonder he was in so much emotional pain.

"Dad." I reached for his hand again. "Was it Brandon?" I puked a little in my mouth.

He turned away. "A guard."

Jesus. Fucking. Christ. I wasn't sure what to say anymore. I didn't even know any guys who had lived through this, and I was terrified I would say the wrong thing. Closing my eyes for a minute, I leaned into my instincts. When Gemma had flashbacks, I held her, stroked her hair, and calmly talked until she settled down. It was one step at a time.

"I'm here. I'm not going anywhere, Dad, but I need you to try to meet me halfway on this. For me. Because you love me." I choked on my words, hoping they were enough to break through all of his pain. "Didn't you have a full medical exam when you were admitted to the hospital? Wouldn't the doctor have talked to you and provided some help?"

Finally, he raised his head. He didn't look at me, but it was progress, and I would take it.

"I declined it. They knew who I was. No one pushed me," Dad said.

"It's okay, but—you need to be checked out."

"No." Tears clung to his eyelashes. "I finally understand how Gemma felt." His voice trembled, and he gulped. "I don't know how she made it through. I want to fucking die. I'm mortified. Embarrassed. I'm so goddammed ashamed."

I wiped my nose, trying not to break down crying. "I'm going to make some phone calls and get you some help."

Dad grabbed my hand with both of his, his expression full of fear. "Don't tell Janice. Please, son. Please."

An uncontrollable ache spread through me I struggled to control my heart from splintering into a million pieces. "Dad, she won't see you as less of a man. Mom loves you so much, and she'll support you every step of the way. As soon as Gemma is home, you've got your biggest ally back. I'm not going to lie—I can't deal with this and help you all by myself. We need professionals. We need our family."

I leaned my head on top of his hands, crying. My shoulders shook. Agony ripped through me, and I allowed Dad to see my pain. For him. For Gemma. For everyone who'd lived through sexual abuse. I wished I could spare him, but he needed to see that even the Harringtons could be vulnerable at times. He'd shared his worst nightmare with me, and I needed to grieve.

Once my tears ran dry, I stood, my knees cracking. "You need to shower. I'll stay here until you're finished."

He slowly pulled himself up into a sitting position, his shoulders slumping. "Thank you."

"I'm not asking for your permission, but I want to let you know that I'm removing all the alcohol and prescription drugs from the house. You're not entertaining guests right now, so there's no reason to have it anywhere around. Plus, Mac is pregnant, so she's not drinking either. You two can have apple cider and other options together. Maybe you won't feel so alone."

He nodded. "I need help getting up, Hendrix." Defeat laced his words.

"Sorry. I forgot about your ribs."

Over the next half hour, I watched over Dad as he shaved and showered. I stripped the bedding and tossed it on the floor. The room was freezing with the fresh air, so I closed and locked the window. At least it didn't stink anymore.

I sank onto the edge of the bed and waited for Dad to finish. As soon as Janice returned from shopping, we needed to talk. First, I needed to know why she'd allowed him to smell so goddamned bad.

Dad finished tucking his blue button-down shirt into his jeans while he entered the bedroom. "I decided I needed to find some semblance of normal again even if it was as simple as not wearing my pajamas all day." He paused. "It's not her fault."

"Whose?"

"Janice's."

I stood. "You look human again. How do you feel?" I wasn't sure if I was ready to discuss Janice yet. I wasn't too happy with her.

"Better." He smoothed his shirt with his hand. "I asked if she would mind sleeping in the guest room, since I was dealing with broken ribs."

I frowned. "And she agreed?" This wasn't making sense to me. At all.

"She was really afraid of elbowing me at night. She hasn't been sleeping well."

Okay, I can understand that at least. "Didn't she spend the day with you?"

"Of course, she did. I told her I was in too much pain to shower or get out of the bed unless I had to use the bathroom."

I massaged my forehead with the heel of my hand. Maybe Janice had done the best she could. I wasn't sure why I was being so harsh with her lately.

Then it all made sense. "Is there a possibility that she didn't call me because she was afraid you were abusing the oxy?"

Dad sighed and carefully sat on the end of the bed next to me. "She's been terrified. We lost our marriage over my addiction once. Now we're so much better together. We've lived and lost and come out stronger. That would devastate her. I think with Gemma gone and no news on that front, it was too much for her to contemplate. It was easier to not look at the situation."

Shit. I was being an asshole for being mad at Janice. Thank God I hadn't opened my mouth and said anything mean to her.

"I think we're all scared right now." My knee bounced up and down, and I made a conscious effort to stop and stay still.

"Hendrix ..." Dad rubbed his chin, then dropped his hand to his lap. "I've had a lot of time to think since I've been home, and the only reason I'm sitting here with you is because of Gemma." He glanced at me, tears welling in his eyes again. "The guard—it was every day."

My jaw tightened. The air around us thickened and closed in until it was too hard to breathe.

"If she hadn't shown up when she did ..." He pressed his lips together. "I sound so weak and pathetic right now."

"Dad." I wanted to hug him, but he didn't seem comfortable with being touched yet.

"I know her decision hurt you and broke your trust, but don't forget that she wouldn't have made her choice lightly. She's the key to bringing the Montgomery family down once and for all. When she comes home, please forgive her. Don't be angry. Say what you need to, then help her feel safe again."

"I will. Promise."

"There was something else. Brandon showed no feelings about his plans to take over the society. When he talked, there were no emotions at all. He was very matter-of-fact about it. The only time there was any change in his body language, or his inflection, was when he talked about Gemma."

A combination of fear and anger dug their rigid talons into my neck and shoulders.

"Hang on, Hendrix." Dad held his finger up to keep me from tumbling down a slippery slope of retaliation. "This is a good thing. He really cares about her in his own screwed-up way. I don't think he's planning on hurting—on forcing himself on her."

I grabbed his hand, and we sat in silence. I scrambled to understand what he'd said. If Brandon was capable of loving another human being, maybe Dad was right, and he wouldn't hurt Gemma. I closed my eyes and inhaled deeply, wishing this nightmare would end once and for all.

I looked at Dad, my heart still in my throat. "I hope you're right. For now, do you want to sit the family down to talk to them, or do you want me to?"

His cheeks grew pale. "I don't think I can." His other hand trembled, and he ran it up and down his thigh.

"Okay. I'll make some phone calls and get some counseling lined up. I'll ask if a therapist can come to the house so it's discreet. Would you like a male or female?"

"Honestly, I don't want to ever talk about it again." He looked at me, his eyes so full of pain it gutted me. I wasn't sure how I was supposed to walk out of this room with my heart still intact.

"I know, but you can't do this on your own. Your family can't wonder every minute of the day if the memories have finally pushed you to drink again. It's no way to live."

"I'll attend therapy. For all of you."

I placed my hand on his back, then squeezed his shoulder. "Love you, Dad."

"Love you, too, son. More than you'll ever know."

I stood and faced him. "Are you okay sitting on the couch and eating some dinner?"

"Yeah. I need to see another place in the house besides the bedroom."

That was a good sign. I collected the dirty linens and his pajamas. I would toss them in the washing machine while he ate. "Is Ruby here? I didn't see her."

"No, Janice gave her the week off. I think she wanted to give me time to heal without someone else around."

I helped Dad stand, then we slowly walked down the hall to the living room. I tilted my chin at Zayne, who had remained near the front door.

After Dad was settled and as comfortable as possible, I walked to the utility room. I stuffed the sheets into the machine and located the detergent in the cabinets above the dryer. I filled the soap dispenser before I closed the lid. The dials were already set, and I pushed the start button. I leaned against the washer as the water kicked on, my knees weak at the thought of talking to Janice and Mac about Dad. I would need to support them, but I was running out of hope that any of us would be able to recover from the devastation.

As I gripped the counter, a white-hot fury blazed through me. *Fucking Brandon.* He might not have hurt Dad, but he'd still allowed it. My mind started spinning scenarios, each one ending with Brandon's body on a spike. Next, I would put a few bullets in that guard's skull, right in the forehead, so I would know that rat bastard couldn't hurt anyone else. A cold sweat dampened my upper lip, and I wiped it off with the back of my hand.

My arms shook as I struggled to process what Dad had told me. Lately, life was an ongoing nightmare that I couldn't seem to wake up from.

"There you are," Janice said from behind me.

"Hey." I took my time before I faced her. "I'm washing the linens from Dad's—your bed. It was pretty rank in there."

"Thank you." Her cheeks pinked. "I should have called you sooner, but I wanted to try to handle things, since you're dealing with the Gemma situation."

Shit. She'd said that like Gemma was dead. I folded my arms, a warning that I wasn't interested in talking about Gemma and for her to tread lightly. "We should talk. First, Dad needs to eat. If you'll get him something, I'll locate Mac. I think the guesthouse will work for a safe place to say what we need to."

Fear flickered in Janice's eyes, and I had a moment of compassion. "He hasn't relapsed, but we need to get the booze and pills out of the house."

"Okay. I can do that. I'll have Mac and Cade help, since they probably know where the liquor is."

Under normal circumstances I would have laughed, but I didn't have it in me. "I'll have Cade keep Dad company while we talk."

"That sounds good. I'll heat Franklin up some soup that Ruby made." She glanced at me. "At least he finally left the bedroom."

"We have a long road in front of us, so if there's any question in your mind whether you want to be here, now's the time to leave. I won't judge you if you go."

Confusion twisted Janice's features. "Hendrix, I'm not going anywhere. I love Franklin with all my heart."

I nodded. "All right. I think you'll need to tell him that later." I slipped past her and into the kitchen. I peeked at the clock. It was a little after seven. "I'll meet you at the guesthouse in fifteen minutes."

9

I wished like hell that Gemma was with me. She would probably know the best way to break the news to Mac and Janice. I had no clue how to tell them about what happened to Dad. *Shit.* I hadn't wrapped my head around it myself.

Pacing the small living room of the guesthouse, I blew out a sigh. I hadn't been here since Pierce had worked as our bodyguard. Everything looked the same—the light-colored hardwood floors, black area rug, and black suede sofa. A flat-screen television hung over the gas-burning fireplace. The kitchen's black-and-white granite countertops were clean of any items except a coffeepot. There were three small bedrooms and two bathrooms. At seventeen hundred square feet, it was cozy yet spacious, exactly what I needed to openly discuss Dad's situation with Mac and Janice.

Although I realized that Mac would support Dad in his healing, I was seriously worried about her stress level. There was no way it was good for the baby. Maybe Dad had been right. Perhaps she and Cade would be safer somewhere else. The moment I had that idea, I kicked it to the curb. Mac needed to be with her family regardless of the chaos.

Personally, I was nearly out of my mind with the possibilities of what Gemma might be living through. If Dad had gone through an assault... "Dammit!" I released a low groan and placed my hands on the back of the couch, bowing my head as the dark thoughts bombarded me.

The door swung open, and Janice and Mac filed in, the chill of the autumn air following on their heels.

"I've always thought this place was so cute," Mac said, attempting a smile until she saw my expression. "Dude." She walked into the living room and hugged me. "Quit kicking yourself in the ass. You got Dad out of his hidey-hole, and that's like a thousand times more than we've been able to do. Cade is keeping him company right now. They're watching a comedy movie."

"Good," I said. Dad needed all the lighthearted fun he could handle. It was scientifically proven that watching funny videos and laughing often reversed depression and anxiety over time.

Janice and Mac sank into the sofa, expectant and fearful expressions on their faces. My nerves were fucking shot, and I hoped I could talk to them without falling apart again.

"What's going on, Hendrix?" Janice asked, unwilling to wait any longer.

I placed my hands on my hips and continued to pace.

"You're pulling a Mackenzie," Mac said. "Spit it out."

I barked out a near-hysterical laugh. She was right. Mac did the same thing when she was trying to process intense shit. I sucked in a deep breath, then ripped off the Band-Aid. "Dad was raped. Repeatedly."

The cold, hard truth crushed my lungs, and I struggled to stop the room from tilting as images of Dad sobbing came rushing back. Time stood still as Mac gaped and Janice's face twisted with horror. It was so quiet I wasn't sure we were even breathing.

I attempted to still my racing pulse, but I couldn't. "It was a guard, and it happened each day that he was gone."

"Dad?" Mac's hands flew over her face as the tears flowed silently. "Oh God."

Janice remained still. Even though the news had torn me in two, a little bit of relief washed over me. I was no longer carrying Dad's secret alone.

My brain kicked into fix-it mode, and I laid out the plan to Janice and Mac. "I'm going to find a therapist who will be discreet and come to us. They might recommend a few sessions a week, but I'll let you know. I'm not sure, but I suspect there will be some family sessions as well. First, we need to clean the house of any alcohol or prescription meds. If they're here, I'm afraid Dad will relapse. He hasn't yet, but this is a lot to deal with. We need to give him every possible opportunity to succeed and heal."

Mac wrung her hands. "I can do that. I know all the good hiding places for the bottles of alcohol." She paused, the stress and concern expanding in the space between us. "How can I help him? What do I do or say? Shit. Shit. Shit." She wiped her damp cheeks and peeked at Janice, who still hadn't spoken.

"Mom?" I asked. "If it's too much, you can still go. No judgement."

I didn't mean it. If she left, I would judge her. Hard. I just didn't want her to pretend that their marriage was fine when it wasn't. Show up or get out—to me, it was simple. Dad needed to be surrounded by people who loved him and believed in him. She'd left once before, and there were no guarantees that she wouldn't walk out the door again.

Janice arched her brow at me. "I'm not walking away from Franklin. Don't keep expecting me to." She released a heavy sigh and folded her hands in her lap, guilt clinging to her features. "He kept crying in his sleep," she whispered. Her voice was raw and thick. "I figured it was PTSD. He'd barely been back home and hadn't even started healing yet. The physical wounds would mend quicker than the inner turmoil he went through, but this ..." She trembled, crying. "He's the strongest man I know, but there's no way he could deal with something so horrific on his own." She shook her head. "I love him so much. I'll help him in every way I can." She hiccupped through her tears. "And, Hendrix, I did the best I could for my daughter when Franklin was drinking heavily. I realize leaving hurt you deeply, but I never abandoned you. I suspected at some point that you would need a safe place to stay, so I did my best to provide that for you. I'm sorry that you got caught in the middle."

"Mom." I knelt beside her and took her hands in mine. Now that I was clear on where she stood, my fear of her bailing on us simmered down. "We're all in this with him. I wasn't sure how you would react. This could affect so many areas of your marriage. Intimacy on every level."

She reached out and placed her palm against my cheek. "Gemma … you went through this with her, didn't you?"

I nodded, afraid to speak.

"How?"

"She was ready to move forward, but I was her first kiss … her first intimate relationship. I had to be patient and let her take the lead. More than anything, I wanted her to feel safe with me. Mac had a lot to do with it too." I glanced at my sister, who was a total mess.

"We were good for each other," Mac said. "Plus, it was easy to brag about how amazing Hendrix was. Is. Oh shit. I can't take all of this. Gemma's with that fucker, and Dad …"

She buried her face in her hands. Her small body shook with her anguished crying. Janice scooted closer and wrapped Mac in her arms. They clung to each other as I watched their world crumble.

"I'll be back. I need some air," It was too hard to witness the people I loved fall apart.

I swung the door open and hurried outside. The cold night breeze stung my chapped skin where my tears had fallen earlier. I linked my hands behind my neck and walked in a circle, taking deep breaths, trying to hold it together. All I wanted—needed—was Gemma in my arms. No matter what else happened, I knew everything would be all right if she were with me.

But she wasn't. The more I understood about Dad's kidnapping, the more terrified I was about what Brandon might be doing to my future wife. The thoughts alone wrecked me. I couldn't imagine what I would be like if I learned the truth.

I was at the end of my rope and realized that inaction was no longer a choice. I didn't give a shit who went with me. I was going to find Gemma. After Janice and Mac returned to the house and settled in for the evening, I would talk to Zayne. He had military experience, and maybe he would be willing to help me make a plan.

Feeling a little calmer, I entered the guesthouse again. Janice was talking to Mac and smoothing her hair. If the situation hadn't been so screwed up, I would have thought it was really sweet—Mom comforting her baby, who was having a baby. There was obviously a bond there that I would never experience simply because they were women. Women who I loved very much.

I leaned against the wall and watched them. Then the reason I'd been so hard on Janice finally dawned on me. Deep down, I was afraid it would be too much for her, and she would leave just like she had when Dad's drinking had escalated. The logical part of me understood why, but a voice in my mind had continually whispered that she'd left me too. She didn't believe she'd abandoned me, but the way I remembered it, I'd been alone and scared. I'd been the only one left cleaning up Dad's messes.

Even then, Janice was the only mother I'd ever known, and the mere thought that she would take off nearly left me breathless. I couldn't do this on my own. Hell, I could barely put one foot in front of the other while I waited for news concerning my fiancée.

"Since you've been through this, how do we act around Dad?" Mac sat up and peered at me through swollen and red-rimmed eyes.

"The same way you always would. Joke around with him. Sit with him and hold his hand, watch his favorite movie. Just love him like you always do. When he's cranky, love him even more. When he pushes you away, give him some space, then snuggle up to him later. Gemma was in a slightly different place when we first started dating. She'd had four years to process her trauma, and she still struggled to move forward. I think family counseling would be best for all of us. We need to be able to talk to someone about the rape. We won't be any good to Dad or each other if we're as messed up about it as he is."

"I was thinking the same thing," Janice said. "In fact, I think I would like to see someone as well. On my own, I mean. That way, I can express my own grief and work through it."

"When Gemma comes home, I suspect we'll be going too," I said. A heavy silence hung in the air. "Speaking of which, I should get everyone settled for the night. I need to get back to Pierce's place and see if Sutton is any closer to locating Gemma."

Janice and Mac stood, then we all embraced.

"I love you, Hendrix. I'm so damned proud of the man you've become," Janice said softly against my ear.

"You're the best," Mac added.

We released each other and the ladies wiped their tears away. I draped my arm around Mac's shoulder and kissed the top of her head as we filed out of the guesthouse. I locked the door behind us, then we all held hands as we trudged up the hill and toward our new future.

HALF AN HOUR LATER, I climbed into the Mercedes along with Zayne.

"Some heavy shit today, huh?" Zayne pushed the button, and the car purred to life.

I arched a brow. "Did you overhear anything?"

"No, dude. It was obvious everyone had shitty-ass day."

I chewed over the idea of telling him. There was no doubt I could trust him, but I wasn't sure how Dad would feel if Zayne knew. My heart played a full-on tug-of-war inside my chest. One person I wanted to talk to was Sutton. She would be helpful in lining up the resources we needed. I also realized that she would speak with Pierce, since he was her husband.

More importantly, I needed to figure out what would help *me*. Even though Janice and Mac knew what had happened, they would work through the trauma differently. I couldn't deal with this shit by myself.

"I feel like you and I have become friends through all of this," I started, still wondering if I was doing the right thing.

"Agreed."

I swallowed the massive lump in my throat. "Dad was—

My phone vibrated in my back pocket, interrupting me. I leaned forward and removed it.

"Weird. Someone is trying to FaceTime me." I furrowed my brows. "What if it's Brandon with another demand?"

Zayne hadn't left the driveway yet, and he slipped the gear into park. "Keep it at an angle so he can't see me."

"Okay." My pulse stuttered. I tapped the green button and waited for someone's face to fill my screen.

The camera on the other end bounced around, then landed on an attractive older lady. Her large blue eyes assessed me eagerly. I didn't recognize her.

"Hello, Hendrix." Her voice was low and hauntingly familiar. I scrambled to identify her but came up blank.

"Uh, hello. I'm sorry, but I don't think we've met." I made sure I didn't look at Zayne as I spoke to her.

"I'm a friend. The reason I'm contacting you is because I have information concerning Gemma. You'll need to act on what I tell you immediately." Her tone held a note of urgency.

My hands began to shake, and I nearly dropped my phone. "How? Have you seen her?" Since I didn't know this lady, I had to be sure not to give any details away in case she was working for Brandon.

"I'll answer your questions another time, but for now, get something to write on."

I flipped my phone facedown on my leg, giving her a view of my dark-wash jeans. Zayne pointed to the glove box. I popped it opened and rifled around until I found some scratch paper and a pen that appeared to be on its last leg. I shook it in case the ink was threatening to dry up. Scribbling on the paper, I held my breath. It worked. I turned the phone over again, making sure the camera wasn't picking up Zayne. She filled the screen again, and before I thought about it, I snapped a picture of her and saved it.

"What information do you have?" I asked, wondering if this was someone's sick idea of a game.

"Gemma is alive. She's in a very secluded house in Montana at the base of White Sulphur Springs Mountain. Brandon Montgomery is with her there, but in the next few days, he's going to move them to Colorado. You need to act fast."

My hand shook as I jotted the information down. "Does the house have an address?" I was stunned that I was able to think clearly enough to ask.

"It's 1125 Mountain Knob Road. It should pull up on Google Maps. I would use the aerial view."

"How do you know all of this?" I knitted my brows together, confused. "And if she's really there, how will I find you again to thank you for helping me?" I still had more questions than answers.

"Consider it a wedding gift. Hopefully, the second one will work out better than the first." She flashed me a warm smile. "I'll be in touch." With that, the screen faded to black.

In shock, I lowered my phone and stared out the window. Within seconds, the adrenaline zipped through my veins. Zayne was already ahead of me. He started the car and peeled out of dad's driveway. I hadn't even realized he'd called Pierce and Sutton.

"Westbrook," Pierce answered.

"It's ZW. We got a lead, man. The address where Gemma is being held is 1125 Mountain Knob Road in Montana. Check the aerial view if the address isn't showing on the map."

"You're on speaker now. Sutton is at the computer. How did you get the tip?" Pierce asked.

"Some older woman contacted me through FaceTime," I finally managed to say. "She said the house is secluded but Gemma is alive. I have no idea who she is, but I took a screenshot of her face. I'm not sure she realized I snapped her picture."

"Excellent. Send it over to me. Hopefully the image will help us identify your caller. Sutton is searching for the address now."

I glanced over at Zayne, who was speeding like an escaped felon. At least we were on the backroads, but they were rough as hell. Spokane was known for its shitty roads.

"Zayne, I'm going to call Brian. The FBI will want to be involved. Get here as soon as you can. We still have to—"

"Got it!" Sutton yelled in the background.

"I'm coming with you. Don't you fucking dare leave without me, Pierce," I said.

"I wouldn't dream of it. Zayne, drive straight to the airport. Now that Sutton can see the property, we need to move out. If anything changes, I'll call you back. Otherwise, we'll meet you there." Pierce disconnected the call, and I clutched the dash.

Zayne nearly gave me whiplash as he whipped the car onto the side of the road and pulled an illegal U-turn.

"Jesus. Should I call Dad and let them know? What if it's inaccurate information and it turns out to be nothing?" My heart stuttered against my rib cage. A false alarm would screw us all up.

Zayne weaved around several potholes, and I grabbed the oh shit handle. I wondered if he'd ever driven a getaway car before. He had some mad driving skills.

"It's hard to say, but my recommendation is to wait until Pierce talks to his FBI contact. They can send men ahead of us and use infrared tools to see if people are really there. Maybe someone in the area has seen Gemma or Brandon. I'd give it a little longer. If it's not Gemma ..." Zayne's voice faltered. "Then at least we didn't drag them through hell again."

"You're right. I'll wait." I stared out the passenger window, replaying the woman's message in my mind. I tapped the home screen of my phone, then selected the photos icon. "Sutton should be able to run facial recognition on this lady, right?"

Zayne's eyes darted to the image. "Never seen her, but yeah. Sutton's fucking magic at digging up people's secrets. If this woman's information pans out, I'm taking a wild guess she either knows Gemma or Brandon. For whatever reason, she wants you to find Gemma. And you know what? That works for me. We can worry about who she is later."

My knee bounced as Zayne sped toward the Spokane airport. "How many speeding tickets have you gotten?" I didn't really care. It was my lame attempt to make conversation while I reminded myself to breathe. Too bad I wasn't a vampire who could flip the switch on my humanity. Having no feelings or anxiety sounded really good right about now.

"Nah. Gotta get caught to get a ticket."

I threw my head back and laughed. "You're full of surprises. I've decided you're all right. At first, I wasn't too sure."

"It's a good thing I don't need your approval to feel okay about myself." The corner of his mouth pulled up, and his chuckle filled the car.

I sank into my seat, suddenly terrified that we wouldn't be able to locate Gemma. Or worse, we would find her, and she would be …

"It's hard riding the emotional roller coaster. One minute, you're so far down the rabbit hole there's no hope of seeing the sunlight again. The next, you've given yourself the best mental pep talk ever and feel like life is going to be all right. Then a tip comes in or some pertinent information that could crack the case wide open. If it doesn't pan out, it's super easy to sink even further down the hole than you were before. My gut tells me we've got something, though. Even if it's not Gemma, I think it's the big break we're looking for."

An incoming call startled the shit out of me. Zayne answered from the button on his steering wheel. "This is ZW."

"It's Sutton. We've got the signal. It's strong enough that I was able to pinpoint her location. Whoever called you wasn't messing with us, Hendrix. Gemma is right where that lady said she'd be. Hang on, hon. We're going to get her, then we're bringing her home."

She sounded cautiously optimistic. My emotions overflowed, rippling through me like a storm over the sea. The push and pull were chaotic and uncontrollable. All I wanted was to touch Gem, kiss her, and hold her. I would never let her go again. In a split second, my thoughts betrayed me. *What if she's barely alive, holding on by a thread? What if Brandon has raped her over and over again?*

My hands curled into fists. "Sutton, promise me after Gemma is safe, Brandon will be taken care of once and for all."

"Let's get her home, then we'll sit down and talk," Pierce said.

I didn't miss the deadly tone to his voice. We were in agreement.

He hadn't forgotten our vow after my wedding had gone to hell in a handbasket. I slammed my eyes shut and pleaded with the universe that I would still be able to marry the love of my life.

83

10

Forty-five minutes later, Pierce's plane was in the air, and we were flying toward Montana.

Pierce leaned back in his cream-colored leather seat, his expression grim. "Here's what we know at this point. We'll land at the Helena Regional Airport. Then Brian has given us permission to accompany the FBI and SWAT to Central Montana near White Sulphur Springs."

I swallowed against the tightness that had suddenly seized my chest.

"Hendrix, this is new to you, so I'm going to go over the rules. If you break them, I'll kick your ass." Pierce removed his black Westbrook Security coat and flung it over the seat across the aisle.

"Understood." I was shocked that I would even be allowed near the home. At this point, I would take any break I could get, which meant not screwing it up.

"First, SWAT will clear the house and area. If there's a threat, they'll eliminate it," Pierce said.

My eyes narrowed. "As in, kill Brandon?"

Pierce's jaw ticked, but other than that small tell, he seemed outwardly cool. "I'm not sure how that will play itself out."

Pierce continued to lay down the rules. I had to remain out of sight until the danger had been cleared. At least I was closer to her. My heart hammered so hard my ears rang.

"Breathe." Sutton placed her slender hand on my arm, compassion filling her blue eyes. "Take some deep breaths, Hendrix. This is scary. Put your head between your knees if you need to."

Grabbing the collar of my polo shirt, I willed my pulse to calm down. This was not the time for me to lose it, but my anxiety was over the goddamned top. I scraped my hands down my face.

"Here." Pierce handed me a tumbler with amber liquid. "It will settle your nerves."

I hadn't even realized Pierce had gotten up. I arched an eyebrow at Zayne, wondering if he was going to snatch the glass away, but he didn't move. I slammed the whiskey down. It burned the back of my throat, but within seconds, my mind sharpened again.

"Thanks." I held onto the empty glass so I would have something to busy my hands with. "I don't know how you guys do it."

"After a while, you get addicted to the adrenaline, but this situation is different for all of us," Pierce confessed. "We've just had more practice not revealing how fucked-up we're feeling."

"So you're human after all?" I cracked a small grin.

Sutton laughed softly. "We're all nervous and excited at the prospect that Gemma will be home soon."

"Tell me more about this FaceTime call," Pierce said, his eyes narrowing suspiciously.

"Shit. I nearly forgot." I removed my cell from my pocket and located my photos. "Here." I handed my phone to him.

Pierce silently stared at the screen. "Can I send this to Sutton and me so we can do some digging?"

"Of course. I meant to send it to you earlier, actually. Hell, I'm happy I thought to snap the picture. I don't know why taking a screenshot crossed my mind under the circumstances, but I'm glad it did."

"She obviously knows Hendrix," Zayne added. "She was very comfortable reaching out to him. Whoever she is, she's not a stranger.

Maybe he doesn't recall meeting her, but there's a connection some-where. She knew that the wedding got screwed up too."

"It was all over the media, though," I pointed out. "I do remember looking at her and thinking she was familiar, but I have no idea from where. What I want to know is why she called me. I mean, did she do it out of the goodness of her heart, or does she want something in return?" My attention bounced between Pierce, Sutton, and Zayne.

"Let me see what I can find out. If she reaches out again, let us know." Pierce ran his hand over his short dark hair and stared out the window.

I stretched my legs in front of me, wondering how close we were to the airport. "How long is the flight?"

"About an hour. Once we land, it's another hour by car to Gemma's location."

"Damn." I leaned forward. "It seems like an eternity. What did you guys do to pass the time in the military?"

"There was a lot of waiting," Zayne said.

A heavy weight descended on my chest as my mind wandered to Dad. "I need to tell you all something."

Pierce draped his arm over the armrest. "What else is going on?"

I tilted my head back, touching the soft leather of the chair. "It's Dad. I saw him today, and it wasn't good." I leaned over and propped my arms on my knees, staring at the tan-carpeted floor. I sat up and flipped my hair out of my face. "When he was gone ..." *Shit, this isn't any easier the third time around.* "A guard raped him. Multiple times."

"What?" Sutton gasped.

Pierce dug his fingers into the leather material, his jaw clenching so hard I could see the tic of his muscle.

"That's fucked-up," Zayne said softly. "I'm feeling a vacation coming on soon, boss." Zayne shot a knowing glance at Sutton and Pierce.

"Vacation?" I frowned. *What the hell kind of response is that?*

"Time off for some ... personal hunting time." Zayne cracked his knuckles.

I understood now. Zayne was ready to take Brandon *and* the guard out. I was okay with that idea.

"Do you have a name?" Pierce asked, gritting his teeth and hardly able to remain calm.

"No. I barely managed to pull the information out of Dad. Actually, I had to keep asking questions until I finally guessed correctly. It fucking gutted me." I stared out of the window, lost in thought as the grief grabbed me by the balls again. "Sutton, if you can help us with a counselor or psychiatrist, I would really appreciate it. I want someone to visit Dad at the house a few times a week, or however often they think is necessary. I'm not sure if he'll feel more comfortable with a male or female, though."

"Neither," Pierce and Zayne said in unison.

"That's what I was thinking. So how do I find the right one?" I asked.

"I know a psychiatrist that works with rape victims, both male and female. It's not only a female problem. The men just rarely report it," Sutton said, her tone gentle and soothing.

"Zayne, this is why I was on the fence about calling them before we left for Montana. It's been a really screwed-up day, and if the information didn't pan out ..." I blew out a breath, imagining how detrimental a false lead would be for Dad. For all of us.

"You made the right decision," Zayne said. "Now that I know, I won't call them until Gemma is in FBI custody and on the way to the hospital."

My heart sank to my toes. Although Dad had been sent to hospital immediately, it hadn't dawned on me that Gemma might need medical care and possibly a rape kit. I slammed my eyes closed and refused to entertain the thought.

The soft voice of the captain floated through the speakers. "We're approaching the Helena Regional Airport. Please buckle your seatbelts and prepare to land. We've got a bumpy descent ahead of us."

"This is my favorite part." Zayne grinned and laced his fingers behind his head. "Sometimes the turbulence is the best part of the journey. Once it's out of the way, it's smooth sailing. I'm ready for something to go right for a change."

The plane dipped along with my stomach. I wasn't afraid to fly—I'd done it a million times on Dad's plane—but unlike Zayne, I didn't enjoy the descent at all. Ten minutes later, the plane had landed, and we joined Pierce's FBI friend, Brian.

"Thank you for your help." I extended my hand to Brian. I'd heard Pierce talk about him, but I'd never had an occasion to meet him.

"Let's get her home and Brandon Montgomery behind bars again, then you can thank me." Brian shook my hand, his alert gaze assessing me.

A nondescript black van rolled up next to us, and Brian ran a hand through his thinning dark hair. It was a wonder he had any left at all. I couldn't imagine the level of stress and lack of sleep an agent went through.

Zayne filed in behind me as we loaded into the van. Other than Brian and Pierce talking quietly, everyone else remained silent.

"Hang in there, Harrington." Zayne nodded at me, then took a seat.

"I'm trying." I sank into a spot near the window, thankful to have something to distract me as we drove. Not that I could see much now that the inky darkness had consumed the last rays of sunlight.

The van pulled forward and I stretched my legs out. Sutton sat in the seat in front of me, her shoulders nearly reaching her ears. She shifted and peered at me over the seat. "I have some headphones in my purse if music will help."

"That would be great." I leaned forward and collected a pair of earbuds in a small clear baggie from her.

"They're clean and sanitized." She mashed her lips together, then faced the front of the van again.

I fumbled for my phone in my back pocket, then plugged the head-phones in. Scrolling through my playlists, I landed on "Running" by Abi Ocia. Gemma had stumbled on this song a few days before we flew to Maine for the wedding.

Closing my eyes, I allowed the singer's silky tone to transport me to a different time and place. Gem had played this song, lit several vanilla cinnamon candles, and turned off the lights to our bedroom. I nearly groaned out loud as the images played through my mind.

Gem dropped her black satin robe to the floor, a shy smile easing across her face. My tongue darted across my bottom lip as my dick begged to be freed from the constriction of my jeans. I gulped as my attention landed on her small but perky tits, the curve of her waist, and the toned legs that should be wrapped around my neck.

Fire burned up my throat, stinging the back of my eyes as I continued to reminisce.

She stood before me, naked and beautiful. The flames of the vanilla-scented candles cast shadows across her porcelain skin, and I closed the gap between us.

"I want to remember this moment for the rest of my life. You're stunning." I traced her collarbone with my fingertips, savoring every touch, every kiss, every inch of her.

She placed her palms on my chest and peered up at me through her long eyelashes, stealing my breath along with my heart. "I love you, Hendrix."

The lilt of her soft voice sent delicious chills through my body.

The van bounced over a bump and jarred me from the safety of my thoughts. I dragged my hand along my jaw, frustrated that all I could do was take sips of memories when she should be next to me. Large drops of rain splattered against the window, and I wondered if Gemma could hear it. She loved the rain and thunderstorms.

"We're twenty minutes out," Pierce called from the front of the van.

I squirmed in my seat, anxious as hell to reach her. "Sutton, do you still have a signal?"

She held up her phone, allowing me to see the bright green dot. "We're almost there. An ambulance will be on site as well … just in case. Brian was saying that a lot of kidnapping victims were dehydrated, so we want to be able to give her the proper care immediately."

I leaned forward, my shoulders and neck tight with nerves. "What else did he say?"

Sutton twisted around in her seat so she could see me. "That each situation was different." A wistful expression flickered across her features.

"Can you … can you keep talking to me, please?" My knee bounced so hard I wondered if my leg was shaking the van.

"We'll do anything to help you." Her attention landed on Zayne.

"I told Hendrix that he and Gemma should tie the knot in England," Zayne said.

"Oh, they have some amazing places to visit and get married," Sutton said, perking up.

"I introduced Hendrix and Vicki over the phone. Since she's a wedding planner, I figured she would have some great suggestions for him."

Sutton arched a brow at him. "How is she?"

"Good. She wanted to know if I would be joining the wedding party if Hendrix and Gemma chose a location there."

Sutton giggled softly in the back of the van. "You should take some time off and visit her, Zayne. She's special to you, and an amazing person."

Zayne frowned. "It's too messy. All that would do is open a box that I closed a while ago."

"Mm-hmm. As you know, it had been nine years since Pierce and I ended our relationship."

An exasperated sigh escaped Zayne. "There's someone else, if you must know."

Sutton gaped at Zayne, and I leaned back in my seat. At least this was getting more entertaining. I desperately needed the distraction.

"Who?" Sutton asked, playfully smacking Zayne on the knee.

"I'll tell you when I know more." Zayne held up his hand to halt any additional conversation about the matter.

"Come on. At least tell me where you met her." Sutton wasn't going to let this go. Apparently, Zayne having an interest in someone other than for casual sex was a big deal.

"I met her at a party. No more questions, because right now I have no answers."

Sutton huffed. "Do you know how many parties we attend for business?"

"Yup." Zayne smirked, then stared out the window.

Under normal circumstances I would have laughed. Zayne was thoroughly enjoying messing with Sutton.

The van jostled, nearly bouncing me out of the seat and onto the floor.

"Hang on back there!" Pierce called.

"We're on the makeshift road that leads to the house," Sutton said, grabbing the armrest.

Zayne and I didn't have anything to hold onto since we were on the bench seat in the back. My attention landed on Brian and Pierce, both hanging on to the oh shit handle as we continued to drive down the dirt road. A growing sense of apprehension nagged at me as the vehicle finally came to a stop.

I leaned forward, trying to see where we were. Brian slid the side door open and climbed out. The cold air whipped through the van. *Shit.* We were definitely at a higher elevation.

"Hendrix." Pierce motioned for me to follow him.

Suddenly feeling boxed in, I was unwilling to spend another second inside the van. I hurried around Sutton's seat. Sickness rolled in my belly, and my heart rate picked up while I exited the vehicle.

"Where are we?" I asked quietly.

Brian folded his arms across his chest, his FBI windbreaker rustling in the unforgiving wind that was whipping through the leafless trees.

I shoved my hands into my pockets, attempting to retain even a shred of body heat. Since the trip wasn't planned, I hadn't grabbed a coat when we left. At least the rain had stopped.

"Here, this should fit." Pierce handed me a blue jacket with FBI printed on the back in yellow.

"Thanks." I wasn't sure where he'd gotten it, but I didn't waste any time as I shrugged it on. "Are we near the house where Gemma is being held?"

"Not yet," Sutton said from behind me. She exited the van, landing lightly on her feet.

At that moment, several armed men with night goggles ran into the woods. *Shit. This is real.*

"The home is right through the trees." Brian pointed in the general direction, but it was too dark for me to see. "They're going in to clear any threats."

Black clouds rolled into my thoughts. The possibilities of shit going wrong flooded my mind, and I shook my head and tried to clear the fear. We were so close. Dry leaves scraped along the ground, giving this location an even more eerie feeling.

Pierce gripped my shoulder. "We'll know more in a few minutes."

"Sutton, can you still see the red dot?" I asked, unable to hide the tremble in my voice.

Sutton held her phone up and stared at the screen. I stood behind her and peered over her shoulder.

She glanced up at me. "Dammit. Her signal is gone. Something's wrong. We're too close for me not to pick it up."

Sutton couldn't mask her vulnerability. Panic held me in its vise-like grip.

"Does that mean—" I stepped backward and stumbled on a sharp rock that jutted out from the dirt road.

Pierce quickly grabbed me by the arm before I landed on my ass. "No. It means the signal has a ton of interference. With the trees and mountains, it all makes sense why we had a tough time picking up her location," he said calmly. Before I had a chance to challenge that, he turned to Brian. "Do we have an update of what's happening inside the house?" Pierce rubbed his jaw. He might have appeared calm, but I could feel the fear rolling off of him in waves.

Brian spoke in a hushed tone, and I held my breath while we waited for an update. Without an explanation, Brian placed his finger to his mouth and motioned us to follow him. My pulse skyrocketed with each step I took closer and closer to Gemma. *Is she alive?* I needed to know.

I shoved the nearly debilitating panic aside. Minutes felt like hours as I trudged across the uneven terrain behind Brian. Pierce and Sutton were on my left side, and I wasn't sure where Zayne was anymore.

We reached the edge of the woods, a large home finally coming into view. Lights from the windows broke through the darkness. It took everything inside of me not to dart around Brian and the other agents to find Gemma on my own.

"They've cleared the house. There's no sign of Brandon Montgomery," Brian said.

Fuck Brandon. I needed to know if they'd found my fiancée.

"And Gemma?" Pierce asked before I had a chance to.

Brian pressed his hand to his earpiece, and once again, we waited. My heart was pounding so hard I was afraid it would burst out of my chest.

"Coming through!" Medics raced by me with a gurney.

"Who is that for? Brian, please." My legs trembled. I wasn't sure I would be able to stand much longer.

"She's there. Gemma Thompson is there. But they can't find a pulse."

My entire world screeched to a halt, and I dropped to my knees. "No. No. No. She can't be gone."

Pierce knelt next to me, but I couldn't make out a word he was saying. An arm slipped around my shoulder, and my hair hung in my face, cloaking me from the outside world. *Gemma, hang on. I'm here.*

When I was boxing competitively, I'd been known for being fast and never telegraphing my next move. Not only did my opponent rarely see me coming, but I could also dodge blows like nobody's business.

"Pulse ..."

I wasn't sure what Brian had just said, but I stood slowly, my eyes never leaving his. Before I could second-guess myself, I stepped backward, darted around Sutton and Brian, then hauled ass to the front door.

"God dammit, Harrington!" Pierce yelled.

I didn't look behind me to see how close Pierce was—I just continued to weave through the people blocking my progress. The moment I set foot inside the house, I took a quick inventory of my surroundings. I hightailed it through the living room, then followed the voices up the stairs. My shoes squeaked on the hardwood floor as I ran down the hall. Glimpsing a lock of red hair, I backpedaled, then entered the room.

"Stop!" An older guy grabbed my arm.

"Gemma Thompson. Is she alive? I'm her fiancé. Please. Someone, just tell me." I attempted to peek around the EMTs, dread seeping into every part of my soul as I glimpsed her limp hand hanging off the gurney.

"I'm sorry, son. She's not breathing. You have to stay back while they work on her," the agent said. He moved over so I could stand next to him.

"Gemma, baby, wake up," I said, hoping she could hear me. *Gemma, I don't want the world to turn without you. Please don't leave me behind.* My breath hitched. *Kendra, I need you right now. Gem needs you. It's not her time, so send her back to us.*

Fat hot tears rolled down my cheeks as I paced behind the agent. My legs grew heavy when I was finally able to see Gemma.

"Hendrix," Sutton said from behind me.

"Sutton," I whispered, my throat raw and raspy.

She took my hand in hers, then her other one flew over her mouth when she spotted Gem. The EMTs placed the paddles against Gemma's small frame, and her upper body arched off the gurney. Sutton gave a strangled cry.

"Oh God." I wrapped my arm around her, and we clung to each other as we watched Gemma fight for her life.

I held my breath and mentally pleaded with Gem to come back to me. We had a wedding to plan, a life to live, songs to sing, and hopefully, babies to make. My attention never left her as I imagined a redheaded little girl running and playing in our yard. If we had a daughter, I hoped she would look just like her beautiful mother and carry herself with the same determination and gentleness as Gemma.

My heart skipped a beat as the EMT warmed up the paddles again, then placed them on Gemma's chest. Time stood still as I stared at her with tears in my eyes, my world shattering into a million pieces. I trembled violently, and Sutton tightened her hold around my waist.

The medic placed two fingers on Gemma's neck, his eyes narrowing as he focused. "We've got a pulse! It's faint, but it's there."

A strangled sob escaped my mouth as the EMT placed an oxygen mask over Gemma's face. "Let's go!" They ran out of the room and maneuvered the gurney down the stairs.

I grabbed Sutton's hand and ran after them. "She's my fiancée. Can I ride with you to the hospital?" My words were filled with desperation and hope.

"We're airlifting her to the nearest hospital. There's not enough room."

I hadn't even realized we'd left the house and were standing in the front yard. "Let me ride with you to meet the helicopter!"

A dark-haired younger EMT finally looked at me and gestured with his head. "Come on." They loaded Gemma into the back of the ambulance, then I hopped in.

"Sit over there." The medic pointed toward the corner, and I quickly settled in. And for the first time, I had a full view of Gem. Pale. Thin. And in a fucking wedding dress. *Jesus. Brandon was going to force her into marriage.* My hatred for him was so strong I could taste it on my tongue.

Bile rose in my throat, and panic ripped the air from my lungs as I reached for Gemma's hand. I'd barely reached her in time. "Babe, it's me, Hendrix."

Her fingers were cold to the touch. I placed them between the palms of my hand. "You're safe and on the way to the hospital." Maybe if I continued to talk to her, she would regain consciousness. Although she was breathing again, I realized she wasn't out of the woods yet. Despair saturated every part of me, drowning me in a dark and turbulent sea of sorrow.

The blonde EMT gasped. "Oh my God, you're Hendrix Harrington. I love August Clover."

"Yeah. She's my fiancée and the lead singer with me, so let's make sure she lives."

The guy's attention landed on Gemma, and his eyes widened with recognition. "Sorry, I wasn't trying to be an asshole. I just finally realized who you were."

"No worries, man. I'm stressed to the fucking max right now." I kissed Gemma's knuckles. "Can you get me onto the Life Flight with her?" If August Clover had a fan, I wasn't above bartering for what I wanted.

"I don't know. It's a different crew, but I can try." He held Gemma's wrist and checked her pulse. "It's strong, man. Hang in there. I can't guarantee anything, but she's on the right track."

I appreciated him giving me an update. "Next time we go on tour again, I'll get some front-row tickets and backstage passes for you and a guest. I appreciate you … and your partner bringing her back …" I choked on my words, unable to finish my sentence.

"We didn't recognize her at first," the other medic said. "But it's not our job to. We saw her and got to work."

"You saved her." *Now I need her to make a full recovery and come back to me.*

The ambulance slowed, then came to a complete stop. "I'm Randy. I'll see if they have room for you on the flight."

"Thanks, man."

The next several minutes were a flurry of activity while they loaded Gemma onto the helicopter. I held her hand until I was forced to let go.

"Hendrix Harrington?" A tall, thin man who appeared to be in his forties approached me.

"Yes, sir." I wasn't sure who he was, but if there was a chance that he could get me on the flight with Gemma, then I wanted to be as polite as possible.

"We've got space for you. Come with me."

I jogged behind him, anxious to be next to her again. After I squeezed in beside her, I planted a kiss on her forehead. "I've missed you so much, babe. You're the beat of my heart …"

I began whispering my vows to her as the blades began to turn faster. My fingers were intertwined through hers while I spoke softly.

The *thump-thump* of the blades accelerating rang in my ears as we lifted off the ground.

Gemma's hold tightened slightly, and a trickle of hope flowed through me. "Babe? It's Hendrix." I felt as though I was yelling at her, but with the noise, I wasn't sure she could even hear me. "You're safe. We're on the way to a hospital."

Her eyes fluttered open, and a look of sheer terror twisted her face. My insides crumbled when she began screaming into the air. It was tortured and heartbreaking. Her whole body was rigid and strained.

The EMT attempted to calm her down, but she continued to cry out and thrash. I moved out of the way and pursed my lips in order to remain silent so the EMT could help her. Yelling at him to do his job wouldn't help the situation. Within seconds, her outbursts stopped, and her eyes fluttered closed again.

"What did you do?" I asked, frantic. *Did she die again? Did she slip out of my grasp once more?*

"Nothing. It seems like she was hallucinating, and now she's out cold again." He placed his fingers against her neck. "Her pulse is good. We're in the air, and it's dangerous to have an out-of-control patient while we're flying. But maybe she'll stay calm until we land. You can come back up now."

I carefully moved next to her again. Her scream had ripped my heart out. She had to be okay. She had to come back to me. Kissing her hand, I swore that I would personally end Brandon Montgomery. I didn't need Pierce or Zayne's permission. It was up to me to protect my family.

The helicopter lurched sideways, and I tried to grab something to hold onto. It felt as though I was being tossed around like a rag doll in the back of a pickup truck on a dirt road.

"What the hell is happening?" I yelled, glancing at my fiancée, who was out cold. I was suddenly grateful she wasn't witnessing this turbulence.

The EMT hurried to check the straps that secured Gemma to the gurney. We pitched forward again, launching me across the small space. "Shit!" The whine of the engines grew louder as I struggled to find anything to hold onto.

"Hang on!" the pilot yelled. "I'm going to try to set her down, but the winds are really bad!"

I glanced at the EMT as he made the sign of the cross over his chest. "Tell her goodbye now, man. We're fucking going down."

My heels dug into the floor as the engines whined. I flung myself over Gemma in order to protect her if the pilot wasn't able to land us safely. Not that it mattered, but if we were going down, at least we were together, and I could die along with the one person I loved more than life itself.

I closed my eyes and silently sent messages to Dad, Janice, Mac, and Cade that I loved them. If Gemma and I didn't walk off this helicopter…

A loud metal screech filled the air, and the helicopter shook violently. I held onto Gemma, and somehow, my mouth found her ear. "I love you, Gemma. I love you so fucking much."

I hoped like hell she wouldn't wake during this shitstorm. If we happened to land in one piece, then I wanted nothing more than to see her beautiful blue eyes open. But not when the helicopter was on its way to crashing.

The next several seconds seemed like an eternity as we bounced around. Then in one quick moment, the chaos stopped, and the helicopter righted itself. I peered at the EMT, afraid to hope that we'd made it through the worst part.

"Well, that was a fucked-up ride," the pilot said. "We made it, though. Prepare to land."

I sat up and sucked in a deep breath, my hands shaking from the near-death experience. Apparently, someone was watching out for Gemma, because she'd cheated death twice in one night.

Smoothing her hair back from her forehead, I hoped I hadn't crushed Gem in my attempt to protect her. The EMT scrambled over to check on her, and I held my breath until he confirmed that she was all right. I ran a hand through my hair as my gaze fell on my fiancée. I wasn't sure what her recovery would look like, but I couldn't wait to slip a ring on her finger and call her my wife. Life was too fucking short to wait much longer.

A few minutes later, we landed on the helipad of the hospital roof. Once again, the EMTs were in action, and I followed them through the entrance doors. Information was exchanged concerning Gemma's condition, and as hard as I tried, I couldn't follow what they were saying. A burly guy walked toward the gurney, and I jogged behind them as they wheeled her to a room.

"One, two, three!" They lifted Gemma's limp form from the gurney to a hospital bed. I remained in the corner of the sterile white room while they cut the wedding dress off her thin body. I wanted to burn that fucking gown, but I also wanted to cover Gemma's nakedness and protect her. Then I realized the medics weren't ogling her breasts. They were focused on saving her. These guys probably saw naked women of all ages, sizes, and ethnicities.

A nurse took Gemma's vitals and drew blood while I watched help-lessly. I'd given the hospital permission to run any tests they needed to. I'd lied and told them I was her husband, which in my mind I already was. When the nurse asked me about the different last names, I told them we were the lead singers for August Clover, and for professional reasons, Gemma had kept her last name. As far as I was concerned, a little piece of paper wasn't going to stop Gemma from getting the right medical care. If the doctor gave me shit about it, I would ask Dad to help me.

The burly guy began to secure leather straps around Gemma's

wrists, and I darted forward. "What the hell? No." I grabbed the restraint and slipped it off her.

"It's only for a little while. We have to make sure she's not a danger to herself or others."

"If anyone restrains her, it will be me." I tapped my finger in the middle of his chest, backing him away from Gemma. "She's traumatized. She's not going to hurt anyone. I'll stay with her, but if you come near her with those again, I'll fucking tear you limb from limb," I growled. *Mess with me, motherfucker.*

Burly tossed his hands in the air and backed out of the room.

"Asshole," I mumbled as I returned to Gemma. I smoothed her hair off her forehead and tossed the restraint into the trash.

I sat on the side of the bed and leaned forward, relieved everyone had left us alone. "I'm going to kiss you." With a featherlight touch, I brushed my lips against hers and attempted to bring her back to me. "I'm not sure why you're still unconscious, but I'll be the happiest man alive when you wake up. I can't wait to see your beautiful blue eyes."

No response. I held my fingers against her neck, checking her pulse. When I found it, I released the breath I hadn't been aware that I was holding.

I placed my ear against her chest and listened to her heartbeat. Seconds later, I finally lost my shit. I crawled into the bed next to her, lay on my side, and wrapped my arms around her while my tears landed in her hair. The anger flowed out of me, and all I wanted was for her to wake up. We could deal with anything else together.

I thought losing Kendra had broken me, but I was wrong. Holding Gemma in my arms after seeing her dead had reduced me to a fucked-up mess. Even though it would be difficult, I could lose everyone else in my life but not her. Not my Gem.

I tightened my grip around her as I muffled my cries against the pillow. "I won't give up on you, babe. I refuse to give up on us."

"Hendrix."

I knew that beautiful voice anywhere.

"Gemma," I whispered and kissed her forehead again. "I'm right here. You're safe."

Her head lolled to the side, and I realized she was most likely dreaming. At least it was my name on her lips. Even in her dreams, I was with her. I wrapped my body around hers, willing her to realize she was safe and warm next to me. Before I knew it, my eyes had closed.

"Mr. Harrington."

I sat up slowly, trying to identify who was speaking my name.

"I'm Dr. Bakersfield."

My attention landed on a lanky man with dark hair who looked as though he was in his late thirties. I slid out of Gemma's bed. "Sorry. It's been a hell of a week." I shoved my hands in my pocket as Dr. Bakersfield approached Gemma's bed. "Is she going to be okay? When is she going to wake up?"

"From the toxicology report, the drug has been in her system for about eight hours. It will have run its course soon. From what I understand, her trauma is extensive."

My eyes narrowed. "Drugged? Extensive?"

"Kidnapping, drugging—it appears that the reason her heart stopped was due to an overdose of ... honestly, we're not sure what it is. It had some similar components to GHB, but this was absorbed through her skin instead of digested. It was most likely engineered in a makeshift lab. Our team here hasn't seen anything like it before. Whoever administered it didn't account for her weight. Or they meant to kill her."

I stared at the white tile floor as my thoughts crashed violently around. Brandon had screwed up. He wouldn't have put her in a wedding dress, then killed her. He was obsessed with her. He wanted her. He was planning a life with Gemma.

I suspected that whatever drug Brandon had put in her system, he had no clue of what he was doing. Folding my hands over my chest, I made a concerted effort not to blow my fuse. A fresh sprinkle of hatred for Brandon crawled over my skin.

Dad's words rang in the back of my mind: "He walked out of there hardened. He's smarter and more dangerous."

I sucked in a deep breath. "My guess is Brandon Montgomery."

Dr. Bakersfield unwrapped the stethoscope from his neck and placed it beneath Gemma's hospital gown, listening to her heart. After a few more minutes, he finished his preliminary tests. "She should wake up soon. If she's hysterical, we'll try to calm her. If we're not able to, we'll sedate her."

I ground my molars. "So you're just going to keep her quiet until you want to deal with her?"

"It might seem like it, but in a few more hours, she should start to orient herself to her new surroundings. If you can be with her, touch her ... talk to her, then she'll come out of her haze more grounded. Once she's awake, we'll run a brain scan and check her heart."

A soft knock at the door pulled my attention away from the doctor. I glanced over my shoulder, tears forming in my eyes. "Dad!" I rushed to him, then gently hugged him. I'd almost forgotten about his healing ribs.

"I'm here, son. It's a short flight from Spokane." Dad wrapped his arms around me gingerly. "I'm here."

I leaned my head against his shoulder, allowing the comfort he offered to settle my frayed nerves. "I lost her. She died right in front of me." My words caught in my throat.

Dad's body went rigid, then he took a deep breath. "She's back, son. That's what we have to focus on." He held me tightly, then patted my back before releasing me.

"Where's Janice, Mac, and Cade?"

"They're at home. If Gemma has to stay more than a day, they'll fly over. I didn't want her to get overwhelmed."

"Makes sense. Pierce and Sutton were still at the house where we found Gemma. I suspect they're on the way here by now."

I loved my sister, but she could be a handful, and I needed some time to process. My heart jumped as the image of Gemma's dead body flashed through my mind. *She fucking died.* The room was beginning to close in on me when Dad's voice broke through my escalating alarm.

"I'm Franklin Harrington." Dad extended his hand to Dr. Bakersfield. "Thank you for taking care of my daughter-in-law."

"Of course." Dr. Bakersfield's brows knitted together. "Aren't you … weren't you kidnapped? You were all over the news."

Dad carefully put a hand on his hip, slipping into full attorney mode. "Yes, and she's the reason I'm alive. I want her moved to a private room. Her bodyguards will watch her door as long as she's here."

"Bodyguards?" The doctor's composure faltered.

"My son," Dad nodded at me, "and Gemma are lead singers for August Clover. They have their own security. Plus, a very dangerous man is still on the loose. He's the same man that kidnapped me."

Dr. Bakersfield scratched his chin. "I understand. Do you need treatment?"

Dad dropped his hand to his side, visibly tensing. "No, thank you. I've already been treated in Spokane. I'm here for my kids."

Even though Dad wasn't anywhere near healed physically or mentally, he was here when I needed him, and that meant the world to me.

"I'll have an executive room prepared right away." Dr. Bakersfield cleared his throat. "Does she have—"

"She has insurance, and any additional expenses should be sent to me. She gets the best doctors and the best care. Do you understand?"

"Of course." The doctor excused himself, then hurried out of the room.

"Thanks, Dad." I shoved my hands into my pockets. "I know you're not up to being here right now, but I sure am glad you are."

Dad squeezed the back of my neck. "A few broken ribs couldn't keep me away, son. Gemma saved my life. I'm going to make sure she has everything she needs to make a full recovery."

Before I could respond, a knock on the door interrupted our conversation. A detective and police officer sauntered in, an air of arrogance surrounding them.

"Can I help you?" Dad stood between them and Gemma.

I nearly chuckled as Dad cut them off. I walked over to Gemma's bed and held her hand.

"I'm Detective Radcliff, and this is Officer Peterson. We were hoping to speak to Gemma Thompson."

I narrowed my eyes as I assessed the men. Detective Radcliff looked like he needed a few meals. The belt on his black slacks was on the last notch, but they were still hanging off him. His thinning gray dark hair told me he'd been a detective for years. I wondered if he'd ever been married or if his job consumed every aspect of his life.

I pegged Officer Peterson as being in his mid-thirties. His dark eyes were alert, and I could tell that he was absorbing every detail as Dad spoke. When I was little, Dad had started drilling into me the idea that body language and tics spoke louder than words.

"She's sleeping. You'll have to come back another time," Dad said in his no bullshit tone.

The detective arched an eyebrow. "And you are …?"

"Her attorney. I'm sure she'll be happy to speak with you when she's awake, but right now, please respect her privacy."

Officer Peterson took a step forward, and Dad blocked him. "Here's the situation. You need to question the FBI who were on the scene, then speak to the medical staff and ask them to notify you when Gemma wakes up. She was drugged and hallucinating. Your presence and attitude could lead to more hysterics and trauma."

"Of course, Mr. Harrington. But we'd love to speak with you as well. From the information that we have, the same man took you and Gemma. Is that correct?"

Dad's jaw clenched. "That depends on who you think it was."

I wasn't sure why Dad was trying to stall them. They needed any help they could get to track that bastard down.

"Brandon Montgomery," Officer Peterson said.

"Let's take this conversation elsewhere, then." Dad turned toward me, fear flickering in his expression.

"Are you sure?" I approached him. "If you wait until Pierce and Sutton get here, then I can go with you." Every time he had to tell someone what happened, I assumed he relived the rape. I also understood that his sexual assault would never make it into a police report. A part of me wanted to protect him from reliving his nightmare, but I also realized that the police needed every scrap of information possible to locate Brandon. Although I wouldn't verbalize it, I hoped like hell I would find the bastard first. Until then, I would enjoy imagining every possible scenario of making him suffer until he took his last breath.

"I've got it. You focus on Gemma. I'll be back as soon as I'm finished." Dad nodded, assuring me that he would be all right.

Within the next half hour, Gemma was transferred to the VIP suite. The tiny hairs on the back of my neck bristled when I laid eyes on the security guard outside her door. At that point, I wasn't crazy about a stranger guarding her. *Where are Pierce, Zayne, and Sutton?*

"Who sent you?" I stood eye to eye with the short, stocky man.

"Dr. Bakersfield and a man named Franklin Harrington." He showed me his ID.

I tipped my chin up at him, then quietly entered Gemma's room, keeping my attention trained on her. Maybe I needed to relax, but there was no way in hell I would leave her alone. I didn't trust anyone except my close friends and family.

My phone buzzed, and I removed it from my pocket. I tapped the screen and answered the FaceTime call.

"You son of a bitch!" Brandon screamed at me. "How dare you take Gemma! How dare you!" Brandon tugged on his hair as he paced the floor in front of his phone. He slammed his palms on the top of a table. "We had a deal, Harrington. She willingly came to me. It was a permanent agreement. The minute I left to pick up her wedding gift and my tux, you stole her!"

My mind scrambled with an idea while I waited for him to stop ranting. I inhaled deeply before I spoke. "You killed her, you sick fuck," I yelled as I managed to produce a few tears.

In an instant, Brandon's expression morphed from fury to shock to fear. "You're lying. She was fine when I left."

"You overdosed her. She was dead by the time I got there. The police and FBI are looking for you, but you'd better pray they don't find you." I ground my teeth.

Wild-eyed and confused, Brandon ran a hand over his short hair. "You don't want me caught?"

"Yeah. Do you want to know why? I'm going to hunt you down and kill you myself. No one takes my fiancée and lives to tell about it. I would start running if I were you."

"I really killed her?" A mixture of awe and remorse hung from his words.

He was a wreck, so I suspected our conversation would take a while to sink in. I hoped like hell I could keep Gemma's return out of the media. If Brandon thought she was dead, it would buy us some time.

I was seething and teetering on the edge of losing control. "You really did. See you in hell, motherfucker." I ended the video call and rolled my shoulders, trying to relieve the tension. The day we were finally free from Brandon and Dillon Montgomery, we would have a huge-ass celebration.

"We're here," Pierce said as he entered the room. "Brian contacted one of his security connections, Michael. He just replaced the guard outside the door. How's she doing?" He entered the room with Sutton and Zayne strolling in behind him.

"She's still not awake," I said. "But Brandon thinks she's dead. At least, that's what I told him to throw him off her trail. I was trying to buy us some time." I massaged my forehead and held up my phone. "The bastard just FaceTimed me, screaming at me for taking Gemma."

Pierce chuckled. "Good call. Hopefully he believes you, and we can keep her hidden for a while."

Zayne approached the foot of Gemma's bed, his attention landing on her. "I'm glad she's here," he said softly.

"Me too."

"What happened after you got into the ambulance?" Pierce leaned against the wall, and his concerned gaze landed on my fiancée.

"It was a nightmare." I reached in the front pocket of my jeans and pulled out a hair band, then quickly gathered my loose strands and pulled them into a man bun. Gemma always loved when I sported that look. Maybe it would help her smile when she woke up.

Sutton pointed at the chair nearest Gemma's bed. "Sit."

I wearily sank down into the chair and propped my elbows on my knees, trying to still my galloping pulse.

"What happened?" Sutton sat in the seat next to me.

"The helicopter almost crashed. We hit some bad winds, and I thought we were going to die. Even the EMT told me to tell Gemma goodbye."

"Holy shit." Sutton grabbed my hand. "But you're both here. You made it." She nodded emphatically as though she were trying to convince herself that Gem and I were safe.

"She woke up in the helicopter hysterical, then she was unconscious again. Thank God she was out cold during the worst of the flight. That would have been really screwed up if she'd regained consciousness right before we thought we were going to crash and die." I leaned back and glanced at Gem, but she hadn't moved. "The doctor hopes she'll wake up soon since the drug should be leaving her system."

Three puzzled faces stared at me. "What drug?" Pierce asked, fury blazing in his eyes.

I updated them on the conversation I'd had with the doctor about how the drug was similar to GHB. "All we can do is wait."

"I'm wondering if Brandon drugged Gemma so he could force her into marriage," Sutton speculated. "It's the only way she would have agreed. Like she'd be confused and not realize what was happening. She could have hallucinated like she did on the helicopter and thought she was marrying you instead. Luckily, we got to her in time."

I stretched my legs in front of me and stifled a yawn. "The doctor said the reason she … died …" My voice sounded haunted. "Was because she'd been overdosed with whatever the hell Brandon gave to her."

Sutton's nostrils flared, and she balled her hands into fists. "That son of a bitch had better hope the police get to him first." Her tone was harsh and lethal.

"I've been plotting his murder for a while now. You're welcome to join me." I tried to give her a playful smile, but I couldn't because I wasn't kidding. I glanced at Zayne, who had a wicked sneer on his face, but he remained quiet.

"We'll discuss this after Gemma is home. Don't think for a minute that we'll let that sick son of a bitch get away with what he's done." Pierce's eyes narrowed, and a vein in his neck bulged.

He was pissed, but not as much as I was. My stomach growled loudly, interrupting my thoughts.

"When did you eat last?" Sutton dug a small paper bag out of her purse and handed it to me.

I opened the bag, the savory smell of carbs tickling my nostrils. A warm croissant caught my attention. "This morning, I think? I can't remember. Oh, man. This looks amazing. Thanks." In three bites, I wolfed it down.

"I'll get you some food and coffee. Anyone else need anything?" Zayne asked.

"I think we could all use a bite to eat and some caffeine." Sutton reached into her bag and removed her wallet.

"I've got it." Zayne left the room before she could argue with him.

I nodded, the weight of the last week crashing into me like a tsunami, but instead of spitting me out on dry land, it was still sucking me under. "Dad's here. He's talking to a detective and officer about Brandon."

Pierce pushed off the wall. "Any idea where they are?"

"No, man. Maybe …" I gave a half shrug, my mind drawing a blank.

"I'll find out. I'm going to check on Franklin, then I'll be back." Pierce strolled over to his wife and kissed her before he left.

"He's protective of Franklin … of all of you." Sutton released my hand and sat back, her attention landing on Gemma.

"Zayne and Pierce will guard Gemma's room tonight. I want you both to get some sleep if you can. I'll stay with Franklin."

A thick silence hung in the air. "Thank you. I don't want Dad to be alone. Although he was relieved to see Gemma alive, the look on his face …" I shook my head, a sharp pain stabbing me in the heart. "I knew it caused flashbacks for him. I fucking hate it. I hate what happened to him." I choked on my words and dragged my hands down my cheeks in an attempt to wake myself from this nightmare. "When is it going to stop?" I glanced at Sutton and wished like hell she had an answer for me.

"Soon."

I caught the confidence in her voice. Maybe she was aware of something I wasn't.

13

The soft light over Gemma's bed hummed in the otherwise quiet room. I stood and stretched, my muscles screaming at me. Apparently I'd given them a workout on the helicopter ride.

I peeked into the hallway and told Pierce and Zayne I was going to try to get a few minutes of sleep. Then I crawled onto the mattress next to Gemma and wrapped my arms around her. "You're finally back where you belong." I smoothed her hair and kissed her forehead.

The warmth of her skin soothed my frazzled nerves, and the gentle rise and fall of her chest reminded me that she was actually alive. A few days before, I hadn't been sure I would ever see her again. Earlier in the day, she'd died. I couldn't lose her again.

Cold fear wrapped its fingers around my chest. The images of her lying lifeless stole my breath, and my palms grew clammy. My world had come to a screeching halt as I watched her body jump from the volts of electricity traveling through her.

A little voice whispered that she wasn't out of danger yet. I kicked that thought in the ass and reminded myself that the medics had revived her. My throat ached with pent-up emotion as I watched her sleep.

I held her hand and stroked her knuckles with my thumb. "I love you, Gem." Suppressing a territorial growl, I realized her engagement ring wasn't on her finger. In my gut, I knew Brandon had taken it. My nostrils flared as I imagined my hands wrapped around his neck, squeezing the life out of him. That ring wasn't his to take. Gemma wasn't his to take. She was *mine*.

"Hendrix?" A whisper floated through the air and reached my ears.

My head shot off the pillow, and I stared into the most beautiful blue eyes I'd ever seen.

"Gemma, I'm here. You're safe."

She scrambled to get free of the sheets, but I was on top of them.

"Babe, it's Hendrix." I placed my hands on her cheeks, hoping to ground her before she became hysterical. "Look at me. You're next to me in a hospital bed. I needed to hold you, so I crawled in beside you. You're safe, Gem. You're safe."

Her gaze connected with mine, and my heart constricted at the sight of her so scared. Her face was full of tears and distress. She was a wreck, and the fear, hope, and dismay in her expression collided and crashed into her all at once.

She grabbed my hands and gripped them. "It's really you?" Her entire body shook against mine.

"It really is."

She gave an anguished cry as she grabbed my shirt and bunched it in her fist.

"I've got you. I'm never going to let you go again," I said softly, attempting to soothe her.

Her hot tears soaked my shirt, then she peered up at me. "Franklin? Is he all right? Did he make it home?" Her voice was raw, and her eyes flickered with a hint of panic.

I wiped the moisture from her skin with the pad of my thumb. "He's safe. He has some broken ribs, but he's healing. Dad has been at the hospital all day, but he's next door at the hotel right now. Sutton is with him."

"Oh God." Her hand trembled as she massaged her temple. "I was so scared he wouldn't make it back. He was in so much pain, and I was worried that he had internal injuries." She tugged on my shirt. "Kiss me, Hendrix. Please."

I didn't waste any time as my lips gently caressed hers.

With a heated frenzy, her mouth dominated mine. "If I'm not dreaming that you're here, then show me. Please." Desperation clung to her words, and I struggled with what to do. Her hand slid beneath my shirt, and my cock jerked and stiffened. Gemma flicked the buttons open on my jeans, and her fingers wrapped around my dick before I realized what she was doing. She'd barely woken up from a drug overdose. We shouldn't have sex.

"I need you inside of me," she pleaded.

"Gem." I hesitated. "Babe. I need to know first." I gulped as dread coursed through my body. "Were you …?" I couldn't force the horrible word out of my mouth.

She shook her head furiously. "No. Brandon didn't hurt me like that."

I released my breath, but I didn't miss what she'd said. Thank God she hadn't been raped, but he'd definitely hurt her. "You would tell me, right?"

"Yeah." She let me go, then slipped out from under the sheet. "I need you. I need to know I'm safe. Make me forget everything else for a few minutes."

Gemma eased her gown up to her thighs, straddled me, then slid my cock inside her. I'd forgotten she was completely naked beneath the thin hospital fabric. Gemma lay down on top of me, and I wrapped my arms around her, careful not to pull on the IV in her arm.

"Thank you," she whispered, her lips grazing my ear.

I gently lifted my hips and elicited a soft groan from her. Although sex with Gem was always amazing, I realized it wasn't about an orgasm. She needed to connect with me again on the deepest level possible. We couldn't be any closer mentally or physically than we were at that moment. I needed this as much as she did.

"I missed you so much, Hendrix." She sat up and slowly rocked against me. "I thought about you every second we were apart."

I slid my hand up her gown, then cupped and massaged her breast.

"Never again. We'll never be apart again." This time, I would make sure I kept that promise. Nothing would rip us apart again.

We found a slow and steady rhythm as everything else in the world slipped away. All of the fucked-up shit we'd just lived through faded into the background, and I made love to the only girl who had ever owned my heart.

THE NEXT MORNING, Gemma had the MRI and heart tests. To our relief, the doctors didn't find any damage. Gem was going to physically recover. After the news, she returned to her room, snuggled under the blankets in the bed, then drifted off in my arms.

The creak of the door jolted me from a deep sleep. I stood quickly and remained next to Gemma. She yawned, and her eyes fluttered open.

"Excellent, you're awake," the detective said. Dad and Pierce were directly behind the officer.

"Franklin!" Gemma scrambled to sit up and jump out of bed.

"Whoa." I wrapped my arms around her and pulled her to me. "Take it slow, babe. Plus, your gown is open in the back," I said as quietly as I could.

Her cheeks flamed red, and she quickly covered herself with the lumpy white hospital blanket.

Dad approached Gem, then carefully embraced her. "Hey, Gemma. Welcome home."

Tears streamed down her face as they held each other in silence. I suspected they were both reliving the moment they'd had to say goodbye before the exchange. The mere thought of it nearly killed me. I couldn't imagine what it had done to them. I understood that since their shared experience, they had a bond that no one else would understand. Hopefully, it would help both of them heal.

Dad released her, tears welling in his eyes. "The authorities have some questions. Are you up for it?" He took her hand in his and squeezed it gently.

Gemma's attention bounced between Franklin, Detective Radcliff, and Officer Peterson.

Pierce waltzed farther into the room, wearing a big grin. "Before you decide, I need a hug."

"Pierce!" A huge smile eased across her face.

Pierce hugged her so hard he nearly jerked her out of bed. Her laugh floated through the air, healing my heart a little bit.

"I missed you tons. Zayne and Sutton are here too. They'll be in shortly. They're in the hallway right now," Pierce explained.

Gemma's arms dropped from Pierce's neck, fear clouding her features. She remained sitting up, her body rigid. Unsure of what had just triggered her, I placed my hand on her back, then rubbed her soft skin in small circles. It had always helped her before, and I hoped it would now.

She nodded at Dad.

"Okay, gentlemen, she's ready to talk to you. Gemma, this is Detective Radcliff and Officer Peterson."

The detective stroked his chin. "We've already spoken with Franklin, and we'd like to hear your version of the story."

"Do you have specific questions?" Gemma asked, her voice calm.

"How did Brandon Montgomery contact you for the exchange?" Officer Peterson asked.

Gemma played with the tie on the side of her gown. "He used FaceTime to reach me. He said he would let Franklin go but he wanted me in his place. He said if I told anyone ..." Gem turned to me, tears streaming down her cheeks. "Brandon said if I told anyone about the trade that he would slit Franklin's throat in front of me, so I didn't take any chances. Franklin is the only real father I've ever had. I had to help him."

I took her hand in mine. With those few words, everything made sense, and the last remnants of my anger about her decision slipped away. She glanced up at Dad, and he placed a gentle kiss on the top of her head.

Detective Radcliff's brow arched as he witnessed Dad's fatherly affection toward Gemma. "So, this is actually a conflict of interest." He pointed between the two of them.

"No. I'm making sure that you question her appropriately and not try to pull any bullshit. If you think she needs to be charged with anything, which would be appalling, she'll have different legal representation."

Officer Peterson ran his fingers along his jaw. "At this time, there's nothing to charge her with."

Every part of my being bristled at his comment, and I wondered how in the hell they would be able to charge her at any time.

"We're simply trying to piece together what happened so we know where to look for Brandon Montgomery. He's all we care about," Officer Peterson explained.

Gemma released a soft sigh. "I obviously made the exchange."

"What happened after that?" the detective asked.

"I spit in his face." She tilted her chin up in defiance as she spoke.

Pierce and I chuckled. Even the officer and detective couldn't hide their grins.

"He knocked me out after that, so I don't remember much. All I know is that we were in Montana, and he is in the process of rebuilding the Dark Circle Society. He showed me the blueprints for the new headquarters. Brandon wouldn't tell me where it was, but my guess was Colorado from the way he was talking about it."

"What were his plans for the society?" Detective Radcliff asked.

"Trafficking of underaged girls, auctions. He had some girls at the house to serve him food and ... sexually. They appeared to be under eighteen, but I wasn't sure."

"Why did he want you?" the detective continued.

Gemma shrugged. "I think he told me, but I don't remember."

"When you were found, you were in a wedding gown asleep on a bed. Do you know why?"

Gemma flinched. "No."

"Where did you stay in the house?" the officer asked.

"I don't know," Gem whispered.

"Were you ever downstairs?" The officer probed again.

"Gentlemen, please get to the point," Dad said.

"Gemma, were you aware that there were prison cells downstairs, and did you ever see anyone in them?"

Unable to control my reaction to that information, I flinched. *Holy shit.* If Brandon had locked her away, then that could explain the lack of a signal. *But in a goddamned cage? Jesus. That bastard keeps getting sicker and sicker.*

Gemma shuddered, and she gripped the bedrail, her breathing becoming labored. She placed the palms of her hands against the sides of her head. "No."

"Are you sure? From your reaction, I'm thinking you did."

"That's enough for today." Dad hurried to the door and opened it. "You can contact me if you have any additional questions. I'll make sure she supplies any details she remembers, but not today. She's too traumatized."

It was good to see Dad's badass side kick in. No one messed with Franklin Harrington. He was a shark in and out of the courtroom and had connections across the country. Dad could pull whatever strings necessary to get what he wanted. I respected the hell out of him because he still played by the rules. I was sure he bent them some, but he never broke the law. At least, not that I was aware of.

Officer Peterson and Detective Radcliff handed Dad business cards before they left.

Gemma collapsed against me. "Take me home, Hendrix. Please, just take me home."

My heart somersaulted. I wasn't sure how to help her if I didn't understand what had happened. For the first time, I realized I might never know the truth. I hoped like hell she would never remember if forgetting the experience helped her heal faster.

After the authorities left, Sutton came in. She sat on the side of Gemma's bed, her gaze filling with love and compassion. "I'm glad you're back."

"Me too. I missed everyone so much," Gemma said.

Gemma sounded like someone who'd been away on vacation

instead of with a monster for several days. She was shutting her emotions off faster than I'd ever seen before.

"Did the serum not work? Is that ..." Gem's eyes had a faraway look. "I thought you would never find me. Although I lost track of time, I remember counting at least two days. By then, I knew something had to have gone wrong."

Sutton glanced at me. Feeling restless, I reached in my pocket for a hair tie and slid it on my wrist. After I lost Kendra, my therapist had recommended I gently pull on it and allow it to pop my skin. It was a fast way to bring myself out of the painful memories and ground myself in the present moment. I hadn't used the technique in years, but this seemed like the time to revive it. Maybe it would help Gemma too.

"I received an anonymous video call. I don't know who she is, but she had the location of the house. Once Sutton was able to determine that the information was accurate, we were on our way." I folded my arms across my chest. "Did you ever meet a woman in her late forties? Blonde, well-dressed, and poised?"

Gemma stared at me. "No. I remember guards, Brandon, and his girls, but I'm missing large chunks of time, so I don't know if anyone else was around or not."

"Don't push yourself, Gemma," Dad said from the foot of her bed. "You need to rest and feel safe. That's the main priority." His concerned gaze connected with mine.

"Dad's right. The important thing is that you're with us again. That's what matters." I leaned over and kissed her on the forehead. "I'm going to find the doctor and see if you're well enough to go home." I strolled toward the door, then turned to face her. "By the way, in order for me to be able to make medical choices for you, I told them we were married. They questioned the different last names, so I explained that you kept Thompson because you were the lead singer for August Clover." I shoved a hand into my pocket. "Also, Brandon thinks you're dead. He contacted me after the FBI found you. I told Brandon that he killed you. Dad will make sure your medical records are sealed so no one will be able to hack into the system and get your information. This is the best way to keep you safe."

With one smile, Gemma reduced me to a puddle of mush on the floor. That girl owned me, and I was man enough to admit it. "Thank you," she said.

"You don't have to thank me, Gem. I love you."

As soon as I left Gem's room, I reminded myself to ask Sutton if she'd learned who my anonymous caller was. More than that, I needed to know why the woman had been willing to give Brandon up and help me when I didn't have a clue about who she was.

I approached the nurse's station and requested to speak with Dr. Bakersfield or whoever could evaluate and release Gemma. Gem wasn't the only one eager to get home. Then I headed outside, desperate for some fresh air. I needed to clear my clouded thoughts.

A bitterly cold breeze greeted me as I walked through the automatic doors to the front of the hospital. I shivered and rubbed my arms and mentally reprimanded myself for forgetting the FBI jacket upstairs. Pulling the band from my hair, I continued to walk and stretch my legs. I hadn't visited Montana before, and I wondered what the view would be like from the roof. If Gemma and Dad hadn't been held hostage in this state, I would have considered exploring the area as a possible place to live. It was obvious that Spokane was becoming too dangerous for us to stay. Maybe it was time to go off the radar for a while.

The more I walked, the warmer I became, so I continued down the sidewalk and around the corner of the building. I took deep breaths, drawing the bitter cold air into my lungs.

My phone buzzed in my back pocket, and I slowed as I reached for it. I frowned at the number. It was most likely spam, but it could be the detective with some new information about Brandon.

"Hello?" I leaned against the brick wall, attempting to hide from the wind. Dead leaves skittered across the sidewalk, scraping the cement like fingers on a chalkboard.

"How is she?"

An introduction wasn't necessary. I recognized the voice of the woman who'd told me where to find Gemma.

"Relatively speaking, she's okay. Alive, so that counts for something."

"I'm sure you're trying to process that the love of your life died right in front of you."

I frowned. Hard. *How the hell could she have that information?*

"Who are you?" I didn't try to hide my confusion. "How do you know that?"

"I've made it my business to know. As for your other question …"

I waited in silence to see if she would tell me who she was and why she had a sudden interest in my life.

14

"We can discuss it later, but please tell Franklin I hope he's well."

"Tell him *who* hopes he's well?"

"In time, Hendrix, you'll learn all about me," she said gently.

I clenched my jaw in frustration. "I don't understand. Just tell me who you are and what you want."

"Hendrix." Her tone was wistful. "Help Gemma and Franklin heal. That's all you need to worry about right now."

Before I could respond, the line went dead. "Shit!" I stared at my phone to make sure the call had actually ended. A mix of anger and curiosity flowed through me. Someone was feeding this woman information. Fear crept down my spine. This lady was apparently well-connected. A niggling thought took shape in my mind. *What if she has a nurse or doctor watching us now, and she is actually an enemy?* I bolted around the corner of the building, then took off running toward Gemma. *We need to leave. Now.*

A few minutes later, I darted down the hall to Gem's room.

"Whoa." Zayne stuck his arm out in front of me.

"I need to get Gem. We need to go," I said, my breathing labored from my near sprint up several flights of stairs. The elevators were too slow.

"Is she in danger?" Zayne dropped his arm.

"I don't know. I—she called me again." I didn't have to explain to Zayne who I was talking about because he was immediately on the same page. "She knew Gemma had died and the medics revived her. Someone is watching us or ..." Frazzled, I ran my fingers through my hair.

"You have to calm down before you go in there, though. You're going to freak Gemma out. Sutton is still with her, and no one else has come or gone. I've been here the entire time."

"The doctor hasn't stopped by yet?"

"Nope." Zayne shook his head for emphasis.

Without another word, I spun on my heel and hurried to the nurse's station. Before I started to quiz the nurse about the whereabouts of Dr. Bakersfield, he rounded the corner.

"Mr. Harrington."

"Doctor." I followed him down the hall toward Gemma's room.

The doctor reached the door, but Zayne was in front of it, blocking him. "Arms up."

"I'm sorry, what?" A look of dismay crossed Dr. Bakersfield's face.

"I'm Gemma's bodyguard, and you have to be searched for anything that could be used as a weapon before you can enter."

"This is ridiculous. I'm her doctor."

Zayne took a step forward and peered down at the man, who barely cleared Zayne's chin. "It's also ridiculous that she was kidnapped and poisoned," Zayne growled.

If the situation hadn't been so serious, I would have laughed my ass off. Zayne wasn't messing around. Dr. Bakersfield's attention landed on me, and I nodded. The phone call from the mysterious woman had me on edge, and I didn't trust anyone other than my family and friends.

The doctor raised his hands in the air and allowed Zayne to pat him down.

"That wasn't so bad, now, was it?" Zayne quirked an eyebrow, then stood back.

Dr. Bakersfield cleared his throat as he strolled into Gem's room as though he didn't have a care in the world. I was right behind him.

"How are you feeling today, Gemma?" he asked.

I closed the door behind me, ensuring our privacy. I hoped. After a thorough examination and tons of questions, the doctor approved Gemma's release. I immediately called Dad and Pierce to let them know. I couldn't wait to get the hell out of there.

THE FLIGHT HOME was much safer than the helicopter ride. Once we reached the airport, Zayne escorted Gemma and me to the Westbrook Security Mercedes that Vaughn had dropped off for us.

Dad had requested that we stay at his place, but I wanted to take Gem to our house for the night. Pierce assigned us an additional bodyguard, Jaxon, who was waiting for us at our place. The property had been searched and secured, and I was eager to crawl into bed with Gem next to me. Once we were in our bedroom, Gemma sank onto the end of the mattress and looked at me.

"I thought I would take a shower. Do you want to join me?" I tried to sound as casual as possible, but I still wasn't clear on what had or hadn't happened to her while she was with Brandon.

Gem stared at the floor. She seemed thinner than before she'd left, and although I had encouraged her to eat, she didn't have much of an appetite. "You seem upset with me." She looked at me briefly.

I wasn't sure if it was a good time or not, but eventually, I had to tell her how I felt. "I do think we need to talk, but it doesn't have to be right now." I took her fingers in mine and kissed the backs of her knuckles.

Gemma dropped my hand, then hopped up and walked across the room. She leaned against the wall and looked out of the floor-to-ceiling window, then folded her arms. It was her favorite place in the house. The view of the Spokane River rushing by was breathtaking.

"Let's get it over with. Say what you need to say." Her tone was clipped.

I blew out a sigh and attempted to formulate the right words in my head before I spoke. "I think the logical part of my brain understands why you chose to leave and not tell anyone, but ..." *Shit, how am I going to say this without sounding like a total asshole?* "It fucked me up. Our relationship has always been built on trust. You made a life-altering, earth-shattering decision without me, and I don't know how to move past it."

Gemma squared her shoulders and her chin jutted up as she turned around and met my eyes with her intense gaze. "Hendrix, if Brandon had wanted you, are you telling me that you would have sat down with me and talked it out? Would you have been able to walk out that door as I cried and pleaded for you not to go through with it? Hell, I would have clung to your arm and dug my feet into the floor, screaming and begging you not to leave. I would have done everything in my power to stop you." Pain flashed across her face. "Would you have been ready to deal with that?" She looked away from me. "If my pleas had worked, Franklin would have died, and you would never have forgiven yourself for not making the exchange. Again, the decision would have fallen on *my* shoulders. If I'd stopped you, Franklin wouldn't be here with us today. He would be dead. I would have carried the guilt around for the rest of my life. With that said, are you sure you wouldn't have made the choice without me because you were protecting me? Protecting Franklin's life?"

My brows shot up. *Shit, I hadn't considered that before.* It would have been impossible to leave Gemma if I'd discussed it with her first. She was right. I would have done everything to stop her, even if it meant sacrificing Dad. How would I have been able to live with myself afterward? Kendra's death still weighed on me. I should have taken Kendra to the kitchen when I cooked dinner that night. If I had ... an ache spread through me as I longed to move backward and rectify that choice. But if I could have changed that day, I doubt I would have ever met Gemma.

"And to the rest of our friends and family, it would have made you a hero, but I'm guessing you and Mac are pissed at me." She stared a hole into my soul. "I love you so damned much I can't see straight. You and your family are also *my* family. It's not like I took a chance of losing everyone I love to pump up my ego." She placed her hands on her hips. "You would have done the exact same thing. You wouldn't have said a word as you did everything in your power to bring Franklin home safely and end Brandon Montgomery once and for all."

I inwardly groaned as my cock twitched. *Dammit, she's hot when she's angry.* I wanted to pin her against the wall and bury my dick inside her.

Frustrated, I ran a hand through my hair. I would have made the same choice. It pained me a little to realize I had a double standard in this screwed-up situation. But I still needed some stability. We both did. I couldn't live in fear that she would disappear again. I wouldn't be able to live through it. She'd taken it on herself to deal with Brandon twice. As much as I loved her, even I had limits.

"Gemma." I looked at her. "We have to be able to trust each other. I can't tell you what it did to me when I watched the goodbye video."

Her arms dropped, her expression twisting into one of frustration. "How do you not trust the person that saved your father?" She tossed her hands in the air, clearly irritated.

My timing sucked ass. I was ready to put it behind us and rebuild our life together. I wasn't counting on Gem's anger, but she had every right to it after spending five days with a monster. Not to mention that some of her memories were gone. This was the wrong time to have this conversation. We were exhausted, and both of our emotions were raw.

"I need to know, Hendrix. Trust is the foundation for every good relationship, so does this mean you're calling off the wedding? That we're over?" Gem's chin tilted up, and although she was trying to be tough, I knew her well enough to recognize the signs that she was about to fall apart.

A heavy silence descended over us. *Wow, how did we get to this point?* Not only was it our first argument, but it had taken a sharp turn in the wrong direction too.

"Babe, I can't begin to tell you how grateful I am that you saved Dad. Your courage alone makes me love you more, but as much as I love my father, my love for you is far greater. My life is with *you*. I'm not saying that we're over at all. We need to talk this through, and I need to know that you won't make big decisions without me anymore. The same goes for me."

I sat on the bed and patted the space next to me. I waited for her guard to drop and sit down. Once she was next to me, I took her hand in mine. "When I was growing up, Kendra's mom, Marion … she and Dad used to have some horrible fights. They yelled at each other, and on occasion, they threw shit. There was nothing healthy about the way they argued. I don't ever want to be like that, babe." I massaged soothing circles in her palm with my fingers. "What I realized while you were gone was that I love you more than I thought was possible. I promised myself …" My heart pounded frantically against my rib cage. "I promised myself that if you came back to me, I would create the life I really wanted. We would create that life *together*. Gem, I can't live like this anymore. We're constantly looking over our shoulders. Our wedding was shot up, and people died. Dad was taken and tortured. All I want is you. All I want is you next to me. But we *have* to make some changes. I've already lost Kendra. I can't lose you too. It would destroy me."

"Like, what kind of changes?" She peered up at me, fear and vulnerability in her eyes.

I reached up and tucked her hair behind her ear, then kissed her gently. "I think we should build our dream house and move. Also, I think for now, we need to step out of the limelight. Put the band on hold. Let's find some property and spend time together. We can travel, write music, or whatever we want to do. I have two goals: to keep you safe and to keep you by my side. I don't think I could ever live through losing you again. I love you so much, Gem." My stomach clenched as I struggled to hold the tears back. "I never thought I would see or touch you again." A sharp pain stabbed me in the chest. Even though she was home, I wasn't sure I would ever recover from the fear and memories of her lifeless body on the gurney.

Her shoulders sagged with relief. "I would love to build our next house, Hendrix. I love you too. I'm so sorry I hurt you. I don't know what I would have done if you'd left instead. What I can tell you is that I had to save Franklin. You and your family are all I have. I love you all so much. I'm sorry I barked at you earlier. I'm so angry. I'm angry with myself for not being more prepared for Brandon. I'm mad at myself that I hurt you. At the same time, I know in every fiber of my being that Franklin wouldn't have lived much longer if I hadn't shown up." She squeezed my hand so hard pain shot up my arm. "I couldn't have his death on my conscience."

I held my breath, waiting for her to bring up Dad's rape. From what she'd just said, I figured she knew. Maybe Brandon had rubbed it in her face and used it to hurt her emotionally. That bastard would do anything for control.

"I can't explain it, but when I saw him on the video call, tied and beaten, alarm bells rang in my head. I didn't have time to make other plans, and Brandon had been a few steps ahead of us for months. If he even suspected I'd talked to you, he would have waited until I showed up, then killed Franklin in front of me. I would never have been able to forgive myself."

Tears brimmed over her eyes and streamed down her cheeks. "I need you to understand that I did the best I could under shitty circumstances. If you think the decision was easy, you're wrong. I've never had to make a choice like that in my life. I hope like hell I never have to again."

She sniffled, then peered up at me. "I know I broke your heart. I hope you can forgive me, but I also need to know that you can trust me. I'm not sure I can live with myself if you aren't able to."

I placed my fingers beneath her chin and kissed her. "All I need to hear is that you'll never do anything like that without talking to me again. We will *always* work out life together, no matter how hard it is. I promise you I'll never make a major decision without talking to you first. All I want is the same commitment from you."

"I promise." She threw her arms around me, and with a long hug, she pieced every shattered part of my heart back together again. I hoped like hell I could do the same for her. I suspected her journey to healing would be long.

"Is the shower offer still open?" she asked, her warm lips tickling the side of my neck.

"Only if you let me wash you from head to toe."

She sat up and smiled. I lifted her off me, then stood and removed my shirt on the way to the bathroom. I felt grungy and exhausted but not tired enough that I didn't want to taste and suck every beautiful inch of her.

Turning on the water, I peered over my shoulder. Gemma stood with her clothes on and her arms wrapped tightly around herself. The color had drained from her face.

I was next to her in three steps. "Babe?" I smoothed her hair.

Fear flashed in her face. "When I woke up, I was ... naked beneath one of Brandon's shirts." Her voice hovered above a whisper. "I don't remember anything else."

I ground my molars, and my pulse pounded in my ears. Gemma had made so much progress concerning her rape when she was fourteen. The idea that Brandon had caused her more harm made me sick. My stomach twisted into knots. He'd seen my future wife naked. He'd dressed her. There was no way he hadn't touched her. I reminded myself not to lose my shit in front of Gemma. The last thing she needed was to deal with my temper.

"Okay. I don't want to trigger you. What do you need? Can I hug you?"

She nodded. "I don't know what happened, Hendrix." She bit her lower lip. "But I think I ..."

She visibly trembled, and I wrapped my arms around her. "When you feel scared we'll take things slow. I want you to feel safe."

I wouldn't force her to talk, but everything inside me wanted to ask her what parts she did remember.

After a few moments, Gemma stepped back and squared her shoulders. "I won't let him destroy me. I won't." She removed her shirt and tossed it on the floor. My eyes were glued to her as she ditched her clothes and stood in front of me, beautiful and naked. "I love you. I trust you. If we need to stop, I'll let you know."

"I love you too. Just say the word." I flipped open the button on my jeans and freed my throbbing cock. "The water should be nice and hot by now." I extended my palm to her, and my pulse thundered in my ears when her small hand fit into mine. I thought I'd lost her forever. I thought I'd never see or touch her again, but she was with me. Thoughts of the strange woman contacting me swirled inside my mind, but I would deal with that later. All I cared about at the moment was the precious time I had with Gem.

I moved under the spray and backed up, allowing Gemma to get in. She shut the door and closed the gap between us. I wrapped my arms around her as the water cascaded over our bodies. I could stay like this all night, skin to skin with her, the beat of her heart against mine.

She peered up at me then stood on her tiptoes, her lips gently brushing mine. Gemma grabbed the bodywash and poured a little into her hand. Her fingers wrapped around my dick, then she cupped my balls. "I've missed you so much."

I groaned as she stroked me, and my fingers dug into the soft flesh of her hips. Gem reached up and unhooked the shower nozzle, then rinsed the soap off of me. She sank onto her knees and looked up at me as her tongue swirled around the tip of my cock. Sucking in a sharp breath, I placed my palm against the wall for balance. Her head bobbed up and down as she slid me in and out of her mouth.

"Oh God, babe." I wasn't sure what she was doing to me. She'd always been good at a blow job, but the moment she hollowed her cheeks, I nearly came. Her hand gave a corkscrew twist as she played with my nuts. "Dammit. You've got to stop."

"Doesn't that feel nice?" Water droplets hung off her eyelashes.

I reached down to help her up. "It's too good. I need a minute. Let me soap you up."

Maybe I could regain my composure while helping her relax. She leaned her back against me as I washed every inch of her. I cupped both of her breasts with soapy hands, then one hand trailed down her stomach and between her legs. To my relief, her pussy was wet. Soaked. I'd been worried the recent trauma would have her too scared, but she was ready for me.

I reached up and adjusted the setting, allowing the spray to become narrower. After I rinsed her off, I aimed the spray on her clit. "Do you like that?" Her hips moved forward as I slipped a finger inside her.

"Yeah." She propped a foot up on the seat, allowing me better access.

I eased a second finger inside her, and she bucked against my hand and gasped. "Mm, baby. I need you to fuck me."

I nearly dropped the showerhead. The last thing I expected for her to say was to fuck her. I'd assumed she needed to go slow and gentle. "Are you sure?" I asked from behind her.

"Please." A little whimper escaped her as I removed my fingers from her slick core.

"Let me finish washing up, then I'll take you to the bed where I have more room."

A few minutes later, we were clean and exited the shower. I knelt and dried her off gently, taking a moment to kiss the inside of her thigh. Unable to stop myself, I sucked on her swollen bud. *God, I missed her.*

I spread her apart and lifted her leg over my shoulder. My dick throbbed while I circled my finger over her wet core. I thrust my tongue into her, and her taste consumed me. Gem moaned as I licked and savored her sensitive flesh. I bit gently at her clit, and she rocked her hips. Her body quivered beneath my touch, driving me crazy. I needed her. I needed her hot pussy clenching me as she shuddered with an earth-shattering orgasm.

Her fingers threaded through my hair as she rocked against my mouth. "I'm going to come." Gemma's hand smacked against the wall as she trembled. "Oh God!"

I stroked my cock as she came on my face. She was hot as hell when she lost control.

After a moment, she stilled, and I stood. Without a word, I led her to the bed. She crawled up the middle of the mattress and lay on her back. Her gorgeous blue eyes connected with mine as her legs parted. Her pussy glistened from her orgasm, and I knelt on the mattress, positioning myself at her entrance.

"How do you want it?" I pushed the tip of my cock inside her, then withdrew. I continued to move in and out of her with only the tip of my dick.

"More." She gasped and fisted the comforter in her hand. "Please."

She squirmed beneath me, but somehow, I managed to hold steady. "More?" My breaths came in short pants, my restraint growing thinner by the second.

Before she could respond, I thrust all the way inside of her. She wrapped her legs around my waist and tilted her hips up. I shifted slightly, attempting to hit her clit as I moved. My goal was to give her as many orgasms as she wanted. She'd been through hell and back, and all I wanted was to reconnect with her and make her feel good.

Her fingernails dug into my ass as I pumped in and out of her. Gemma's upper body arched off the bed, and her lips parted as she moaned. "Fuck me, Hendrix."

I propped myself up on one arm and drove into her, losing myself in her slick walls. "I love you," I whispered. My body tightened as she trembled beneath me, and we released together.

I collapsed on top of Gem, then kissed her cheek. Her breathing was labored as she ran her fingers over my sweat-slickened back. Although the sex had been mind-blowing, something was missing. Gemma might be home physically, but she wasn't with me in every other part of herself. Whatever had happened, she'd walled herself off from the memories ... and me. It was almost as though she'd flipped a switch inside of herself when she swore she wouldn't allow Brandon to destroy her.

I nipped at her bottom lip and looked at her. "Come back to me, Gem." I pressed my mouth to hers before she could respond. There wasn't anything she could say anyway. I felt the absence of her mentally and emotionally.

1 5

The following morning, Jaxon brought Gemma a new phone. After she was settled at the kitchen table, setting up her new cell, I made a pot of coffee and cooked pancakes and bacon for breakfast. Gem needed to eat, and I was craving comfort food. She nibbled at her bacon until I sat next to her.

I gave her a lopsided grin as I removed the fork from her hand, then cut a piece of her pancake. "Open."

Gemma gawked at me, and I took advantage of the opportunity and fed her.

"What are you doing?" she asked around her bite of food.

"You're not eating, so I thought I would help." I sliced off another piece for her with the side of the fork and waited while she chewed.

"You're being a little overbearing, don't you think?" Mischievousness flickered in her eyes. "What are you going to do to me if I refuse? Spank me?"

I was stunned by her question. My fingers fumbled, and the fork dropped from my hand and clattered to the floor. "Um, do you want me to?" *Where is this coming from?* Gem had gradually entertained the thought of expanding our sex life, but spanking had never been on the agenda before. Apparently it was today.

Her palm slid up my jeaned thigh and to my now hard cock. "That's what I thought. You do like the idea of bending me over your knee or over the kitchen table and smacking my ass."

Struggling for the right words, I bent over and picked up the fork along with the pieces of pancake. "If you want to explore, then we should talk about it."

Gemma stood and ran her fingernail down my chest. "What's off-limits for you?" She nipped at my earlobe. "Do you want to watch me with another girl? Would you watch another couple together and finger me until I come?"

Yes! Hell yes! I scrubbed my face with my hands, attempting to rein in my fantasies. This wasn't the same girl who had left me nearly a week before. My brain scrambled for the reason she was suddenly interested in new sexual activities, but I was clueless.

"I tell you what. Let's get settled in again and make sure whatever drug was pumped into your system isn't going to have long-term side effects. Then we can talk about any desires you have."

"At the bridal shower, I received a gift card to The Lily. From what Avery told me, it's a safe place to explore fantasies. They mostly cater to women, but they've expanded to include couples. I thought it might be fun. Claire and Vaughn have gone, so maybe it's an option."

That made a little more sense. At least I understood where the conversation came from, but I couldn't dismiss the nagging thought that something else was going on.

"Were you really serious about all of those fantasies you rattled off?" I stared at her, searching for clues.

Gemma sat down at the table. "I'm not sure. While I was gone, I think something inside me snapped. I can't really explain it because I don't understand it. I promised myself that if I made it back home, I would try new things with you if you wanted to. Brandon—" Gemma slammed her mouth closed as a dark expression clouded her features.

"Gem." I sat next to her and took her hands in mine. "Hey. Stay with me. I'm right here."

Her cheeks paled as her body snapped to attention. "I'm okay," she mumbled. She remained quiet, then she squeezed my fingers. "I want to explore with you. I've never had any of those experiences, and I'm tired of living in fear. And ever since I've been back, I'm so … horny." She glanced at me shyly and laughed.

"I can definitely help with that." I'd missed her so damned much.

She straddled my lap and threaded her fingers through my hair. I snaked a hand beneath her shirt and trailed it up her stomach. She moaned as I moved the soft lace material of her bra and pinched her nipple. "What do you want, Hendrix?" She ground her hips against my painful erection.

Shit. We were supposed to be leaving for Dad's, but there was no way I was going to deny her.

"Do you want to fuck me with the vibrator? Or do you want to watch me fuck myself? Will you wrap your hand around your cock and stroke yourself? I get so turned on thinking about watching you."

I gulped. "All of it. All of it sounds amazing." *Screw going to Dad's. If she's asking me what I want, I'm going to request it all. Why ruin a good thing?*

I lifted her off my lap, and she set her feet on the floor. "Let's go," I said, then took her hand and led her upstairs to the bedroom. Since Jaxon and Zayne were outside and had access to the house, I closed and locked the door behind me.

Before I could say a word, Gemma pulled her top over her head and tossed it on the chair. Her bra, G-string, and jeans were next. She strolled over to the nightstand, knelt, and gave me a view of her ass in the air as she reached for something under the bed. It took everything inside me not to fuck her right there.

She produced a rectangular container and set it on the mattress. "It's my goody box. I only have the handcuffs, blindfold, heated lube, and vibrator right now. I guess it's a start, though."

I unbuttoned my jeans and knelt next to her. "Have you been thinking about this for a while?" I picked up the handcuffs, my thoughts immediately returning to the only time we'd used them.

"Yeah. I guess so. I think I'm going to talk to Claire. She's had a lot more experience than I have."

Holy shit. Gemma was incredibly private about our sex life. She obviously trusted Claire.

"I've never talked to anyone about this type of thing, so I hope it's okay?" Gemma glanced at the items. "I guess if we get some more toys, you'll have to teach me." Her tongue darted across her bottom lip, and I resisted the urge to suck on it. She smiled at me. "Why are you still dressed?"

I chuckled as I ditched the rest of my clothes. "Come here." I took the vibrator out of her hand and set it next to me. "Let's try something. If you don't like it, let me know. There's no right and wrong here, so talk to me. Let's figure out what you … we like."

"Okay." A dusting of pink graced Gem's cheeks. She was nervous, and it was adorable.

I grabbed the heating oil out of the box and squeezed some into my palm. I wrapped my fingers around my shaft and stroked myself for her. Desire flashed in her eyes as she watched me. She sank her teeth into her bottom lip, and I groaned. I leaned back on one hand, my cock twitching in the other. Her undivided attention sent ripples of desire through me. It wouldn't take long for me to come if she continued to stare at me, but I had other things in mind.

I released my dick and moved to the edge of the mattress. "Bend over my lap."

Without hesitation, she walked toward me, then lay across my legs.

"Just relax." I traced a path over the curve of her ass, then between her thighs. I teased her clit as her juices glistened my fingers. "Spread your legs a little bit."

She did as I asked, and I picked up the vibrator and turned it on. The toy hummed as I ran it across her slick entrance. "Does that feel good?"

"Yeah." Her reply was a bit breathless, and my cock throbbed against my stomach.

She whimpered while I eased the vibrator inside of her. With a full view of her pussy, I thought I was going to lose my mind. I spread her ass cheeks apart as I fucked her.

"Do you want my finger in your ass?"

"Yes." Her hand grabbed my lower leg, and she dug her fingernails into my skin.

Making sure my fingers were wet with her desire, I slipped one of them into her tight little hole. I stilled, waiting for her to tell me to stop or to continue.

"Oh God. Why does that feel so good?"

Jesus. "Your ass is so goddammed tight." She writhed beneath me and moaned. My cock itched to be inside her, but watching her squirm on my lap was hot as hell.

"I'm going to come. Harder." She bucked against my hand, then shuddered as she released.

The second she was finished, I put the toy aside and placed her on the mattress. "Bend over the bed." She got situated, and the moment her legs were apart, I shoved my cock inside her. "Did you like that, babe? Did it feel good in your ass?" I thrust into her deeper.

"Yes. Do it again," she pleaded.

I did as she asked and fucked her as hard and fast as I could. She begged for more, and I was suddenly worried I would hurt her. This was the roughest sex we'd ever had. Even though I enjoyed it, I couldn't dismiss a nagging feeling that I should slow down.

My balls tightened, then the most intense orgasm I'd ever had ripped through me. I emptied myself inside of her, shuddering as I dug my fingers into her hips. Once I finished, I continued to move inside her. I wanted her to come again.

"Wait." She glanced over her shoulder at me.

I pulled out and stepped away. She flipped over onto her back, then scooted to the edge of the bed. She handed the vibrator to me. "Will you finish me off with this while you lick my pussy? I want to watch."

This woman is going to undo me. "You're going to make me hard again." I knelt and buried my face between her thighs. I swirled my tongue around her clit as she placed her legs over my shoulders.

"That's it, baby." She tugged my hair, forcing my head back a little bit.

I licked up her slit and sucked on her bundle of nerves. She lifted her hips up and moaned. I grabbed the vibrator, slid it inside her, and flipped the switch.

"That feels so good." She smoothed my hair back, her attention trained on me as I continued to lick her. "Next time we go to a restaurant, I think you should get under the table and shove your tongue inside me. Bring me to the edge, stop, then sit down again. I'll be begging for you to take me to the restroom or outside and fuck my brains out." She squeezed her tit, her eyes never leaving mine.

My cock hardened again. *Jesus, what is she doing to me?* I hadn't been expecting any of this when she came home.

She leaned back on the bed, squirming, as I set the vibrator on a higher speed. "That's it, baby."

I looked down. Her upper body was arched, and her tits were pointed in the air, begging for me to come on them. She jerked beneath me, and she tensed while her fingers dug into the comforter. Her lips parted as she gasped.

Once she'd finished, I switched off the toy and tossed it onto the bed. "Gem, will you suck me off and let me come on your tits?" If she were open to new things, I would ask for some of my fantasies too.

She smiled and motioned for me to move up next to her. I straddled her upper body as her mouth parted and licked the precum off the tip of my head. She grabbed my cock and stroked it as she eased it between her lips. Her hold tightened, and I rocked against her.

"That's it." I pinched her nipples, and her pace quickened. My eyes fluttered closed as I allowed the sucking sensation to consume me. A low moan escaped me. "I'm going to come."

Gemma leaned back, and I gripped my shaft and pumped it until I came all over her tits. She looked sexy as shit with my load all over her. My body shook with the remnants of my orgasm. I gazed at her, wondering if she would regret our romp now that we were finished. Her silly smile said otherwise, though.

"I'll be right back." I hopped off the bed and made my way to the bathroom, where I turned on the sink faucet and let the water warm up. I washed my hands and mouth, then soaked the washcloth and wrung it out.

"Here. Hopefully, it's not cold." I wiped off her chest, then focused on the insides of her legs and pussy. "I made a mess." I grinned at her.

She giggled. "Thank you. Thank you for understanding, Hendrix. I wasn't sure how you would take it when I told you I wanted to try some new things in our sex life." She sat up and crossed her ankles.

"First of all, I could stare at you like this all day. You're so beautiful I forget my name sometimes."

Gemma glanced away, her cheeks flushing.

"Second, I'm flattered that you feel safe enough with me to experiment." I took her hand. "What I really need you to hear, though, is that I love you. If I think at any time that I'm hurting you mentally or physically, then we stop. You're more important than sex."

She leaned over and kissed me. "I'll tell you. I promise."

I tucked her hair behind her ear. "One more thing. I would like to take you to the doctor for a checkup in the next few days. I want to make sure you're doing all right." Something inside me wasn't going to let this go. Gem wasn't herself, and although I didn't expect her to be normal after everything she'd lived through, her sex drive was insatiable, and she wanted to push boundaries she'd never even talked to me about before. Other than the first night we made love at the hospital, there'd been zero emotion on her part. It was purely physical. Sex between us had always been more than physical before. Without an emotional connection, it felt empty.

Her change was more than wanting to explore. Something was off, but I couldn't put my finger on it. Maybe other men wouldn't care as long as they got laid, but I knew her too well, and I wasn't other men. I was her fiancé.

"A checkup would probably be smart." Gem gave me a tentative smile.

I quickly dressed and handed Gem her clothes. "We need to get to Dad's. Do you have everything packed?" I tugged my polo shirt on, then smoothed the burgundy material.

"Yeah. I think so. If we forget anything, we can pick it up." She pulled her long hair from beneath the collar of her green top.

I released a sigh. "Before we go, I need to talk to you." Her eyes filled with fear, and my heart plummeted to my toes. "It's about Dad."

"No." She shook her head, furiously. "Please tell me it's not true." Her hands flew over her mouth as tears welled in her eyes. "I knew something was wrong, Hendrix. God dammit, I'm going to hunt the motherfucking guard down that hurt Franklin, then I'm going to bury him alive. What sick bastard hurts someone like that?" Her lips pressed together, and she paused. "I obviously feel strongly about what happened."

I gathered her in my arms. "No one had any idea. Dad refused to tell anyone. I found him curled up in bed, sobbing. Even then, I had to pry it out of him. Honestly, I thought he was using or drinking again. It never crossed my mind that he'd been raped." My voice cracked with pain as I recalled the afternoon Dad had told me. "The family knows now, and I talked to Pierce, Zayne, and Sutton."

Gemma peered at me through red-rimmed eyes. "You did? Don't you think Franklin would have wanted that information to remain private?"

I nodded. "I wasn't going to tell anyone. It sure as hell wasn't my place to share his experience. But Gem, I can't manage all of this on my own. If Dad is with Pierce and has a flashback, they need to know how to handle the situation."

"The flashbacks are crippling. You have no sense of time, and you're not aware of your surroundings." Gemma stared off into space, her eyes unfocused. "If you're around him enough when he's having them, you might learn to spot the physical signs. But you're right. If he were walking across the street and the memories bombarded him, it could be dangerous."

I stroked her hair. "I think you'll be able to offer him support in a way the rest of us can't, babe. I hate to ask if you can help, but you've been through this. No one else is going to understand like you will."

Gem placed her warm palm on my cheek. "You never have to ask me. He's my family. I'll do whatever I can, but I would highly recommend counseling. Hendrix, I was raped by a man, which was horrible. Franklin was raped by a man too." She frowned and paused. "I'm not explaining this very well. Franklin might struggle even more than I did because it was a same-sex assault. I would think there would be other mental complications, but I'm not sure. Please don't misunderstand me—it's a horrifying experience to live through regardless of who you are. I just don't think society hears about men being raped as often."

I kissed her gently. One minute I was terrified something awful had happened to her while she was with Brandon. The next, she was soothing my soul with her kindness. This was the Gemma I knew.

"Counseling sessions are already set up. Sutton helped me find a woman who deals with sexual assault for men and women. Dad will have a therapist come to his house twice a week. I also took the liberty of scheduling some appointments for us." I swallowed, preparing myself for her objections. "It was before you came home. At the time, it was wishful thinking that you would be back. Honestly, I thought I would have to cancel the appointments. You're here, though. What do you think of going together?"

Gem frowned. "Is something wrong with us?" She jumped off the bed and wrapped her arms around herself.

"No. Not at all. I have no idea how to help you or Dad, babe. I'm not clear on what happened while you were gone. What if you have flashbacks too? I've already seen you teeter on the edge of dark memories. I want to be able to support you." A blanket of silence stretched over us, and my pulse pounded in my ears. "I love you, but I can't fix whatever happened. Hell, I don't even know how to process this shit show myself. I'm only one man. Granted, I'm *your* man, but I can't do this on my own."

Gemma stared at me, her expression void of any emotions. I wondered if I'd screwed up when all I was trying to do was piece my family back together.

"It was Ada Lynn that helped me," Gem said softly. "Mom and Dad didn't believe in therapy, so I never spoke to anyone after the rape and pregnancy." She paused, tucking her red hair behind her ear. "I'll try it because I love you. I love you for believing that I would come home. I love you for making the appointments. I love you for not giving up on me." She closed the gap between us and placed her hands on my chest. She peeked up at me through her long eyelashes, and my cock immediately sprang to life. "I need to ask you a few things, though."

"Of course." I rubbed her arms, encouraging her to continue.

"Are you sure you're up for the challenge of whatever I might put you through?" Concern filled her beautiful face.

I couldn't hide my frown. "I don't understand, babe."

"I don't have all my memories back. What if something so horrific happened that I'll never be the same? I told you Brandon didn't rape me, but I honestly have no idea. It flew out of my mouth because you were so scared, and I needed you. I'm sorry, Hendrix. I shouldn't have told you he didn't when I can't remember. What if ..." Her forehead creased as she visibly struggled to articulate her thoughts. "What if Brandon put a shock collar around my neck and forced me to do things against my will?"

Gemma quickly jerked her hands away from me and stumbled backward, smacking her ass on the floor.

"Are you okay?" I knelt next to her, my heart beating frantically against my rib cage. Even the barest hint of what she'd gone through hit me like a freight train, almost knocking the wind out of me.

She stared at me with a blank expression.

"What is it, Gemma?" Dread and horror seeped into every crevice of my soul, nearly leaving me breathless with the idea that Brandon would torture her as though she were a savage animal. Because of what I'd learned about Dad, though, I knew that Brandon was capable of anything. Shocking girls into submission was right up Brandon's alley.

"I don't know. Why would I say something like that?" Fear flashed in her big blue eyes, and the color drained from her cheeks. My stomach flip-flopped.

I pulled her into my arms. "Whatever it is, I'm not going anywhere. We'll get through it, but that's why I want to talk to someone." I kissed the top of her head. "Moving forward, you have to be honest with me as well as the doctors. We should get you tested for any …" *Shit, never in my wildest dreams did I think I would have a reason to say this to Gem.* "STDs." I internally cringed as I waited for her response.

"We've already had sex, so I guess you should be tested too." She gave a small cry, then she covered her face with her hands. "I'm so sorry, Hendrix. When I woke up in the hospital, my mind was vague, as if everything was a dream. Otherwise, I would never have put you in that position."

I heaved a sigh. I'd been a dumbass for not thinking about the testing while she was in the hospital. I'd been out of my mind with fear and grief after seeing her lifeless body, and I hadn't been thinking straight either. All I'd wanted was to be with her and help her feel safe.

I hoped like hell we were both clean. The entire situation was messed up, but I realized it wasn't Gemma's fault. She hadn't been thinking clearly when she was at the hospital. It had been my responsibility, and I'd been so shaken with her death it hadn't crossed my mind.

"It's okay. I'm to blame too. We'll get tested and figure it all out."

She stood, then paced the bedroom, wearing a path in the plush, beige carpet. "Hendrix, I don't think I'm okay. I don't know what he did to me, but …"

Her words punched me in the throat, and I struggled to speak. It was one thing when I'd suspected something horrible, but when it was finally said out loud, there was no turning back or talking myself out of it. The truth could be as vicious as a rabid dog, chasing you down until it stared you in the face.

"It puzzles me that I can't remember, Hendrix. Wouldn't I have realized I was losing chunks of time when I was with him?" She approached me and clutched my shirt, bunching the soft fabric between her fingers.

"No. I don't think you would. He could have drugged your food or drink. You could have faded into oblivion. I'm no expert, though."

Gem closed her eyes and dragged in a deep gulp of air before she opened them again. "I feel like there are two parts of me right now. Whatever happened, maybe it split me into two people. Is that possible?" Fear and sadness twisted her expression.

In my college psychology class, I'd learned about how the brain protects a victim after trauma. From what I'd studied, split personalities could happen, but Gemma wasn't flipping from one personality to another. It seemed like something else was driving her behavior.

"I don't think so. Please try not to stress about it. There's no doubt in my mind who you are, babe. I suspect a therapist will be able to soothe any of your concerns too."

"Do you still want to get married?" Her voice was so soft I wasn't sure I'd heard her correctly.

"Of course. I thought we'd already discussed that."

"That was when we first got home." She worried her bottom lip with her teeth. "And before we both realized that something is wrong with me."

I could see the pain in her eyes. My entire body buzzed with churning emotions, my fear bubbling to the surface. The concern that I'd lost her for good and that we wouldn't be able to recover from what Brandon had done to her terrified me.

"Gemma," I whispered. I cupped her chin and tilted her head up. "We belong together. Nothing in this world can tear us apart." Although I'd already proposed, I wanted to reassure her that she was the only one for me. I dropped to one knee and gazed up at her. "I want to marry you, and if you'll let me, I eventually want to have a baby with you. The idea of a little girl that looks exactly like you melts me. *You* melt me. Marry me, Gem."

Tears streamed down her face. "Even if I'm broken for the rest of my life?" Deep concern was embedded in her features.

"If you're broken, so am I. We'll have our entire lives to put our broken pieces together." Gemma collapsed against me and I smoothed her hair. "You're stuck with me, babe. The sun doesn't come up in my world if you're not next to me."

Once her tears had run dry, I realized she hadn't noticed her finger yet. "I need to buy you a new ring." I squeezed my eyes closed and wished I could take the sting out of my words.

"That son of a bitch." She released me and held her hand up. "I've been so messed up I didn't even notice." Desperation flashed across her face. "I should have realized it was gone." Her pitch rose with each word, and I was worried her anxiety was escalating.

"It's okay. I would rather buy you a new one to symbolize that no matter what, we're moving forward together. A ring to remind you each time you see it that we're indestructible."

"I would love that. Maybe it would help remind me that I'm living in the present with you, not in the past with that sick bastard."

"Let's talk about some ideas." I kissed her forehead, grateful to be having a more positive conversation.

"Okay." She attempted a smile while she wiped the moisture from her cheeks.

Suddenly, an idea occurred to me. It had been two years since August Clover hit it big. Gem and I were in a much better financial place than when I'd proposed to her. "What do you think about designing your engagement ring and wedding band? It will be a one of a kind, just like you."

Gemma's face lit up. "That would be absolutely amazing. And your band, too! Can we make it a top priority?"

"Yeah. I'm ready to marry you. We can plan our wedding and our new house." I kissed her gently.

"Me too," she said against my lips.

We stood in silence as we held each other. "Are you okay to go to

Dad's now?" I finally asked. "Mac needs to see you. She's most likely going to cry, then let you know how hurt she was that you left. Are you up for it? Mac's hormones and emotions are all over the place, babe. I just wanted to mention it in case she's verbally aggressive." A protectiveness rose inside me. I wouldn't leave Gemma alone with Mac. Not that Mac would be hateful, but she was emotional, and shit flew out of her mouth before she realized it. "If not, I'll tell Dad we're staying here tonight."

"No. I have to work things out with Mac. Let's get it over with. Hopefully, she won't be angry with me for too long. I need my bestie. Plus, I want to talk to Franklin." She played with the hem of her shirt, then tucked her hair behind her ear.

Gem wouldn't admit it, but she was scared to see Mac. The last thing she expected was to come home to an angry best friend. Even though I understood where my sister was coming from, I also knew that her emotions were flip-flopping every few seconds. I wasn't sure what to expect, but I doubted Mac did either. It was difficult to be upset with someone who had saved your father's life.

"She needs you too. I've stalled as long as possible, but I know everyone wants to see you. Mac started blowing up my phone at seven this morning, and I turned it off. It's a good sign, though."

Gem laughed. "She did? That's crazy early even for her."

"Yeah, it is. She's anxious, but you and I are exhausted. Besides, I didn't want to share you yet." A lopsided grin tugged at the corner of my mouth.

"Me either. I'm glad we stayed here last night." Gem glanced at the rumpled comforter on the bed and began to straighten it.

"Dad made sure we were coming to his house. As long as Brandon is still loose, it's the safest place for us." I wouldn't admit it to Gemma, but internally, I was kicking and screaming like a little kid. She and I owned our home, and I was tired of not living in it.

"I want to grab a few things from our office before we leave." I kissed her gently. "I love you. Please don't ever doubt that."

"I love you too." She took my hand and threaded her fingers through mine as we made our way downstairs.

Gemma called the doctor and scheduled appointments for both of us later that week. After I collected a sketch pad from the office, we let Zayne know we were ready to go to Dad's. My phone buzzed, and I removed it from my pocket as we slid into the back seat of the Mercedes.

"Hey, Dad. We're on our way over now."

"No! Don't. Have Zayne drive you to Sacred Heart Hospital." His words oozed with worry.

"What?" I couldn't hide the alarm in my voice. "Are you okay?"

"It's not me, son," Dad said.

"Then who is it?"

1 7

I leaned forward so I could speak to Zayne while I listened to Dad. "Zayne, please take us to Sacred Heart as fast as you can." I frowned as I glanced at Gemma. "Dad, what's wrong?" I asked, panicked as the car started to move.

"It's Mac. Somethings wrong with her and the baby."

Fuck! "We're on our way," I said. "I'll call you as soon as we get there." I disconnected the call and turned to Gem, my stomach twisted in knots. "Mac is on the way to the emergency room by ambulance. Something is wrong with the baby." I diverted my eyes, attempting to calm my overactive imagination, but this wasn't good. At all.

"Hendrix, what did Franklin say?" Gemma asked.

"That something was wrong, and everyone is on the way to the hospital." My hand balled into a tight fist. "I should have asked more questions, but he was driving."

"Hendrix …" Gem released her seatbelt and slid over next to me. "How long was I gone? I mean, remind me how far along Mac is now."

"Twenty weeks."

"Did Franklin say what her symptoms were? It could be absolutely nothing. Some women spot or bleed during pregnancy, even cramp. Mac might be one of them."

I realized Gem was trying to help me stay calm and not jump to conclusions, but I didn't have any other information. "He didn't say."

"Is it all right if I call Janice?" She rummaged through her purse for her phone.

"Yeah, she might be more helpful." I massaged my temples, willing myself to wake up from this nightmare.

Gemma kissed my cheek, then reached up and squeezed Zayne's shoulder. She tapped her cell's screen and Janice's phone began to ring.

"Hi, Gemma. I should have called you already," Janice said.

"It's okay. Your main focus should be on Mac. I have you on speaker so Hendrix and Zayne can hear, if that's all right with you."

"Of course." Janice blew out a soft sigh.

"What happened?" Gem chewed on her thumbnail as Janice began to explain.

"This afternoon, she got a horrible headache, and her vision was blurry. At first, I thought she needed to eat, so I grabbed her a piece of fruit, then made her a sandwich. By the time I had her food ready, she was doubling over with stomach pain."

"Mom, who is with her in the ambulance?" I asked.

"Cade. We're not far behind them, but we're hitting every damned red light possible." Janice sniffled. "I'm trying to stay calm, but Mac has been under so much stress. I'm terrified she's going to lose …"

She didn't need to finish. I was already thinking the same thing, and from the expression on Gemma's face, she was too.

"Zayne, what's our ETA?" Gemma asked, leaning forward so Janice could hear his response.

"Forty minutes, but I'll take any shortcuts I can," Zayne offered.

"We love you guys, and one of us will call when we get there," Gem said.

"Please be careful, Zayne. You have our other two kids in your hands," Janice pleaded.

"Yes ma'am."

Apparently, that request hit home with Zayne because he slowed down a little.

"Mom? How's Dad holding up?" I leaned against the leather seat and closed my eyes, attempting to shut out the shit show that was my life, if only for a moment. Every time I thought we would catch a break, crap hit the fan again. I was over it.

"He's very focused at the moment. I think he's hanging on as best he can under the circumstances. The last few weeks have been hell for all of us."

"No shit," I muttered. "I'm right there with you."

"Mac's strong, which means the baby is too. She's going to be fine," Gemma said.

"I hope you're right." Janice couldn't hide the anxiety in her voice.

"We'll see you in a little bit," I said.

After Gem disconnected the call, my attention landed on her. "What do you think is wrong?" It wasn't that I expected her to have the answer, but she'd been pregnant before.

"I don't know. It's hard to tell. It could be a miscarriage or preeclampsia, maybe." She tapped her manicured fingernails against her iPhone case.

"What's preeclampsia?" I wasn't familiar with the term, but I hadn't been around many pregnant women either.

"High blood pressure, which is really dangerous. Hopefully they can get it under control, but Mac will have to reduce her stress and hang out in bed." Gemma looked over at me. "Babe, I'm not a doctor. I don't know if I'm right or not. The only reason I even think it might be preeclampsia is because my mom had it while she was pregnant with me. She told me all about it when I was carrying Jordan. I think she was scared I would get it, too, but I didn't."

"Can they fix the condition with medication?" I was scrambling for any shred of information that would give me some hope.

"According to my mom, yeah. We need to wait and see because I could be totally wrong."

I slid my arm around her shoulders and pulled her closer. "Let's hope you're right." I kissed the top of her head, then stared out the window for the duration of the ride.

❤

I'D BEEN in a damned hospital three times in the last week and a half. I gave the universe a big *screw you* as we hurried down the hall toward Mac's room. Gem's grip on my hand was almost painful, but at least we were together. This could have happened when Gemma had been gone.

Zayne's footsteps slapped the tile floors behind us, and I slowed as I identified the numbers.

"There." Gemma pointed a few doors down the hall. "Hendrix, I think I should wait out here with Zayne. Mac is upset with me, and I don't want to cause more harm to her and the baby."

Shit. I wasn't sure I could leave my fiancée in the hall when her best friend needed her.

We stopped in front of Mac's room, and I gently tugged on Gemma's hand. "Give me just a minute to see if we know what's wrong with her yet. I would think that she would be relieved to see you, but you might be right." I wrapped a few of her beautiful red strands around my finger. "I love you more than anything else in this world, Gemma Thompson."

"I love you too." She pushed up on her tiptoes and pressed her mouth to mine. "Go see your sister." She worried her bottom lip, then a mask of coolness slipped over her face.

"I'll be right back, babe." I glanced over my shoulder at Zayne. "Gemma is going to stay with you for a few minutes."

"You go on in. I'll make sure Gemma is safe." He nodded at me, then walked closer to her.

I knocked and poked my head in. "Hey, Mac."

"Hendrix." Tears flowed down my sister's cheeks, breaking my heart.

The soft beep of machines filled the sterile white room. A small television hung on the wall, and although it was on, the sound was muted.

"Come on in." Dad waved me over, and I closed the door behind me. I gave Dad and Janice a brief hug, then joined Mac.

"Dad says you're causing trouble again." I gave her a playful smile.

"Yup, that's me." She leaned back on the pillow, fear in her gaze.

"Hey, man." I nodded at Cade. "How are you holding up?"

Cade looked like hell. His hair was ruffled, and dark, half-moon shadows made his eyes appear sunken. If life didn't settle down, I suspected he would end up in the hospital from a nervous breakdown.

"Hanging in there. The doctor came in, and they're running tests and bloodwork. Waiting makes me anxious." He laced his fingers behind his head and inhaled sharply.

"I can't lose the baby, Hendrix." Mac's chin trembled.

I gently squeezed her shoulder. "It's going to be okay. Take a deep breath and let the nurses and doctor take care of you."

She nodded and wiped her nose.

"I'm going to steal Cade for a few minutes, since Mom and Dad are here with you." I held her hand in a vain attempt to help her.

"Please take Cade for a walk. Maybe some fresh air will be good for him. He's been taking care of me twenty-four seven, and he needs his best friend." Mac hesitated. "Speaking of best friends, is Gemma with you?"

"Yeah. She's out in the hall with Zayne. She didn't want to take a chance on upsetting you more. Gem knows you have mixed feelings about her making the exchange for Dad, so she offered to stay out there."

Mac sat up in her bed. "Tell her to get her ass in here. I need my bestie."

I chuckled. "All right, but keep your stress level down."

"Hang on, Cade. Let me grab Gem, then we can get some fresh air." I opened the door and stepped into the hall. "Babe, Mac wants to see you."

"She does? Are you sure?" She looked hopeful.

I waved her over, then gave her a reassuring kiss. "Yeah."

Gemma nodded and plastered on a sweet smile. She squared her shoulders and followed me into the room.

"Bestie!" Mac burst into tears.

"Mac!" Gem hurried to her, and they threw their arms around each other. "I love you. It's going to be okay."

"Oh my God. I thought I would never see you again. I'm so happy you're back." Mac sniffled loudly.

The girls released each other, and I handed them the box of tissues from the bedside table.

"Thanks, babe." Gem took a few and handed one to Mac.

"Franklin and I are home, and you and the baby are going to be okay," Gemma assured my sister.

Mac blew her nose, then collapsed onto her pillow. "Don't leave." She grabbed Gem's arm.

"I'm not going anywhere. I'll stay here as long as you need me to. As soon as you're better, we'll go to the house, crawl into bed, and watch some romcom movies."

"And pizza?" Mac asked between her tears.

"Every kind you can possibly imagine." Gemma took Mac's hand in hers.

A silence fell between them, and I held my breath.

"I was really mad at you," Mac whispered. "At the same time, you're the reason Dad is alive." Mac placed her palm on her forehead, her attention landing on Dad. "That trumped me being furious at you. Now that you're home, all I want to do is talk and hang out. I can't tell you how much I cried while you were gone."

"I'm so sorry, Mac. I didn't do it to hurt you—please understand that," Gemma said. "I missed you more than you'll ever know. I thought about you and the baby every day. I'll answer any questions you have later, but for now, let's catch up. I want to—"

"Oh my gosh, look!" Mac rolled the blanket down to her waist, then raised her gown, revealing her stomach.

"Oh my God, Mac. You have a tiny baby bump." Gem pulled Mac in for another hug. "I'm so happy to be back. Life wouldn't be the same without you. I love you so much."

"Same, bestie, same."

The room grew quiet other than Mac and Gemma's sniffles. "I'm going to get Cade out of here for a few minutes, but call me when the doctor comes in if we haven't returned yet," I said. "We won't be gone long."

Janice patted my back. "Cade needs some air. He's a bit pale. Now that Gemma is here, Mac will begin to calm down."

"I don't want to leave Mac," Cade protested.

"Son, you need a break. This isn't up for discussion, since we're right here," Dad said. "The second we see the doctor, I'll call. Just stay close."

Even Cade understood not to argue with Dad when he put his foot down. My attention landed on the girls, and I was secretly relieved that Mac hadn't ripped Gemma's head off. Maybe the scare with the baby had put life into perspective for her.

"Let's go, man." I left and waited for Cade in the hall.

"Babe, I'll be back in a few minutes." Cade kissed his future wife, then joined me.

The moment we were out of earshot, I nudged my best friend in the ribs with my elbow. "Dude, you look like shit. Other than today, what gives?"

He ran his hand through his short hair. Cade peered over his shoulder before he spoke in a hushed tone. "She's having nightmares about Brandon every night, Hendrix. I hold her until she falls asleep, but she gets too hot and pushes me away. I'm exhausted. She was a wreck when Franklin was kidnapped, but when Gemma disappeared … she went dark. It scared me, man."

"First, why the hell didn't you call me? Second, how dark?" I stopped in front of the elevator and pushed the button for the main floor. The bell chimed, and the doors whooshed open.

"Because I'm not a dick. Your dad was kidnapped, then Gemma. Hearing my bullshit problems was the last thing you needed." Cade folded his arms.

I narrowed my gaze at him. He'd been my best friend since middle school, and I should have checked in with him sooner. "I'm going to kick your ass."

A flicker of surprise crossed his face, then he clamped down on his emotions. "Bring it on. I need to hit someone."

I chuckled. Cade and I had threatened to beat the hell out of each other for years. It was our way of blowing off steam. I had only punched him once, and that was when I found out he was sleeping with my sister. After I realized how much he loved her, it was easy to come to terms with their relationship.

"Maybe Gemma can help now that she's back. We'll be over at Dad's for a while. I think Mac does better when we're all together." I stared at the elevator panel and watched the numbers tick off floor by floor. The doors opened, and we walked into the hall.

"Definitely. Like, she loves our alone time, but she does best when she's surrounded by family." Cade trained his focus on the floor as we walked through the lobby. "I really love that about her. I've always wanted a houseful of kids." He gave me a sheepish smile.

"So, you're already planning on knocking my sister up again?" I arched an eyebrow at him.

"As many times as she'll let me. I love kids." Cade chuckled as we exited the building and stepped into the cool evening air.

"I get it. I've always wanted kids too." I shoved my hands into my pockets, and we continued to walk down the sidewalk. "I told Gemma I wanted kids today. I have no idea why. It just flew out of my mouth."

Cade stopped in his tracks. "No shit? How did she react?"

I kicked at the concrete with the toe of my tennis shoe. "She didn't. That's what I'm worried about. She's home, but there are times she's so disconnected it scares me."

"Like how?" Cade ran his fingers across his stubbled chin.

I focused on the nighttime skyline, allowing the twinkle of the Spokane lights to soothe my raw, frayed nerves. I'd always loved the city in the evening. I debated whether I should tell him what was going on. "I don't know what happened while she was gone, and neither does she."

"She's lost her memories?" Cade sounded worried.

"Yeah ... but she asked ..." I cleared my throat. "She asked if I would spank her or watch her with another girl."

"What. The. Fuck?" Cade tossed his hands up in the air and laughed. "And this is a problem why?"

A grin pulled at the corner of my mouth. "Yeah, I know. It's not Gemma, though—not with her past. She's always been timid in the bedroom. Granted, before our fucked-up wedding, she was making a lot of progress. But not this kind of progress. Something is wrong. Gemma has gaps in her memory. She remembers some things, but not all of it. I'm worried those blanks are hiding events she can't face." I removed the hair tie out of my pocket and slipped it on my wrist. "You're worried you'll lose your baby, and I'm terrified I lost Gemma." There, I'd said it. My fear was so intense I could smell it, a foul pungent odor that soured my stomach.

"Has she told you *anything* that happened?" Cade stared a hole right into my soul. One reason we'd been friends for so long was that each of us had the ability to see through all the bullshit the other one hid behind.

"She made an off-the-cuff remark about what if Brandon put a shock collar on her ..." I coughed into my hand, hiding my grief from Cade. "She doesn't have any clear memories, though. It's random comments out of nowhere."

Cade nodded. "Jesus. That's just wrong." He shook his head. "Maybe it would be best if she never remembered, ya know?"

"I couldn't agree with you more. If she ever recalled what happened, I'm worried it would break her. I think that son of a bitch did some warped crap."

Cade's nostrils flared. "The FBI hasn't found him yet, right?"

"I haven't heard anything, so probably not."

"Then let's end the psycho bastard. Let's talk to Pierce, Zayne, and Vaughn, then hunt this sick piece of shit down and put ourselves out of our misery. There comes a point when a man has to make a decision to protect his family. I know Mac will sleep better if Brandon no longer exists."

This was what I loved about my best friend. He was loyal and protective of everyone he cared about. "I'm thinking the same damned thing. After Mac is home, let's meet with the guys and figure this shit out. If I had the opportunity to slit that piece of shit's throat right now ... I won't lie, man. I would take it."

"Same."

Cade and I stood in silence for a minute, the bitter cold seeping into my bones. "Are you ready to check on Mac?" I asked, shivering.

"Yeah. It was good to get some fresh air, though."

"Maybe Mac won't have to spend the night, but regardless, we'll all be at Dad's again, so Gemma and I can give you a break." I smacked him on the back and laughed.

Cade arched a brow at me. "There wasn't a single thing that was funny about that comment. Are you cracking up and laughing at nothing now?" He chuckled.

"Do you know what I would give to get my hands on a joint?" I gave him a silly grin.

Cade's eyes cut over to me. "I've got some at the house. Mac and I would chill on occasion, but now that she's pregnant I haven't indulged."

"We totally should. I don't think Gem has ever tried it either."

"That might be a really fun evening." Cade shivered. "Dammit, it's cold out here."

"We can't do it around Mac, though. That would be mean." I glanced at him. "We could sneak off to the guesthouse when she's with Janice."

"As soon as Mac is safe and at home, I guarantee you, I'll figure out a time to meet you and Gemma." Cade looked eager to relax. I didn't blame him.

In the back of my mind, I wondered if the pot would help Gemma remember what happened. Maybe it was a bad idea to include her. Cade and I should sneak off without the girls. Or perhaps it would suck ass to open the floodgates and let my thoughts run rampant. *Forget it.* I was barely hanging onto sanity as it was. I didn't need to be dropkicked off the edge.

Cade's phone chimed, and he grabbed it out of his pocket. "Hello? We're on the way." Cade broke out into a run, and I jogged after him. "The doctor has the test results already."

1 8

Breathless after running up four flights of stairs, Cade and I burst into Mac's room. The doctor glared at us, but I didn't care. We needed to know if Mac and the baby were all right.

"What's wrong? Are they going to be okay?" Cade hurried to Mac's side and grabbed her hand. Gemma stood near Janice and Dad with her arms folded. I joined her and slid my arm around her waist.

"I'm glad to see you have so much support. Since we have some new faces, I'll introduce myself. I'm Dr. MacMillan." The doctor peered over his black-rimmed glasses and smiled at us.

He appeared older than Dad, possibly in his mid-fifties, which I was grateful for. It meant he'd been taking care of moms and their babies for years.

"Mackenzie, you have preeclampsia. Most of the time, we don't see it until later in the pregnancy, but on a rare occasion, it will show up sooner. In a nutshell, your blood pressure is dangerously high. We're going to administer magnesium sulfate, then medication. You're officially on bedrest. The goal is to allow the baby to grow more, then we will reevaluate the situation and see if we need to deliver early. It's imperative that you reduce your stress."

Gem tugged on my shirt sleeve and glanced up at me, sadness

159

twisting her expression. If I had to take a wild guess, she was blaming herself for sending Mac's stress level over the edge.

"This isn't your fault. It's Brandon's," I whispered in her ear.

She chewed on her bottom lip and nodded.

Until we had some time alone, I couldn't help her think this through logically. My attention returned to the doctor as he rattled off Mac's restrictions due to the high blood pressure.

"We're going to run a few more stress tests to check on the baby while you're here."

"Excuse me," Janice said. "I'm Mac's mother. Wouldn't her legs and arms be swollen with preeclampsia?"

"With rare cases, the swelling is more internal and not noticeable. Mackenzie is an exception to the norm. Diet is really important. I recommend lining up some Netflix shows and finding some fun projects to do from bed," the doctor explained.

"Well, great." Mac smacked her forehead and released a shaky breath. "No pizza."

Although the circumstances were serious, we all laughed.

"Can I go downstairs to the kitchen?" Mac's eyes widened. "And shower?"

"Yes, you can, but keep it limited. You'll need to stretch and have a change of scenery, which is important to your mental health." The doctor patted her arm.

"What about an occasional car ride? Like an hour tops?" I asked, trying to think of ways for Mac not to lose her mind over the next several months.

Dr. MacMillan pursed his lips. "Bedrest right now." His attention bounced between each of us. "Are there any other questions?"

"No. Thank you for helping her," Cade said. If I thought he looked like shit earlier, it was nothing compared to now. I could have sworn he'd aged ten years in the past twenty minutes.

"You need to check his blood pressure too," Janice said. "These two … our family has been through some very traumatic events in the last few weeks."

You could almost see the switch flip in the doctor's mind. "I'm sorry to ask, but are you Franklin Harrington?"

Dad cleared his throat. "Yes. Mac is my daughter."

The doctor's gaze swept over us, his expression growing grim. "I didn't put it all together at first. I tend to have laser focus when it comes to my patients."

"As it should be." Dad nodded.

"I would like to send a therapist in to see you, Mackenzie." The doctor faced Mac. "Your father being kidnapped is … I can't even begin to imagine how traumatic that was for you and the family."

"We're all going to therapy," Dad assured him. "Since Cade is the lead guitarist for August Clover and my son is the lead singer, along with Gemma, I had my security team check into a psychiatrist for us."

Dr. MacMillan moved toward Dad, and they shook hands. "I'm glad to hear everyone is going to talk to someone. If there's anything I can do, please let me know."

"Thank you." Dad shoved his hand in his pocket. It was trembling.

"When can I go home?" Mac asked.

"I want to keep you for forty-eight hours, then we will reassess the situation," the doctor said kindly.

Tears slipped down Mac's cheek. "Okay. Thank you." She placed her palm on her tummy. "While I'm here, is there a possibility I could have the test to find out the gender?" She peeked up at Cade.

"Are you sure?" Cade asked.

The room grew quiet. He didn't have to verbalize his thoughts. We were all hanging onto a thread, hoping the baby would make it.

"I need to know," she whispered.

Cade looked at the doctor. "Is it possible to have that done?"

"We can actually do the blood draw here and process it. I'll order the stress tests and bloodwork, then." He approached the computer in the room and entered the orders. "You should find out the sex of the baby in a few days."

"Wow, that soon?" Janice grinned. "Things certainly have changed since I was pregnant with you." She winked at Mac.

"That's because you're old, Mom." For the first time in way too long, Mac laughed.

"You might want to order something to eat before the kitchen closes." Dr. MacMillan handed her a menu. "You should get some rest, and I'll see you in the morning."

"I'll try," Mac said.

After we all thanked him, he exited the room.

"Dammit." Mac rubbed her face. "How the hell am I going to manage bedrest?"

Gemma walked over to Mac and sat in the chair next to her. "I'll be there. We should work on some scrapbooks and a baby book. You can still go to the game room and kick Cade's and Hendrix's asses at video games too."

Mac stared at her. "If you leave again, Gemma Thompson, I will get out of the bed and find you my fucking self." Her tone was sharp.

There it was. I suspected some unresolved anger would pop up.

"Mac ..." I joined Gemma and placed my hand on her back. "Maybe you should say what you want to, then we should move on."

"I agree," Dad said. "But make sure you choose your words wisely. Once you say them, this is over. When you get home, we'll talk about how we're going to move forward as a family."

Mac blinked several times. She was no stranger to that no-bullshit tone of Dad's.

"Why couldn't you tell me? Why did you leave without telling any of us? What the hell were you thinking? What happened?" Mac launched questions at Gem like they were torpedoes with heat-seeking radar.

"You can be upset with me, Mac. I guess I hoped ... Brandon made it clear that if I told anyone he would kill your dad. Although you're my best friend, I couldn't risk Franklin's life. He was already in danger." Gem's expression filled with grief. "It was a horrible decision I had to make. Please try to understand."

"I do understand, but I can't seem to let it go. Your decision affected everyone in this room."

Gemma pursed her lips. "How do you think it would have affected this family if we'd lost Franklin?"

Tears welled in Dad's eyes. His body was rigid. I suspected he was trying his best to stay out of the argument and allow the girls to resolve their differences.

"I wouldn't have blamed you," Mac whispered. "It would have been on Brandon, but it would have devastated me." She lifted her gaze to Dad. "I feel like I finally have a family. It's all I've wanted for years." Her chin trembled with that confession.

"We've all wanted a family, Mac. It's what brought us together." Gem offered her a smile.

"I understand that it's difficult trying to sift through conflicting emotions, Mac," I said. "I've wrestled with the same thoughts, but Gem and I have an agreement that from now on, no more major decisions will be made without the other one."

"We can do the same," Gemma said. "Would that help if I swear I'll talk to Hendrix first, then you?" Gemma reached for Mac's hand. "I love you. You're my sister, and I'll protect you at all costs. At the same time, if this will help us heal, then you have my word."

Mac closed her eyes briefly. "You've never outright lied to me, just omitted information." She looked at Gemma. "Yeah, and you have my word as well. No more secrets."

"No more secrets." Gem stood and gave Mac a big hug.

I looked over at Dad, but he hadn't relaxed yet.

A knock on the door broke through the silence. "Hi, I'm Annie. I'm going to draw your blood for the gender and perform an ultrasound." We all cleared out of the way except for Cade. "As soon as this is finished, we'll start the magnesium drip."

The tension eased when we all saw the baby on the screen and heard the heartbeat.

"Everything looks good," the nurse said.

AN HOUR LATER, the nurse started Mac's IV drip.

"I feel like I'm on fire," she gasped. "Oh shit, it hurts."

"I'll get a nurse." Dad hurried out of the room and seconds later came back with the nurse.

"Let's grab you some ice packs, hon. Some people have a tough time with the treatment."

"Please hurry," Cade said, smoothing the hair off Mac's forehead. "I'm here, babe. Hang in there."

The nurse rushed back in with ice packs that she placed along Mac's spine. "Is that helping?"

Mac nodded but didn't speak, which told me she was in a lot of pain.

"Mac, would some music help? I have my phone and AirPods," Gemma suggested.

"Yeah," Mac whispered.

Gemma rifled through her oversized handbag, then produced the items. She selected her Spotify app as she approached Mac's bed. "Do you want something upbeat to take your mind off things or ..."

Mac gave her a thumbs-up.

Gemma gently placed the earbuds in Mac's ears and started a song.

"Thanks, bestie," Mac said softly.

An hour later, Mac's nurse entered. "Hon, how are you feeling?"

Mac removed an earphone. "I'm okay. The music is helping distract me."

"Good. Visiting hours are over, so I have to kick everyone out. Normally, we don't allow anyone to remain in the room after hours, but if the father of the baby wants to stay, I'll bring in a recliner so you can try to get some rest too." She smiled at Cade.

"Thank you. No disrespect, but you would have to physically pry me away from her, and I'm guessing my bodyguard is bigger than your security guy."

I hid my grin.

The poor nurse's cheeks turned bright pink. "I did see him."

Gemma grinned and winked at me.

"Yeah, every female in here will agree with you. Not that you said anything, but your face flamed red," Mac whispered. "But you should see the other one."

Gemma began to giggle, then everyone in the room laughed.

"She must be feeling a little bit better," I said.

Dad chuckled. "We do have security, and as long as Cade can stay, then the rest of us will follow the rules and leave for the night. What time can we return?" Dad glanced at his watch.

"Eight in the morning." The nurse smiled while she held the door open for us. "Mac should get some sleep."

We all hugged Mac, then I pulled Cade aside. "Call me if you need anything. I mean anything. Hell, I'll tell you dirty jokes if it will keep you mentally occupied. And of course, if Mac …" I couldn't force the words out of my mouth.

"You'll be my first call, man. Thanks." Cade gave me a quick hug.

"Bye, sis." I kissed Mac on the forehead and removed the AirPod from one ear. "I love you. I'll be back here if you need me. Just call and Dad will make it happen."

A smile tugged at the corner of her mouth. "Gemma forgot her phone, but I'm going to keep the earphones and pair them to my iPhone."

"Ah, she's pretty preoccupied." I peered over my shoulder, but Gem, Dad, and Janice were in the hallway.

"One more thing," Mac said.

"Yeah?" Worry flooded through me.

"You're sounding more and more like Dad."

A huge grin eased across my face. "He gets shit done, even when he's in pain mentally. He's my hero, so you gave me a hell of a compliment."

"It was meant as one." Mac squeezed my hand. "I'm really tired, so go away."

I chuckled. At least her sense of humor was returning.

"Later, guys." I waved before I joined my family in the hall.

The first thing I noticed was that Jaxon was standing next to Zayne. Jaxon's blonde hair was a stark contrast to Zayne's light brown locks. He cleared Zayne by a few inches and was just as muscular, but that wasn't the feature that caught my attention. His eyes were the color of golden honey. I would have to mention it to Mac under different circumstances since she drooled over the bodyguards. Surely, she'd noticed. Chuckling to myself, I approached him.

"Hey, man. Thanks for being here with Mac and Cade." I shook his hand. I'd only met Jaxon twice and hadn't spoken to him, but if he was one of Pierce's men, I trusted him.

"I'll keep you updated if there's any concerns," he said.

"I appreciate it." I looked at Zayne. "We're ready to go to Dad's."

"How is she?" Zayne asked.

"She's going to be fine, but she's on bedrest and has to chill on the stress," Gemma said with a ton of confidence.

"She has preeclampsia. Basically, it's really high blood pressure," Janice explained.

"If she does all right tonight, she'll come home the day after tomorrow." I gently snapped the hair band on my wrist, reigning my fear in before it escalated. Mac and the baby had to be okay.

Zayne's focus followed my movement, then he nodded. "I hate to add additional chaos to the evening, but Sutton and Pierce need to speak to you after you get settled. They're waiting at Franklin's."

Shit. This can't be good. "Dad, do you know why?" I asked, frowning.

"No, but they want to talk to you and me privately," Dad replied.

"We'd better go so we can find out what the hell is going on." I slipped my arm around Gemma's shoulders as we followed Dad and Janice to the parking garage. My thoughts took a chaotic turn as I scrambled to figure out why Pierce and Sutton were waiting for us. *What is so important it warrants a visit after Mac's hospitalization?*

I left Gemma and Janice in the living room as Pierce, Sutton, Dad, and I walked straight to his office. Dad smoothed his button-down blue-and-white-plaid shirt while he sat down in his executive office chair.

"What's so important it couldn't wait?" he asked with a subtle note of irritation.

I had the same question.

Dad's desk was tidier than I'd seen it in a long time, but he hadn't returned to work yet. My attention landed on the picture on the wall with Dad, Janice, Mac, Cade, Gemma, and me. It had been taken the Christmas I'd proposed to Gemma.

Pierce stood to the left of Dad, and Sutton sank into one of the wingback chairs. She crossed her legs and adjusted her beige sweater. Sutton didn't fidget unless she was stressed, which told me this was serious.

"We know who contacted you with the information on Gemma's location when she was with Brandon," Pierce said in a soothing tone, his biceps straining against the sleeves of his blue polo shirt.

Confusion clouded Dad's features as his attention bounced to each of us. "Hendrix, what are they talking about? Someone contacted you? I thought the serum worked."

"Not exactly. Since Gemma is safe at home now, and you had a lot on your plate, I didn't want to tell you until I learned more."

"Well, someone should start filling me in." Dad folded his hands on top of his desk, his blue eyes narrowing at us. His expression was all business.

"I was contacted by a woman I've never met. She knew who Gemma and I were, but at first, I didn't think much about it since the band has grown so popular. Zayne was with me when she used Face-Time to contact me. During our conversation, I snapped a screenshot of her and sent it to Sutton or Pierce. I honestly don't remember who."

"It took some digging, but we found out who she is," Pierce said.

Sutton flipped open a notebook, removed a photo, and handed it to me. "This is her, correct?"

"Yeah." I didn't need to think about it. The image was definitely the woman who had helped me save Gemma. "Who is she?"

"Her name is Allison Collier. Well, today it is. We suspect she has more aliases than we found."

My forehead creased in confusion. "Aliases?"

Sutton released a soft sigh. "Hendrix, she's your mother."

I white-knuckled the arm of the chair as her words penetrated my exhausted thoughts. "What? There has to be a mistake." Leaning forward, I handed Dad the photo. My eyes never left him as he stared at the picture.

"She's had some plastic surgery, but it's her." He dropped the image on his desk and leaned back in his seat.

I shot out of my chair. "My mother has aliases? More importantly, how the hell does she know Brandon Montgomery?" Pacing the small room, I placed my hands on my hips. "What haven't you told me, Dad?" My temper flared. "Nope. Forget it. Never mind. Pierce, your timing sucks. This could have waited."

Pierce remained silent, which meant he was holding his ground.

"Hendrix," Sutton said from behind me. "We're well aware that the timing is shitty, but …"

My pulse spiked. "But? Dad, you don't have anything to say about this? Would you back me up here?"

"I'm waiting for the rest of the information son, like I recommend that you do." Dad's chin tilted, which meant he was about to pull rank on me. He didn't do it often, but when he did, there was no compromising with him.

Dammit, he is being an ass.

"Let's get this over with, then." I played with the hair tie on my wrist.

"Allison is one of the world's most wanted criminals," Pierce said. "She makes Dillon Montgomery look like an angel."

My world spun. The information took me to the edge of reality and threatened to push me over the goddamned cliff. "What? I don't understand. Dad, were you aware of this?" I sat down again, the news crushing my chest like a tidal wave. What baffled me more was the fact that she was worse than Dillon Montgomery. *How is that even possible?*

Dad scratched his stubbled chin, then dropped his hands in his lap. "After she left, I had no idea where she went. I had no desire to find out either."

"Was she already involved in—whatever the hell it is?" Doubt and denial teetered on the edge of my thoughts.

"At the time, she was dabbling in running drugs. I was in law school, and in no way did her activities line up with my goals in life. I made her choose. The next day she was gone, and it was just you and me."

I slumped in my seat. A part of me understood why Dad wouldn't have shared this information unless it was necessary, but I still resented him for it. I'd spent years thinking she'd left because I'd been born and that she wasn't cut out to be a mother.

"What is she involved in exactly?" I asked Pierce.

"It's more like what isn't she involved in. Drugs, trafficking, weapons—nothing seems to be off-limits for her. She's managed to piss off the Mexican cartels, so she's laying low right now."

"The Mexican cartels?" I whispered. "*This* woman is my mother?" I dragged my hands down my face. "*Her* blood is in my veins." I inhaled sharply. Suddenly, an unexplainable blanket of calm shrouded me. Every emotion rippled through me, then receded into a dark corner of my soul.

"Hendrix, I had no idea that she'd continued her *career*. Her name was Pamela when we were married. After she left, I never heard from her again," Dad explained.

"She obviously knows who I am. Gemma is now in danger from Brandon as well as being in a relationship with me ..." I trailed off, hoping Dad would get the impact of my statement. Tension snaked down my neck and back, and I massaged my shoulder, willing the corded muscles to loosen. "I'm done. I'm taking Gemma and we're leaving. We're moving off the grid. I've got a crazy criminal for a mother and Brandon is loose." I shot out of my chair. "I. Can't. Take. Anymore." I spun on my heel, flung the door open, and hightailed it down the hall. "Gem!"

"Hang on, Harrington." In a few quick strides, Pierce grabbed my arm. "We need you, then we'll move if it's still necessary."

"Who the hell is *we?*" I spat.

Pierce dropped his hold on me. "The FBI."

I stared at him numbly. "They want me as bait, don't they?"

Pierce's facial features remained stoic and unresponsive. I'd guessed correctly. After this was over, I was going to tell him he needed to switch up his expressions on occasion because I was able to read him now.

"Please come back so we can talk this out and not scare Gemma. She's been through enough." Pierce's gaze bored into mine.

He was right. I couldn't drag her through any more hell, especially when I wasn't clear about what path we should take.

"Okay." I massaged my temples as I followed him into Dad's office. Apparently, Gemma hadn't heard me yell for her.

Dad stood up from behind his desk. "I'm on your side, son. Unfortunately, the FBI trumps my wishes."

I remained standing as my attention landed on Pierce again.

"They would like to know when she contacts you, and any details you can provide them concerning where she is," Pierce explained. "That's it, but you can't move or leave the country. She obviously knows where you live, and the FBI doesn't want to tip her off in any way."

My eyes narrowed. "What if she doesn't reach out anymore?"

"She's contacted you twice in a week, and chances are she will again. In the meantime," Sutton added, "if you and Gemma want to move, then we'll do everything to help make it happen."

"There's a few seriously screwed-up things about this situation. I'm about to be an uncle for the first time, Dad needs me nearby, and I need my best friend. I need all of you." I ran my hand through my hair as my emotions pushed and pulled me in a heated game of tug-of-war.

"Son, I think we've all worn out our welcome in Spokane. We won't have to separate, and I suspect Mac and Cade will be on the same page. We can find a new city and lay low but still be in the same area."

"Are you sure? We've played around with this idea before and never left. Besides, I don't want you to give up your practice. You've rebuilt your life." Even though Dad got on my nerves sometimes, I loved and respected him a ton. I couldn't imagine not seeing him on a regular basis. My heart ached at the mere thought of not being able to spend time with him whenever I wanted.

"I have more than enough to retire early and live at the same level I am now. My family is more important to me. Honestly, after … after the kidnapping, I made the decision it was time for us to go. I wasn't even sure I would ever see you again, but the idea kept me going." Dad's face twisted in agony.

"Dad?" I hopped up and hurried around to his chair.

He held his hands up. "I'm okay. The memories tend to sneak up on me, but I guess that wasn't really out of nowhere this time."

I hugged him before I returned to my seat. "We don't have to talk about it anymore. I'll work with the FBI, but while I'm waiting for Allison's call, I'm going to figure out where to move. Gemma and I want to get married, design our home, and lay low."

"Janice and I have discussed the same. It's time for a fresh start," Dad agreed.

"One more thing," Sutton said. "Hendrix, you can't tell anyone else what's happening."

"Not even Gemma? What if my mother approaches her in public? I'm sorry, Sutton, I won't risk it. She needs to see a picture and be aware of what's going on."

Sutton glanced at Pierce. "Are you sure she can handle more stress right now? We don't even know what happened when she was gone."

The shit kept rolling down the goddammed hill. "No, but we just promised we wouldn't make any major decisions without talking to each other."

"You're not making the decision. The FBI is," Pierce explained.

I chuckled. "It will still count, man." I stood, my body groaning as I stretched. "I'll talk to her after her doctor's appointments and our therapy session later this week. I need to make sure she's mentally able to deal with this. Hell, I'm not even sure I am, but it looks like I don't really have a choice." My gaze cut over to Pierce. "Thanks for your help. I really do appreciate it."

"I realize it's business, but we're family." Pierce patted me on the back and squeezed my shoulder.

Sutton stood, then embraced me. "We're all in this together. Please let me know how Gemma's appointments go."

"I'll catch you later, Dad." I was too exhausted to talk anymore. All I wanted to do was curl up next to Gemma in our bed and kiss her.

After searching the kitchen, I meandered upstairs. A soft light came from our bedroom, and I walked toward it. I leaned on the wall, the scene making me smile. A wave of protectiveness washed over me. Gemma had fallen asleep on top of the comforter, wearing her oversized Billy Raffoul T-shirt. Her red hair was splayed out on the pillow. She looked angelic, and there was nothing in this world that I wanted more than to keep her safe.

I toed off my tennis shoes and quietly closed the bedroom door. After pulling out a pair of gray sweats from the top drawer, I shed my clothes and replaced my jeans with a more comfortable option. It was a cold night, but I chose to sleep without a shirt. Gemma was a little heater.

I stifled a yawn, then grabbed a blanket off the chair in the corner. Hopefully, I wouldn't wake her up when I tucked her in. A smile eased across my face, and she didn't stir as I gently placed the throw on her. I rounded the bed, then slipped under the covers.

"Hendrix?" Her sleepy blue eyes gazed into mine.

"Yeah, babe. I'm right here."

She smiled at me. "Is Mac okay?"

"I haven't heard anything, so I'm assuming she's doing fine."

Gem scrambled to get beneath the comforter. She snuggled up to me and placed her head on my chest. "This is my favorite place to be." She yawned.

"Mine too." I wrapped a few strands of her red hair around my fingers and played with it until she drifted off again. "Peaceful dreams, babe."

A BLOOD-CURDLING SCREAM jolted me from a deep sleep, and I bolted upright. I struggled to see through the darkness, but there was no mistaking that Gem was huddled in the corner of the bedroom.

Nearly tripping over the covers, I climbed out of bed and knelt beside her. I made sure to keep a little bit of distance so she wouldn't feel cornered. "Gemma. Babe, it's Hendrix. Are you awake?"

She jerked away from me, her eyes wide and alert. "Don't touch me. Stay away from me."

What the hell?

Her body trembled violently as her attention darted around the room. "I won't do it, Brandon. I won't. I love Hendrix, and nothing you ever do to me will change that."

A mixture of relief and anger swirled in the pit of my stomach. At least she was dreaming, but I wasn't sure how to safely bring her out of it when she appeared to be awake.

"Gem. The first song we sang together was 'I Can't Breathe' by Bea Miller. Do you remember? Cade, John, and I had performed at the college that night, and I walked you and Mac to the dorm that evening." I thought it would be best to leave Brandon and the campus police out of the picture. "Mac talked me into singing before you two went to your room."

There was no way that Brandon had those details, and I hoped that fact would reach her. I hummed a few notes as Gemma frantically backed up against the wall. "Sing with me, Gem. Listen to my voice." I began to whisper the lyrics. Although I was grasping at straws, music had always kept both of us sane. Maybe it would help her now.

The first time Gemma and I had sung together, I'd fallen head over heels in love with her. That moment had always been special to me. We'd never discussed it, but I assumed Gemma felt a deep connection to the memory as well.

Her gaze locked on mine as I continued to sing. A soft squeak came from her lips as she began to form the words. Recognition settled over her expression, and I slowly extended my hand to her. Her icy cold fingers gripped mine. God, I missed hearing her sing. I missed us on stage together and writing new music. I wanted my fiancée back. All of her. Not just her body, but her mind and soul too.

Gemma lunged at me, knocking me backward onto the carpeted floor. "Hendrix." She kissed me. "You're here."

I held her tightly as her kiss grew more desperate. Needy. My cock was wide awake in seconds.

She didn't waste any time as she nearly ripped her sleep shirt off. Before I realized it, she'd flipped my dick out of my sweatpants and moved her G-string out of the way. She wrapped her fingers around me, then practically shoved me inside of her. Gemma's tight walls hugged my throbbing shaft, and I moaned.

"Fuck me." She guided my hands to her breasts. She bounced up and down but only grew more frustrated.

"Babe, let's take a break and slow down." I grabbed her wrists and held them together.

"I can't …" She crawled onto the bed. Once she was situated on all fours, she peered over her shoulder at me.

I climbed off the floor and stared at her. Every part of my body pulsated with desire. She'd just come out of a night terror, and turning her down for sex when she was this fragile would cause more issues that I didn't know how to handle.

"Shove your dick in me and fuck me hard," she pleaded.

Dammit. She wasn't going to take no for an answer. I ran my finger up her wet slit and spread her folds apart. Precum beaded on the tip of my cock, and I stroked myself firmly.

She bit her lip as she watched, then she rolled over on her back and propped herself up on her elbows. Her hand slid between her thighs and she began to massage her clit.

"Do you want to taste me?" Her eyes were full of longing.

I knelt and spread her legs apart. "Always." I peered up at her as my tongue swirled around her bundle of nerves.

She grabbed some of my hair and tilted her hips up. "That's it, baby. Fuck me with your mouth." Her lips parted, and she moaned as I eased two fingers inside her. Within seconds, her body shuddered beneath my touch, and she orgasmed.

Damn, Gem was primed and ready to go. She's never come that fast.

"More, Hendrix. I need more."

Crawling up on the bed, I positioned myself between her legs, then thrust deep inside her. She rocked against me, and her slick pussy clenched around my shaft. I growled as I picked up my pace.

"I'm going to come again, but I need one more thing." She glanced at me, then took my hand and placed it on her throat. Gemma tilted her head back. "Squeeze."

I stopped moving and looked at her. "Gemma."

"Do it," she demanded. "Choke me and fuck me at the same time."

I jerked back like I'd touched a hot stove. "No. I won't do that."

She glared at me. "Don't be so dramatic. It's just a little fun."

Jesus. Gemma would never have considered this appropriate, and I sure as hell didn't. I didn't get off on hurting people, especially her.

"I said no." My words were clipped and firm. "It's a hard boundary for me, Gemma."

"Speaking of hard, you're not anymore." She turned away from me.

I stood up and walked to the bathroom. After I washed my face, I peered at my reflection in the mirror. Exhausted eyes stared back at me. *How am I going to reconnect with Gem when all she wants to do is fuck?*

"Hendrix?"

I returned to our bedroom. "Yeah?"

"I'm sorry. I don't know why I asked you to do that. Can we forget about it and finish?"

No, I couldn't forget about it, but I wasn't up for a big discussion either. "We can continue on my terms." My gaze connected with hers, and silence filled the space between us.

"Okay," she whispered.

Maybe Gemma realized she'd gone too far and would settle down, but the voice in my mind said otherwise. I joined her on the bed, and over the next twenty minutes, I did everything in my power to remind Gemma of how good our sex life was when we connected on all levels. I wasn't sure if I reached her or not, but at least I'd taken control of the situation and made love to her.

Two days later, Mac was released from the hospital. She seemed a bit calmer than the other day, but I suspected she was super happy to be at Dad's. Not only was I glad she was home, but helping Cade keep her busy was a welcome distraction for me as well. Between Dad, Gemma, and my mother, I was spinning out of control.

I'd attempted to talk to Gem concerning the choking episode, but she played it off as if it were no big deal. Confused and at a loss about what was driving her behavior, I decided not to bring it up again unless I had to. Maybe she needed more time to adjust.

After Mac ate a healthy breakfast that Ruby had cooked for her, Dad called a family meeting. We all gathered in the living room. I wasn't sure what he wanted to talk to everyone about since we'd discussed Mac's health, moving, and my mother the previous night.

I sat next to Gemma on the couch and threaded my fingers through hers. Mac sat next to Gem and Cade. Dad stood in the middle of the floor, and Janice took her regular seat near the window.

Dad rubbed his hands together, his attention sweeping over everyone. "Mac, it's great to have you home. I think it would be best to get some things out in the open. As we all know, hiding feelings can complicate matters. First, if anyone else would like to express their thoughts or say anything to Gemma concerning Brandon, say it now." Dad placed his hands on his hips as his gaze shifted between each of us. The room remained silent, which was a good sign. "No one? This is your last chance. If you're angry with Gemma, get it off your chest now." Dad paused, allowing us time to speak up.

"Excellent. If you don't have anything you need to share, I do." Dad cleared his throat. "Let it go. I'm alive and our family is together because of the sacrifice that Gemma made. Also, the FBI has valuable intel because of it. Maybe you didn't agree or support Gemma's choice, but it wasn't yours to make. It was hers. If she hadn't done what she did, I wouldn't be standing in front of you. If Brandon had contacted you instead, I have a sneaking suspicion each of you would have made the exact same decision. I would have." His jaw tightened, the muscle tensing briefly.

Mac and I exchanged a guilty look. Gem and I had already had this conversation, and I had come to terms with the fact that Dad was right. I would have made the same choice Gemma had. I didn't think Mac had thought it through, though.

Janice slipped her arm around Dad before she spoke, making it clear that they were a united front. "As screwed up as this situation is, it's brought us all closer. Personally, I've learned not to take a minute with any of you for granted. I love and value every person in this room. We're family, we're going to make mistakes, but we'll always show up for each other and put the pieces back together again." Janice smiled at Gemma. "I think everyone has forgotten how incredibly brave and heroic Gemma's actions were. She was willing to sacrifice herself because she loves us. Her intention was to once and for all free this family of the Montgomerys. How in the world can you hold a grudge over that?"

Janice's words hung in the air. I placed a kiss on the side of Gemma's head. "Mom's right. You are a hero."

Mac's chin began to tremble. Suddenly, she flung her arms around Gem. "I'm sorry I was pissed at you. If I was really honest about it, I wasn't mad at all. I was scared shitless I'd lost you forever."

Gemma hugged her back. "You can't get rid of me that easily." She stood and approached Dad. "Franklin, thank you for your support and for welcoming me into the family when we first met. I love you, and I would trade myself again if it meant you would be safe."

Tears welled in Dad's eyes as he wrapped Gemma in a warm embrace. "Love you too. I couldn't be happier to have you as my daughter."

Dad released Gem, and she hugged Janice before she sat down next to me. The tension began to lessen.

"Mac, you should get back into bed," Janice said.

Mac groaned loudly. "Fine. I have to remember it's not about me— it's for the baby. I still don't like it, though."

"I'll help you." Gem hopped up and extended her hand to Mac. "I bought some scrapbooks too. Do you have your ultrasound images?"

Mac nodded enthusiastically. "Upstairs."

"I also found a great website. We can look at nursery colors and designs. I understand that the decision will be up to you and Cade, but I thought it would be fun."

Mac stood and placed her hand on her tummy. "I don't think I could do this without you, bestie."

"We've got this." Gemma offered Mac a genuine smile, then the two of them left the living room.

"Thanks, Mom. Your support means a lot to Gemma and me too." I hugged Janice.

"I meant every word." Janice patted my cheek.

"Dad, can I have a minute?" I asked. It was nice to see him take charge again. I hoped it meant he was beginning to heal.

"Of course. Let's meet in my office." He placed his arm around my shoulder and guided me toward the hall.

I stopped and turned to Cade. "Catch you in the game room afterward?"

"Yeah, I need to blow off some steam and shoot something." He chuckled, then followed the girls up the stairs.

"Thanks for having a family meeting. I think it helped clear the air. Gemma was really nervous about coming home." I sat in the leather wingback chair in Dad's office while he closed the door.

"Mac had verbalized her frustration several times, so I wanted to get it out in the open and move on. Gemma doesn't deserve to be punished for making her decision. At the same time, everyone has a right to their feelings. It can be a delicate balance." Dad sank into his chair and leaned back.

"Mom had some good points too." My focus landed on Dad's assortment of pictures on his bookcase, including one of Mac and me at the beach when she was two and another of my first on-stage performance in middle school. Those times seemed so much simpler.

"She did. Janice is great in difficult situations. It's one of the many things I love about her." Dad folded his hands in his lap and offered me his undivided attention. "What's on your mind, son?"

I suppressed a chuckle. If Dad hadn't told me he'd been sexually assaulted, I would never have known anything was wrong with him. "I wanted to see how your first therapy appointment went yesterday." I focused on his reaction to the question and hoped for an honest answer.

Disappointment flickered through his eyes. "Difficult, but I told her what I could."

"Did she give you any suggestions on how to handle the flashbacks?"

I was well aware that Dad wanted to change the topic. His shoulders had tensed as the word *therapist* floated off my tongue.

"I'm not sure I want to discuss this anymore." Dad spun his chair around and toward the window, blocking my view of him.

Inwardly, I sighed. I wasn't sure if I should push him or not. I was just checking in to see how he was doing.

"Sorry. I don't remember asking what you wanted," I said. That smart-ass comment did it. He turned slowly, anger flaring in his expression. "I don't need every detail, Dad, but we should get one thing clear—I'm going to check in. I'm going to push you to talk to me at times. Not just for you, but for me. Otherwise, my thoughts will visit some really dark places. I've been through your sloppy-drunk days with you and I won't do it again. I don't deserve it."

I paused, waiting to see if he would respond, but he remained quiet. "And … I don't want to lose you, Dad. We're in a good place, and I need you. The thought of you not staying sober guts me." I choked on my words, tears threatening. "So I have to know how you're doing. No bullshit, no attorney front, no head-of-the-household tone, and no pulling rank. I just need Franklin Harrington to talk to me for a minute and tell me how he's doing as a grown man that went through a traumatic experience." More gently, I added, "Is that too much to ask?"

Dad placed his hands on his desk and leaned forward. "You're definitely my son." A genuine smile slipped into place. "I'll try, Hendrix. It's difficult to discuss."

"I get that, and I don't need to hear any more about what happened. I'm not even sure if talking about it is healthy. I just want to know how you're doing. Like, did you sleep last night, or did you have nightmares? If so, what about working out together a few hours before bed? Maybe that would help us manage the stress. I'm in this with you. I love you, Dad."

Dad's attention landed on me again, then he nodded. "I don't know about working out. My ribs are doing better, but they're still healing. I can ask the doctor if I can at least get in the pool. I was considering asking Pierce to teach me some self-defense after I'd been … taken." He rubbed his chin. "I can throw a solid punch, but when you're lying on the floor getting the shit kicked out of you … what should I have done?"

The sound of my heart breaking rang in my ears. "You curl up and protect yourself as best you can," I said quietly. "You did everything that you could have done in the moment."

A frown furrowed his brow as he stared at me. "That's just it. We're not out of the woods, yet. Not by a long shot. What if … what if?" Dad rubbed his hands together.

"Don't." I held my hand up. "You've got a fortress here, and we're protected."

Dad tapped his fingers against the black ceramic mug on his desk.

"As soon as I'm done with the FBI bullshit, Gem and I are ready to move," I said. "Are you sure you and Janice will want to go with us?"

"Yeah, we've already discussed it. Right now, we're just trying to keep Mac calm, but I think Janice is planning to talk to her in the next few days."

"Sounds good. In the meantime, Gemma has a doctor's appointment. Brandon stole her engagement ring so we're going to design one together. I want a rush job on it if possible."

Dad grimaced. "That son of a bitch took her ring?" He shook his head. "Why am I surprised? The best thing to do is move forward." He opened the top drawer of his desk, then produced a business card and handed it to me. "You should reach out to Kent MacPhee and see if he has availability. He designs as well as owns a jewelry store chain across the US. His rings are stunning."

"That sounds great. Zayne suggested we get married in the UK. He introduced me to a wedding planner he knows over there. Gem would probably be on board, but Mac can't make the trip now."

"I'm sorry, son. You and Gemma can have the ceremony there if you want, but either Janice or I would have to stay home with Mac."

"No, we want you all there." I closed my eyes briefly, attempting to come up with a safe place to get married. "I don't want to wait, Dad. At the same time, I need to." A half-hearted chuckle rumbled through me.

"That was a bit contradictory, son."

"Right?" I sighed and scrubbed my face with my hands. "Hopefully, I'll have more information after the doctor's visit. There are signs that Gem was ... I can't even explain it. She's not herself. Whatever Brandon gave her is either still in her system, or it's caused permanent changes." A sharp pang stabbed me in the chest. "She needs some bloodwork done. I don't know what other tests they might want to do."

Dad's forehead creased. "It's bad?"

I pursed my lips. "At times she's fine, then she'll do something so out of character for her it terrifies me."

"I won't push, but maybe you can tell me more after the test results are in."

"All right. I'll play it by ear for now."

I stretched my legs in front of me and ran a palm across my faded blue jeans. "Maybe we could get married here or at Pierce's place. We would have security. It's not my first choice, but I'm ready to make her my wife. Plus, Mac's complications with the baby changes things."

"It does. It would probably be best to have something small here. I think Mac could manage getting out of bed for a little while."

"I haven't talked to Gem about it yet, but I wasn't going to have any groomsmen. After the last time, I would be more comfortable with me, Gem, and whoever is marrying us at the altar, and that's all. It was bad enough that everyone was in danger when we were in Maine."

Dad's face clouded with sadness. "I'm sorry, Hendrix. Your wedding day is supposed to be special. Happy."

"It will be. It's just going to be a lot different from what we thought it would." Inwardly, I heaved a sad sigh, then I swore I would make it up to Gemma.

I looked at the clock. "I need to catch up with Cade and afterward take Gemma to her appointment, so we'll be out for a while. I wanted to check in and see how you're doing, though."

"I appreciate it, son." Dad and I stood. He gave me a quick hug, then leaned against his desk and crossed his ankles. "Let me know about the ceremony. I think it would give everyone something to look forward to."

"I will. I'll catch you later." I left Dad's office, and instead of going upstairs to find Cade, I meandered down the hall and to the closet and slipped on my coat. I walked through the kitchen and out the back.

The crisp cold air greeted me, and I inhaled deeply, hoping to clear my mind. I needed a few minutes to myself before I checked on Cade. Jaxon rounded the corner of the house after me, and I gave him a small wave. I suddenly missed my solitude, but as long as Brandon was on the loose, I would have to suck it up.

My phone buzzed in my pocket. I removed it and stared at the screen. It was a text from an unknown number. I tapped the icon, then my heart skidded to a screeching halt.

I nervously glanced around me, then ran down the hill toward the guesthouse. There was no way I was going to open this message until I was completely alone. I fumbled for the spare key I kept in my pocket, then unlocked the door.

Nearly tripping over my own feet, I hurried to the couch and sat down, then glared at the text Brandon Montgomery had just sent me. My pulse pounded in my ears, and I took a deep breath before I selected the link.

His ugly sneer filled the screen, and hate crawled beneath my skin. "Hello, Hendrix. I thought you would enjoy this video. I was going to hold onto it until the perfect time, but since Gemma is dead … I hope it fucking crushes you. I hate you, Harrington. Your family made my life miserable. After Franklin turned Dad down for a loan and we ended up homeless, I swore I would live the rest of my life making yours fucking miserable." Spittle flew from his mouth, his eyes wild with revenge. "At least with this video, you'll understand that you didn't win."

The screen flickered, then the video started. Brandon's lip twitched before he walked into the living room where Gemma was sitting in a dark-brown leather chair. I could immediately tell something was wrong with her, and my pulse broke into a gallop.

"Gemma, how do you feel?" Brandon asked and reached out to caress her face.

She jerked back and glared at him. "Don't touch me." She attempted to slap at him but missed. "I belong to Hendrix," she slurred. "Nothing you can ever do to me will change how much I love *him*. I hate you!"

Mentally, I cheered for Gemma. At least she was still fighting that monster.

"I've decided to use you as my guinea pig." Brandon placed his hand on her shoulder and squeezed.

Gemma glared at him. "For what?"

"It's a new drug that makes you compliant, but it also wipes your memory."

"Compliant?" Confusion and fear morphed her features. She attempted to stand, but he easily pushed her back into the seat.

"Sex." Brandon grinned at the camera, his maniacal brown eyes glimmering. "The drug stimulates the pleasure center of your brain and boosts your sex drive. Under normal circumstances, you would be begging to get fucked, but this particular concoction also ... hmmm. Let's just say it will take the fight right out of you."

I lurched backward, gasping for air as though he'd punched me in the throat. *God dammit. Gemma's change in the bedroom was due to the drug that psycho piece of shit gave her.* My stomach churned as the information sank in, and I wondered if this was the same drug that had killed her.

Brandon tapped his watch. "Any minute now, you won't have the strength to fight back. Let me explain things to you. You're the guinea pig for the future girls that will be taken and trained as sex slaves for the Dark Circle Society. Once I have you broken into submission, then you'll run the society with me."

"Never." She shook her head adamantly, then glared at him. "You roofied me?"

"No." Brandon chuckled as his hand snaked up her thigh. "It's so much better," he said in a matter-of-fact tone, a smirk tugging at his features.

Brandon remained kneeling and moved to the side of her. "But just in case the experiment doesn't work like it's supposed to …"

Brandon moved her hair and ran his tongue up the length of her cheek, sucking on her ear lobe. His chuckle rumbled through the room as he slipped a shock collar around her neck. He pushed a button on a remote control, and Gemma's body shook while a horrified scream burst from her. He winked at the camera, then unbuttoned her shirt and slid his hand into her bra. My stomach churned as he grabbed Gemma's breasts. She tugged at his wrist, attempting to make him stop, but she was too weak. Her eyes glazed over, and her face held a faraway look.

"She has the most perfect tits I've ever seen." Brandon stared at the camera. "Hendrix, who is she with now, you fucking prick?"

Logically, I realized I should turn off the video, but the other part of me needed answers. My blood froze in my veins as clips of Gemma being spanked and fucked by Brandon and another girl flashed across my screen. It didn't stop there. Brandon had recorded her with two men in a bed as well as her with two men and a girl on another occasion. He'd filmed her at least three times. Unable to take anymore, I reached for the stop button when that bastard's face appeared on the screen again.

His laughter sent chills up my spine. That son of a bitch was scary because he was insane. "As you can see, the drug is a success. The beautiful part about it? She'll never remember her sex-slave days." He winked. "Soon the sweet Gemma Thompson you knew will no longer exist, and she'll sit by my side and help me run the society. She's mine, Hendrix." His nose flared with anger. "You will *never* get her back. And in case you're curious, there might be long-term side effects from the drug. Who knows what kind of sex fiend she could become?"

Brandon faded away and my screen turned black.

I gasped for air as my knees buckled and I collapsed to the floor. A tortured cry escaped me, and tears streamed down my face. Rage sizzled beneath the surface, battling with sorrow and fear. Brandon had used her as a sex slave and passed her around. *My* Gemma.

Jesus. This is why she's acting so bizarre. Whatever he'd drugged her with was still in her system. Dark thoughts rolled into my mind. *What if it changed her permanently? Worse than that, what if her memories return?* I shook my head, my hair sticking against my damp cheeks. She couldn't remember. It would destroy her.

Blistering anger licked through me as I scrambled to my feet. My vision blurred and I wiped my eyes. I had to keep my shit together. I grabbed my phone off the floor and called the one person I knew I could confide in.

"I'm in Dad's guesthouse, but I need to get the hell out of here," I said, my voice raw and strained.

"I'll start the car. Come on out when you're ready," Zayne replied.

Somehow, I had the clarity of mind to text Gemma that I would be with Zayne for a little while, then we'd be back in time to go to the doctor's appointment. I messaged Dad next, then locked the guesthouse and walked up the hill to the company Mercedes. A crushing weight pushed on my chest and I struggled to breathe. My brain continued to play the images of Gemma that Brandon had sent. She'd worn a shock collar, been drugged, and was made a sex slave. *My God, he used her in every way imaginable.*

I choked back a cry. *How am I going to handle this?* Gemma had been with Brandon, but also other men and at least one girl. She would be mortified and hate herself if she ever found out. That motherfucker had stripped her of every choice and raped her over and over.

Nearly stumbling to the ground with grief, I was grateful when I reached Zayne's car. I hopped in. "Go. Please. I don't care where we go, just drive." I stared out the window as Zayne eased down the driveway, then turned onto the road.

"Dude, what gives? You're a goddamned mess." Zayne glanced at me, but I refused to look at him.

"I didn't know who else to talk to, man. What I learned a few minutes ago is beyond messed up. If I tell Cade, he might slip up and repeat this to Mac. I can't risk it." An unbearable ache crushed my chest. All I wanted to do was scream at the world and shove Brandon into a deep dark hole.

Zayne flipped on his turn signal and drove out of town. "Spill."

"I'll wait until you're not driving. I don't want you to wreck and kill us. Take me somewhere I can lose my shit."

Images of the video crashed through my mind. *God dammit.* I attempted to flip the switch on my emotions, but it wasn't working. Too much had happened too fast.

Half an hour later, Zayne parked at a secluded turnout over the city. I climbed out of the car and walked to the edge of the four-foot-tall brick wall that kept people from tumbling down the cliff. I ran my hand through my hair, then removed the hair tie from my pocket and slipped it on my wrist. I pulled the band tight and gave it a few hard pops, my skin turning red almost immediately. It wasn't helping.

Zayne approached and folded his arms across his broad chest.

"Brandon ..." My attention landed on Zayne for a minute, then focused on the scenery before me. Pine and fir trees covered the landscape with groves of Aspen and maple trees mingling with them. Bursts of red, orange, and yellow cascaded down the mountainside. "Brandon sent me a video. I know what happened to Gemma when she was with him." I shoved my hands into my pockets, my shoulders shaking as I cried. "I saw what he did to her."

Zayne remained quiet while I explained how Brandon had drugged her and shocked her and why she didn't have any memories. I told him about how some of the effects of the drug were still messing with her and she was acting out part of what she'd lived through.

I couldn't look at Zayne yet. I'd just revealed intimate details of what Gemma had experienced, and I had no fucking clue what he was thinking.

"Are you ready?" he asked, his steely voice quiet.

"For ...?" I arched a brow at him.

"To end the problem," Zayne said.

I didn't need time to consider what he'd said. I wanted to take matters into my own hands and end Brandon Montgomery, but I still had to confirm what Zayne meant. "Are you saying what I think? Kill him?"

Zayne nodded. "For the record, you're not involved. Gemma needs you …" Zayne hesitated. "You're right. This is some messed-up shit." He quietly stared over the landscape. "Are you going to show her the video?"

I blanched. "No. I can't. I hope like hell she never remembers either." I wiped my eyes.

"Good call. It would destroy her, man. She loves you, and if she saw the clips, I'm not sure she would be able to recover from it. But you need to *tell* her about it *after* the video has been verified. Since you can't crawl into her head, you have no idea if she's having nightmares or memories that she's not telling anyone about." Zayne paused before speaking again. "I know you're fucked-up right now and not thinking clearly, but it could have been manipulated or Photoshopped. I have a girl that can see if it's real or fake, so you don't need to give it to Sutton. You have my word I won't watch it."

I struggled to swallow against the dryness in my throat as I pulled up the text and forwarded it to Zayne. "I hope like hell the video is fake. While it's being confirmed, I'll figure out how I'm going to tell her, just in case. All I want to do is protect her. Honest to God, it's taking all of my control not to pack our shit and leave. We can find a cabin in the mountains overlooking a lake. All I need is her."

"If I were in your shoes, I would bury Brandon Montgomery, then I'd make that safe place happen. You gotta take time to put your life back together, man."

A cold wind kicked up and I rubbed my arms. "The FBI won't let me leave yet."

"Yeah, I was in the room when Pierce spoke to Brian on the phone. I wouldn't stress too much—Allison will call soon. Once they have an idea of where she is, you'll be finished and free to go."

I realized Zayne was trying to give me some encouragement, but my instincts told me it most likely wouldn't be that easy.

"For now, I'm going to fill Pierce and Vaughn in. I'm not going to tell Sutton. We should keep the ladies out of it." Zayne tilted his chin up, an ornery glint in his eyes. "Once we have a solid plan, we hunt that motherfucker down. And, dude, just to let you know, part of my military training is torture. All I ask is that before we kill the son of a bitch and put him ten feet under, I have some time alone with him."

"You can have as much as you want. As long as we end this, I don't give a shit. He's done ruining my family."

A wave of dread washed over me as I looked at my watch. "Gemma and I have a doctor's appointment. We need to drive back to Dad's."

Without another word, Zayne and I climbed into the car and headed home.

The next twenty-four hours passed slowly as Gemma and I waited for our test results. When her phone finally rang, we nearly jumped out of our bed.

"Hello?" Her attention landed on me while she listened. Her facial features shifted from tense to relieved. "Thank you very much." She disconnected the call and turned toward me. "I'm clean. Whatever happened to me, I …" Sadness filled her expression.

"Hey, it's over. I suspect if you're clean I am too. You're the only girl I've been with since before we met." Seconds later, my phone rang. I glanced at the screen. "It's my doctor." I kissed her before I answered the call. "Hello?" Relief flooded me as the nurse let me know the tests had returned normal. I disconnected the call and smiled at Gemma. "I'm good to go."

Gemma flung her arms around my neck. "I love you."

"Oh, babe. I love you so much." I embraced her as I struggled with the anger and fear of the abuse she'd endured from Brandon. It took everything inside me not to grab our suitcases, pack them, and get the hell out of here. But I couldn't. The FBI needed me, and so did my family.

Gemma's shoulders shook, and I rubbed her back. "What is it?" I kissed the top of her head and leaned against the headboard. She snuggled up to me.

"I'm so tired." She peered up at me, tears hanging off her eyelashes. "Something has to give, Hendrix."

I frowned. "What do you mean?" Smoothing her hair, I waited for her to speak again.

"I can't live like this. Everything is crashing down around us. All I want is to get married and leave. At the same time, Mac is pregnant and on bedrest, so we can't. When is it going to stop, Hendrix? Are we ever going to get to live our life and just be us?"

I gazed into her grief-stricken eyes and wondered if she would ever feel whole again. "I'm working on it. Can you give me a little longer? I'm already talking to Dad about us moving."

Gem sat up and wiped the moisture from her tearstained face. "Really? We can rebuild our lives, sleep all day, and hide from the world for a while so we can catch our breath?"

I placed my palm against her cheek and stroked her soft porcelain skin with the pad of my thumb. "Yeah, babe. Don't say anything to Mac, though. Janice is going to talk to her. Right now, Dad and Janice are planning to relocate with us."

"Seriously?" her voice squeaked, and I realized she was holding the floodgates back on her emotions.

"We need a little more time to plan." I kissed her gently.

Gem offered me a sweet but exhausted smile.

"Since Mac is on bedrest, what do you think about a small wedding here where she can attend and we'll be safe?" I asked.

Gemma worried her bottom lip with her teeth, her forehead creasing while she considered the option. "We would be protected inside Franklin's house. The ceremony doesn't need to be long, so Mac should be okay." Gem's expression softened. "I'll get married anywhere you want to. After Mac has the baby, we can always have a reception or ... I don't know. We can figure it out." She looked away from me and sat up, her features growing sad.

"I have something to show you." I rolled over and opened the drawer in my nightstand. "I was going to wait to give it to you until after our therapy session, but I think now is a good time."

"What is it?" Her gaze followed me as I pulled out a sketch pad. I patted the space next to me, and she moved closer.

Flipping the tablet open, I kept my attention trained on her. I needed her initial impression.

She gasped. "Is that my ring?" She touched the paper with her fingertip and traced the design, then peered at me from beneath her long eyelashes, awe filling her beautiful face.

"What do you think? We can change anything you don't like."

She paused, then smiled. "It's gorgeous."

"The largest diamond signifies that we're unbreakable. Our love is solid. The slightly smaller one represents the past. We're remembering all of the good things but leaving what no longer serves us in the rearview mirror." I pointed at the stone on the right side of the central solitaire. "This diamond represents our future. It's slightly bigger and brighter than the left, but only we will know there's a size difference. All three stones signify the journey of our relationship and that we're stronger together."

Her chin trembled, and she blinked rapidly. "It's perfect."

"What do you think about a small row of sapphires or emeralds on either side of the diamonds? It would represent the path we're on. Mine will have the same stones, just embedded into the band."

Excitement flashed in her eyes. "Sapphires would be beautiful."

I flipped the page. "Then sapphires it is. Depending on how thick of a band we want, I thought inscriptions would be nice. What do you think about *always and forever?*"

"Yes!" Gemma laughed, healing my brokenness a little more.

I tossed the notebook onto the floor and gathered her in my arms, pulling her on top of me. "I'll check and see how fast we can have the rings made. As soon as they're ready, let's get married." I kissed her gently.

"I'll call Lydia about a new dress. She had several designs meant for stores that she'd already mocked up for before we got in touch, so I'll see if one of them is still available."

I lifted my hips, pushing my erection into her leg. "Show me how much you love me, Gem." I nipped at her bottom lip, eliciting a soft moan from her.

She straddled me, her gaze filling with love and desire. *God, I need this.* I longed to connect with her, heart to heart. I rolled us over, then took my time undressing her. For the first time since she'd been home, she held eye contact with me.

As I eased into her, she moaned and rocked against me. "I love you, baby," she whispered against my ear.

"I love you too." Hope rose inside me as we made love. Although Gem appeared normal, there was a part of me that was too scared to think much about it.

AFTER A LONG SHOWER TOGETHER, Gem and I dressed for our first therapy session. I wasn't sure what to expect with Dr. Bernstein, but I was grateful that Gem and I had finally connected on a deeper level.

"Are you nervous?" I asked, taking her hand.

She looked stunning in her emerald green top and boyfriend jeans. I'd noticed since she came home that she'd been wearing the baggiest clothes she owned. I wondered if she realized it or if it was a subconscious choice. At least she wasn't buying them as big as when I'd first met her. Back then, she'd drowned in them. I had no idea how beautiful she was until I was already invested. When I'd picked her up at the dorm for our first date and saw her in a dress and makeup with her long red hair flowing down her back, I was breathless. Her external beauty was as incredible as her loyal and loving personality.

"Yeah, I'm a little nervous. I'm not sure what to say, actually." She grabbed her purse off the dresser, and we left the comfort of our bedroom.

"Don't worry, babe. It will happen exactly as it needs to."

Voices drifted down the hall from the game room, and I poked my head in. "Hey, guys. Gem and I are leaving for a while."

After a much-heated debate with my dad about us leaving the safety of his home to go to counseling, he finally gave in. It wouldn't have mattered if he'd forbidden it. Gemma and I needed to have a safe space to talk without anyone else around. I didn't want us to make progress, then overhear someone in the house and have Gemma retreat into her shell again.

Mac turned around and grinned at us. "I'm kicking his ass in *Mortal Kombat.*"

Gem snuggled up next to me and placed her hand on my stomach. "You're supposed to let him win on occasion," she said, giggling.

I looked down at her. She'd laughed more in the last few days, and each time I heard her, I felt as though she put another piece of my heart back together. Although I'd lost sleep over the video, in my mind, it wasn't Gemma with those people. It was someone else. She'd fought until that son of a bitch shocked and drugged her. Plus, I'd also seen some encouraging signs that she was becoming more and more herself. That's what I had to focus on.

We said goodbye, then hurried down the stairs. Zayne had the car running and we hopped into the back seat.

"I'm really glad to leave, even if it's only for a few hours." Gemma smiled at me. "Hi, Zayne. I feel like I haven't seen you in a while."

"You haven't." He chuckled. "Good to see you too."

He peeked at me in the rearview mirror, and our eyes connected briefly. He was most likely checking to see if there had been any new developments. There had been, but the fact that Gem and I had made love and she hadn't pleaded with me to fuck her wasn't something I was willing to share. It was between us. Gemma's secrets had already been shared enough, and I hated myself for telling Zayne about what happened. But I'd needed a friend to talk to after I saw Brandon's video. *I guess what they say is true—desperate people make desperate choices.*

Gemma pulled out her phone and connected her Spotify app to the car. She played some upbeat, fun songs and sang along to them.

Each laugh, each song she sang, and each love-filled glance she gave me was encouragement that we were moving in the right direction. She was finally seeing *me*, not some guy to get her off or to be afraid of.

Half an hour later, I opened the door to the counseling office and allowed Gemma to enter first. Zayne trailed in behind us. I was so used to him being there that I forgot to warn the doctor. Dr. Bernstein greeted us, then gaped. Zayne was a big-ass dude, and the ladies nearly creamed their panties when they saw him.

Dr. Bernstein cleared her throat, then looked at me with big brown eyes. "Is he with you?"

I stifled my laugh. "He's our security. He'll stay in the lobby while we talk to you, though. I'm Hendrix, and this is Gemma. Thank you for meeting with us." I extended my hand to her, and she beamed up at me.

Dr. Bernstein appeared to be in her mid-forties. She was well-dressed in slacks and a white sweater with her dark hair pulled into a tight bun. Her voice was warm and friendly, and I immediately liked her.

She shook Gemma's hand next. "I'm Dr. Bernstein. It's lovely to meet you both."

She nodded at Zayne again, her cheeks turning red. "Excellent." She diverted her attention away from him and waved Gemma and me into her office.

Gem and I sat on the beige loveseat, and Gem grabbed my hand. "It's okay, babe," I whispered against her ear.

Dr. Bernstein's space was light and open. White bookcases lined two of the walls, and a soft-yellow accent wall brightened the room even more. I appreciated that it was cheery.

"Why don't we take a few minutes to get to know each other?" Dr. Bernstein smiled warmly at us. "Hendrix, you mentioned that you and Gemma are lead singers for August Clover, right?"

"We are." I smiled at Gem, the recollection of our first time on stage together warming my chest.

"I've lost some memories, and I'm scared," Gemma blurted. Her smile faded as she fidgeted in her seat. "Sorry. I'm really nervous. I thought I should get that over with."

"Can you tell me what happened?" Dr. Bernstein crossed her legs and placed her notebook and pen on the table next to her. "I won't take any notes while you talk. There's no judgement here. You're safe."

I wanted to hug Dr. Bernstein. If Gemma had seen her scribbling madly, it would have freaked her out.

Gemma dropped my hand and tucked her hair behind her ear. I slid my arm around her and gently massaged her back. I realized that she sensed something was off inside her, but I silently begged the universe never to restore her memories.

"At our wedding," Gem started, "Brandon Montgomery had someone kidnap Hendrix's dad. There were helicopters and men shooting … people died. Brandon got in touch with me a few days later and offered to trade Franklin for me. I did."

Gem chewed on her bottom lip. "I remember spitting in Brandon's face when I first saw him. I remember sitting at the kitchen table with him while he talked about rebuilding the society that was behind the rape I experienced when I was younger. How he was going to continue to traffic and auction off young girls. The house where I was held was in Montana, and he was planning on moving us, but he wouldn't tell me where." She pursed her lips. "That's it." Gem glanced up at the ceiling, looking like she was about to fall apart. "But inside …" She placed her hand over her heart. "Inside, I know he did something to me. I get these blurry flashes, then I'll say something totally off the wall and out of character." Fear clouded her beautiful features. "I'm not sure I want to know what happened."

"Hendrix, can you fill in any gaps for me?" Dr. Bernstein asked gently.

"She was drugged. The doctor said he'd never seen the drug before, but he compared it to GHB, except worse. The doctors had no idea how long it would affect her." I paused, weighing my next words carefully. "The drug wiped her memory." Brandon's twisted videos assaulted my mind, and my hand began to tremble. My attention darted to Gemma, but she hadn't noticed. I wished I could have said the same about Dr. Bernstein.

"Hendrix, what's different about Gemma now that she's home?" Dr. Bernstein asked.

Dammit, I was hoping she wouldn't ask me that in front of Gem. I coughed into my arm, scrambling for what to say. Embarrassing my fiancée wasn't on my agenda. She wouldn't want to schedule any more sessions.

"She's, ummm … more adventurous in the bedroom." I hoped like hell that came out with some tact.

"Is this the opposite of how she was before she left?" Dr. Bernstein's attention bounced between us.

"I've always been shy in our intimate life. Hendrix is the only man I've ever been with, other than my … rape."

Rage, blinding and terrifying, took hold of me, and I hung my head, my hair cloaking my face. Gemma had no idea that she'd been with other men. My hand made a tight fist, and I willed myself to pull it together before Gemma saw that something was wrong. I peeked at Dr. Bernstein. If she'd seen my reaction, she was masking her thoughts well.

"Hendrix and I have been together for a while, so I've gotten better, but he's right. This is different. I don't feel like myself, and I've asked for things in the bedroom that I wouldn't ever feel comfortable with."

"Hendrix? Is she suddenly crossing boundaries with you?"

I stared at the floor. "Sometimes."

Dr. Bernstein folded her hands in her lap. "I'm really proud of both of you. This is your first session, and you're being kind and honest with each other and me. That's the foundation of good relationships."

"I love her so much." I clenched my jaw in order not to break down. "It nearly broke me when she was gone."

"I can see that. Have you been able to forgive her yet?"

I hesitated, then I answered honestly. "Yeah. She saved my dad's life. When Gemma came home, we sat down and talked about not making any more life-altering decisions without talking to each other first." *Except for the secret I am keeping about the video, but I'm still not sure if it's real or not.*

"My exchange for Franklin's life was never meant to hurt anyone," Gemma said softly. "It was a decision based on how much I love Hendrix and his family."

"You two have a lot going on. I'll say this before I weigh in on the other matter. Forgiveness is also key to a good relationship. I understand that you have come to an agreement you both can be comfortable with, but some residual anger might pop up on occasion. If it does, it's normal. Talk it through, and don't beat yourselves up over it. Be gentle with each other."

Gemma and I looked at each other and nodded.

"I would like to back up and talk about the drug and memory loss. Losing memories is very common during trauma and might be contributing to the picture. Since the drug isn't on the market, and we're in unfamiliar territory, I would suggest that you consider coming to terms with the possibility that you may never remember, Gemma. Also, it might be best if you don't."

"I suspect you're right." Gem placed her hand on mine.

"This new sexual fascination could be lingering effects from the drug. Do you feel safe with Hendrix both physically and intimately?"

Gemma's face burned bright red. "Yeah."

She focused on the floor, embarrassed. All I wanted to do was scoop her up in my arms and kiss her until she was breathless. She was so damned adorable.

"If you're in a safe and healthy relationship, then define what you're both comfortable with, and enjoy it. There's no right or wrong. Every couple has limits. Find yours with each other."

Although I understood what the doctor was suggesting, it would take some time to adjust to Jungle Gemma on steroids.

"I need to use the restroom." Gemma stood.

"Down the hall and to the left," Dr. Bernstein directed.

Gemma left, and I spotted Zayne near the door.

"You love her very much." Dr. Bernstein said after Gemma disappeared.

"She's my world." I sat on the edge of the love seat and scrubbed my cheeks with my hands.

"Hendrix, do you know what happened to Gemma while she was gone? Your reaction when she mentioned she'd only been with you after her rape was intense."

23

---

ammit. She'd seen me. I'd suspected she might have, but I was hoping she hadn't.

Dr. Bernstein tilted her head and assessed me with her kind brown eyes.

"She was raped multiple times by men and women," I whispered. The weight of the confession nearly crushed me, and I gripped the arm of the seat to steady my spinning emotions. "She can't remember, Dr. Bernstein. I'm not sure ..." I hesitated. "If she does, I'm afraid it will destroy her."

"Hendrix, how do you know what happened to her?" Worry lines creased her forehead.

"Brandon Montgomery sent me a video. It contained clips of Gemma drugged and ..." I ground out, past clenched teeth as I held my hand up, unable to say any more. "I'm having the video evaluated to see if it's real before I talk to Gem."

"You saw this?" Shock laced her tone.

I nodded, afraid I would break down if I spoke.

"Let me help you get through this, Hendrix. Please call me and schedule a private appointment."

I nodded as the door swung open and Gemma strolled back in. She appeared more composed than when she'd left.

I arched an eyebrow at my fiancée, and she gave me a shy smile. There was one more thing I wanted to discuss. "Dr. Bernstein, do we still have a few minutes?" I slipped my arm around Gemma's shoulders, reassuring her. The last thing I wanted was for her to bolt on the session. If there was a chance that she wished to come back, I didn't want to screw it up.

Dr. Bernstein checked her watch. "We do. What else would you like to talk about?"

"When the FBI located Gemma, I was supposed to wait outside of the house, but they were taking too long to let us know if she was alive. I managed to get inside and followed the trail of the paramedics. When I found her … Gemma was on the gurney … dead." My heart raced, and my breathing became erratic and labored. I swallowed over the tightness in my throat as the images of Gem's lifeless body barreled through my mind. I massaged my neck, attempting to pull myself back to the present moment before it plunged me into the darkness. I wasn't sure if I would ever move past thinking I'd lost her.

"I'm here." Gem smoothed my hair, then threaded her fingers through it.

I squeezed her hand and took a minute to regain my composure.

Dr. Bernstein's eyes widened, then she sat on the edge of her chair.

"They used the paddles, but it took a few times. Gemma was gone for at least five minutes." I glanced at Gem and her face grew sad. My attention landed on the doctor again, but I wasn't sure of what else to say.

Dr. Bernstein straightened. "That could certainly play into any personality changes, Gemma."

"I was told I'd died, but I hadn't realized Hendrix was there. That must have been horrible," Gemma whispered. "I'm sorry you had to see that."

My head ached from the grief I'd shoved back down. So much had happened that I hadn't had time to process the fact I'd seen Gemma dead.

"It wasn't your fault." I ground my molars together. "It was Brandon's. He's the one that overdosed you."

I stared at the floor and closed my eyes. Clutching my chest, I attempted to get my thundering heartbeat under control. Finally, I looked at Dr. Bernstein again. "I hadn't thought about that. The change in personality might be from Gemma dying."

"It's a possibility that I think you both might want to consider." A peaceful silence hung in the air. Then Dr. Bernstein grabbed her notebook. "It's been an intense session. I'm not sure if you two would like to come back, but I would highly recommend that we schedule an appointment for next week. However, regardless of whether you set up additional sessions or not, I have two assignments for you."

Gemma's eyebrow arched. "Like homework?"

Dr. Bernstein's kind smile eased across her face. "Yes. First, I want you to find something fun to do together. It should make you happy, make you laugh, and remind you that you're alive and together. Leave the darkness behind, even if it's only for a few hours."

"Gem?" I asked, our gazes connecting.

"That sounds amazing actually," Gemma responded. "What's the next one?"

"Second, if you're open to the idea, take some time to touch each other."

Gemma frowned, and so did I. What did Dr. Bernstein think we were doing?

"I'm not following," I said.

"Sit or stand, whichever you're comfortable with, and take a few minutes to place your hand over each other's heart or maybe give a massage. It works best if you're skin to skin. If it leads to intimacy, that's fine, but the goal is to reconnect. Take your time and savor each other."

The lightbulb went off in my mind. I wasn't sure what Gemma thought about it, but I was all in, not just because I could touch Gemma but also because we would slow down and appreciate each other. It might be exactly what we needed to break through Gem's trauma.

"We'll definitely talk about it." I stood and extended my hand to Gem. "Thank you. I know we'll need some time to speak privately, but we'll reach out if we feel another appointment would help."

"It's been wonderful to meet you both." Dr. Bernstein shook our hands.

I opened the door, and we joined Zayne in the lobby. The doctor hadn't followed us out, so we made a quick path to the car. It was imperative that we stay out of sight as much as possible. The last thing we needed was the media snapping pictures and Brandon catching wind of it.

We rode in silence on the way home. I wasn't sure what was going through Gemma's mind, but I was thrilled with the session. Not only did Dr. Bernstein offer some alternatives to Gemma's behavior, but she gave us a tool to try out as well. I'd never been a big believer in therapy if all patients did was complain about their problems. A therapist was supposed to provide possible solutions.

My dick gave a salute at the thought of Gem and me touching each other. I understood that the point of Dr. Bernstein's exercise was for us to reconnect on another level, but my hormones had a mind of their own. Gem was beautiful, and I loved being with her. I could imagine standing behind her and tucking her hair over one shoulder. The curve of her slender neck would be exposed to me. I would nip on her earlobe and trail my fingertips over her soft skin. *Dammit. I need her now.*

"What are you thinking?" Gemma asked.

I wondered if she'd noticed the bulge in my jeans that was growing more and more painful by the second.

"About the homework." I tried to hide my grin, but I couldn't.

She gave a soft giggle from the back seat, and I wanted to pull her into my lap and kiss her. "Are you planning something …" She bit her lower lip and peeked at me through her long eyelashes. "Fun?"

"We definitely need a date. What sounds good to you?"

I didn't miss the slight twitch of her upper lip. I could tell this wasn't the conversation she wanted to have. I didn't feel like we were on the same page yet.

"Do we have to stay in Washington?"

I wondered if we could leave the country for a weekend. As amazing as that would be, Dad would never loan us the plane. If I had my way, I'd take Zayne and Jaxon and fly to the UK to meet with Vicki. Even though Gemma and I had agreed to get married at Dad's, it didn't mean we couldn't honeymoon or buy a vacation home in a nice, secluded corner over there. I would at least like to check it out.

"Probably. I think since Brandon is running around loose, we need to lay low. Hell, for all I know, he saw us today."

Gem jerked back as though I'd slapped her.

"I'm sorry. I shouldn't have said that." I mentally scolded myself for mentioning Brandon.

"It's okay. Sometimes I can push all the darkness into a corner of my mind. If I try hard enough, I can forget. At least for a little bit." She tucked her hair behind her ear.

"Let's talk about some ideas later this evening." I took her hand and kissed her knuckles. "I'm going to order your ring when we get home. I emailed the sketches to the designer, and he said he can make it happen. I'll put a down payment on it, then he can provide an esti-mated delivery time."

Gemma's face lit up. "As soon as you talk to the jeweler, I'll call Lydia. I know what dress I want."

"Yeah?" Images of her on our wedding day flashed through my mind. She'd stolen my breath. She had radiated happiness … then the bullets started. With a slight shake of my head, I attempted to clear away the past.

Zayne rolled up to Dad's garage and parked.

"I'm going to find Mac. I'll catch up with you in a few minutes." Gem leaned over and kissed me.

"I'll let you know about the ring."

She smiled before she hopped out of the Mercedes. For the first time since she was home, she had a little pep in her step.

"How's she doing?" Zayne asked as soon as her door closed.

"Okay. I'm seeing some signs of her returning to normal, but I have no fucking clue about what to expect. Dr. Bernstein gave us some things to try. Plus, she explained that since Gemma had died, it could have changed her personality. The thought never even crossed my mind."

Zayne and I exited the car, and I inhaled the clean, cold air into my lungs.

"I had a buddy in the military that died for almost ten minutes. It definitely changed him." Zayne scrubbed his chin with his fingers, appearing deep in thought. "It took a long time, but he found his footing. Gemma will too. The best thing we can do is end the problem."

"I couldn't agree more."

As soon as those words slipped out, Pierce's car appeared. "Pierce and Vaughn are here." Zayne grinned and sauntered over to his boss's vehicle. "Let's go chat while Gemma is occupied."

"Did you call them?" I asked, following Zayne.

"Yeah. They were available this afternoon, so I took the liberty of telling them to come over. I didn't think you wanted to wait much longer."

He was right. I didn't want to wait. After the video, I'd made my mind up. The psychotic bastard had to die. Not only would it free my family from his evil grip, but it would save young girls in the future as well.

"Hey, man." Vaughn hopped out of the car and gripped my shoulder. "We've got this."

"I appreciate you guys showing up." The realization that I wasn't alone settled over me, calming my nerves.

"We would never flake on you, Harrington," Pierce said, a mischievous grin easing across his face.

"Let's go to the guesthouse, where we'll have some privacy." I pulled my phone out of my back pocket, checked the time, then texted Gemma where I would be if she needed me. Although I didn't want her anywhere near our conversation, too much had happened recently for us not to communicate with each other. She would freak if she wasn't able to find me, and I wouldn't blame her.

Her return message lit my screen up. *Good, you need to hang out with some dudes.* She included a wink emoji. At least she had Mac to keep her company.

I unlocked the door and led everyone inside. "Cade wants to be a part of this. Does anyone have any objections?"

"Nope. Tell him to hurry his ass up." Pierce made himself comfortable in the living room. It was strange how he'd lived here while he was our bodyguard, and now he was one of my closest friends.

I messaged Cade, and within a few minutes, he flew into the house. "I wasn't sure I was going to be able to ditch Mac." He chuckled. "Gemma helped, though."

After everyone said hello to each other, we all settled in. I grabbed an extra chair from one of the bedrooms and sank into it, ready to get down to business.

Pierce rubbed his hands together. "I've got news."

2 4

Silence filled the room, and I gave Pierce my undivided attention.

"We've got a location on Brandon. I'm not sure how long he'll stay there, but he's in New Mexico."

Inside, I shook with anticipation, and my body hummed with the need to get my hands on the piece of shit. "What's the plan?" I stood and paced behind the chair, my anger churning beneath the surface.

"Are you sure you really want to do this? If so, we'll confirm, then ship out tomorrow," Pierce explained.

"Do you?" My attention bounced from Pierce to Zayne to Vaughn and finally to Cade.

"Hell yeah. It's why I'm here," Vaughn said.

"Sometimes you gotta break the rules to protect your family. You and Gemma are our family," Zayne added.

"I'm done, man. I can't have that fucker running around scaring Mac and threatening the life of my baby. I'll do whatever I need to do." Cade's eye twitched, a telltale sign that he was trying to keep his shit together.

"Same," I said. "I just hope I get to pull the damned trigger. After what he did to Gemma … I wouldn't shed a tear over Brandon Montgomery." My stomach twisted into knots. I hadn't said anything to Cade, only Zayne. I wasn't sure if Pierce and Vaughn knew the details.

"Do they know?" I tilted my chin up at Zayne and waited for his response.

"Zayne filled us in." Pierce tapped his fingers on his jeaned thigh.

"Filled who in on what?" Cade asked.

I hesitated as I pondered whether to tell him or not. I wasn't sure it would be fair to ask him to keep the secret from Gemma and Mac.

"If you can keep this between us and never tell Mac or Gemma, I'll tell you. They can't find out. Neither can Dad or Janice."

Cade's forehead creased with concern. "Why would you keep something from them?"

"To protect Gemma," I explained. "If you can live with a big secret, I'll share it. If there's even a slight question in your mind, no hard feelings, but we'll just keep you in the dark about this."

Cade nodded. "Dude, we've been friends since middle school. You never make decisions like this unless it's some serious crap. I trust you. You have my word I won't tell the girls. Hell, it's not like I'm going to tell them about the plans we're discussing in this room."

Once Cade made up his mind, I knew he was good for it. "Brandon sent me a video a few days ago," I said. "He put a fucking shock collar on Gemma and drugged her. There was clip after clip of her being raped by men and women. He used her as a sex slave."

The color drained from Cade's cheeks, and his hands balled into fists. "She doesn't remember any of it?" he whispered, his voice shaking with anger.

"Not right now. I don't think she will. Brandon said the drug would wipe her memory."

Cade shot off the couch and massaged his forehead with his fingers as if he could make the pain of what I'd told him disappear. "I hope like hell she never remembers. Shit!" He faced me, his features clouding with concern. "Jesus, Hendrix. How in God's name are you dealing with this?"

I waved my hand at my friends who were gathered in the room. "All of you." I frowned. "I'm sick of the FBI and cops losing track of

Brandon or allowing him to bargain his way out of prison. They always have an excuse to allow the piece of shit to roam free. When we catch him, I'm ready to retaliate. No one does that to my future wife and lives to talk about it."

"Tell me when, where, and what to do. I'm so fucking in," Cade said.

"Excellent, here's the plan," Pierce said.

Over the next hour, we strategized about how to capture Brandon and where we would take him afterward. Maybe I should have felt some guilt over my decision to murder another human, but Brandon was barely human, and I had a family to protect. I would worry about the consequences later. From what Pierce, Vaughn, and Zayne said, though, Brandon would never see us coming, and there wouldn't be any proof left behind. I bet these guys were machines once they mentally flipped the switch and went into combat mode.

One thing I was sure of: I was ready to end Brandon and the Dark Circle Society. From what Gemma had told me, he hadn't rebuilt it yet. At least we weren't too late. I hoped. Gemma's fake death might push him over the edge. The son of a bitch was scary, and I was well aware that no one could reason with insanity.

After we were finished discussing the details, I offered to feed everyone. It would be good to kick back for a little while. A beer would have been nice, but after Dad had told me about his assault, all of the alcohol had been removed from the house and been given to Pierce and Sutton.

I led my friends to the kitchen in the main house, and Vaughn headed straight to the refrigerator and started collecting ingredients for dinner. I laughed when I saw that he'd taken over the counter and stove. As far as I was concerned, he could cook anytime he wanted to. The dude had mad chef skills. Even better than Ruby, which was a huge compliment to him.

"I'm going to get the rest of the family. I'll be right back."

Laughter rang out across the main floor, and I was grateful we were all having some fun. It was a welcome change. Five minutes later, Dad, Janice, Mac, and Gemma joined us in the kitchen and dining room. Cade sat down and pulled Mac into his lap. She was grinning so hard I wondered if her cheeks hurt. It was good to see Mac happy and out of bed, even for a little bit.

Janice played hostess while we all joked around and enjoyed each other's company. I glanced at the clock on the wall, then took Gemma's hand and led her into the living room. Before she could ask any questions, I removed my phone from my pocket and located the jeweler's number. I kissed her as I waited for Kent to answer. I turned the speaker on so Gem could hear the conversation.

"Kent MacPhee, how can I help you?"

"Hi, Kent, this is Hendrix Harrington."

"Hey, how are you doing?"

"Good, but I'm hoping even better after our conversation." I winked at Gem.

Gemma's expression filled with excitement as she listened.

"I've got your sketches in front of me actually. I think the design will be absolutely stunning." Kent rustled some papers near the phone while he talked.

"How soon can we have them made?"

"Let me check my calendar," Kent said. "I'm pretty booked up, so about four weeks."

Gem's shoulders slumped in disappointment.

"And it's the price you quoted in the email?" I asked.

"Yeah."

"I'll double the money if we can have them in a week."

Gem crossed her fingers and squeezed her eyes closed like a little kid, and I stifled my chuckle.

"It will be tight, but I'll see if I can move some orders around," Kent said. "Let me check on something, though. Hang on."

"A week?" Gemma did a little happy dance, and my heart sang.

"Yeah, I'll make it happen," Kent said. "I'll need half down, then the remainder when you pick it up."

"I can pay you half right now if you want." I tugged my wallet out of my pocket, then identified my credit card.

"Perfect. I'm ready."

I rattled off the information, and he agreed to email me a receipt as soon as we hung up.

"I'll call you if there are any problems, but I don't foresee any. Otherwise, I'll contact you in seven days from tomorrow to pick up the rings. That would be ..."

I could almost imagine him peering over his glasses at his calendar. Once Dad had mentioned him to me, I'd checked out his website. Kent had designed and created some amazing jewelry for celebrities. Kent was also younger in his picture than I'd imagined him to be.

"November first."

"That sounds great. Thank you very much." I hung up and grinned like a fool. Gem jumped into my arms and peppered my face with kisses. *God, why didn't I do this sooner?* I hadn't seen her this full of happiness since before we'd learned Brandon was being released from prison.

I swung her around, her giggles filling the room and breathing life into my soul.

"Call Lydia." I nipped at her ear. "Buy the dress you want, but let's get married the weekend after the rings are in. November seventh or eighth. I'm done waiting. I'm so damned ready to make you my wife. I'm about to drag you off to Vegas." I grinned at her and laid a searing kiss on her mouth.

She moaned softly, and it took all of my control not to scoop her up into my arms and take her to the bathroom. If I had my way, I'd bend her over the counter and ... Pierce's low chuckle interrupted my fantasy and jerked me out of my lust-filled thoughts.

Dark desire lit Gem's eyes. My dick deflated immediately as panic twisted my stomach in knots. She couldn't flip on me. I cupped her chin gently. "Look at me. I love you more than I can ever express. I'm going to join everyone in the kitchen, and I need you to call Lydia right now." I kissed her so she would understand that I wasn't angry with her. She wasn't in control of her actions when the lingering effects of the drug were still present—not to mention I would never disrespect my dad and Janice in their home that way. Plus, I wouldn't risk Gemma embarrassing herself around our friends. She would be mortified.

She blinked multiple times, then nodded. "We're getting married," she whispered.

"We're finally getting married, babe."

I backed away slowly, my attention not leaving her until she sat on the couch and called Lydia. She gave me a sad smile, but I promised myself that I would make it up to her that night.

Ten minutes later, she joined the rest of us and slipped her hand into mine. Tears stained her cheeks, and my heart skipped a beat.

"What's wrong, babe?" I asked softly.

"When Lydia heard about the first wedding and Franklin being kidnapped, she went ahead and made the dress that was my second choice. It's already waiting for me. She said there's no charge. It's a gift."

Gem's eyes filled with tears, and I pulled her into a hug. "Are you happy?" I smoothed her hair, loving the feel of the silky strands in my fingers.

"More than you'll ever know." She sniffled and wiped the moisture from her face.

I kissed her and grinned. "Hey everybody, November eighth is a Saturday ..." I glanced at Gem, and she nodded her consent. "Gem and I are getting married right here. Since Mac is on bedrest, and we need to stay safe, we decided to have the wedding at Dad's house."

Mac covered her mouth. "Ohmigosh," she said. "Ohmigosh." She dropped her hands and looked at us. "It's about damned time." She pumped her fist in the air.

Everyone burst out laughing and the planning began. I explained that we didn't want to take any chances, and since all of our family would be with us, we weren't going to have groomsmen or brides-maids. They all seemed content with our decision.

Hopefully, I could serve Brandon's head on a platter as a wedding present to Gemma. I couldn't imagine any greater gift than freedom.

2 5

That evening was the best I'd had in a long time. Too long, really. Family and friends surrounded our table, and Dad and Gemma were actually engaged in conversations. After their experiences with Brandon, it was often difficult to gauge their moods. I was well aware that moments like these healed us. I cherished them. Gemma and I definitely needed more fun, just like Dr. Bernstein had suggested.

She leaned her head against my shoulder, and I played with her hair. I wondered if we were making progress, since I'd been able to snap her out of her daze earlier. Cade thought I should take advantage of the experimental time in the bedroom. Maybe he was right, but Gem and I had to agree on where our boundaries were first. No way in hell would I choke her. Ever.

A little after midnight, Pierce and Vaughn left. Zayne resumed his post outside. I offered to help clean up since I didn't want Ruby to come to work the next day and have to deal with a huge mess. It would be good to have her back, though. At least Dad had paid her for the time off. He took good care of her, which I appreciated.

Dad and Janice hugged everyone and told us all goodnight.

"I need to get Mac back in bed too," Cade said. He and Mac stood.

"Well, I stayed put, but my ankles and legs hurt. It was nice to have a break, though." Mac's smile fell, and she stifled a yawn.

"We'll see you guys in the morning," I said.

"If you want snacks or something to drink, text me. I'll bring it up in a little while," Gemma offered.

"Thanks, guys. It was a great evening." Mac brushed the stray hair out of her face. "I'm super excited about the wedding too."

Cade scooped her up in his arms, and she yelped. "You've been out of bed long enough. I'm carrying you up the stairs."

Mac kissed him, then snuggled up to him. "You'll be rewarded for your efforts." She wiggled her eyebrows at him, and we all laughed.

Gemma and I walked hand in hand to the kitchen. "That's a lot of dishes." I removed a band from my pocket and pulled my hair into a messy bun.

Gemma grinned. "I'll help."

We dug into the pile of plates and silverware. I rinsed and Gem loaded. It had been good to see her smile while everyone was here. It felt normal.

Twenty minutes later, the kitchen was clean and I started the dishwasher. We made our way up the stairs to our bedroom. I wondered if Gemma was interested in trying the exercise Dr. Bernstein had given us.

When we reached our room, Gemma picked up her sleep shirt and hurried into the bathroom without saying a word. The click of the lock reached my ears, and I blew out a frustrated sigh. Anxiety coursed through me, and my chest tightened. I wondered if I'd said something that made her mood change quickly.

Opening the dresser drawer, I removed a clean pair of sweats and boxer briefs. I needed to clear my mind so when she was ready to talk, I could help. Frustration swirled inside me. We'd had an amazing night for the first time in weeks. Now ... not so much, but I wasn't sure what had happened.

I heard her turn the shower on, then the bathroom door swung open. Naked, Gem leaned on the doorframe with her arms folded across her breasts.

"Hendrix?"

I stood. "Yeah?"

She held her hand out to me, and my heart beat a little easier. She wasn't mad at me.

I joined her, then she tugged my shirt off. After ditching the rest of my clothes, I followed her into the shower. Steam filled the room, and I inhaled the warm air through my nose and into my lungs. Hot water cascaded over her, and she peeked up at me. I stroked her cheek with my thumb.

Gem pushed up on her tiptoes and kissed me gently. She wrapped her arms around my waist and placed her head on my chest. "While I was gone, imagining the beat of your heart against my ear kept me from losing my mind."

I embraced her. "This is where you're supposed to be, babe. With me. Always."

"I've missed you." She stared straight into my soul. "I've missed us being close." She swallowed hard, her fingertips lightly trailing over my back.

Gemma didn't need to explain. I understood exactly what she was saying. Her words reached inside me and massaged new life into my soul.

As we stood skin to skin, holding each other in silence, an unexplainable calm cloaked me. I wasn't sure how often Gemma would have moments like this, but the possibility that she was returning to me emotionally … my breath stuttered in my throat with the prospect.

"I love you, Hendrix."

I tightened my hold on her. "Love you too. The sun doesn't come up in my world without you, Gem."

I rested my chin on the top of her head, and we stood under the water until it turned cold and our fingers pruned. That scene would forever be burned into my brain—the moment that my baby came back to me.

26

The early-morning sunlight streamed through the window curtains, offering the promise of a new day. I rubbed the sleep from my eyes, then I glanced at Gemma, who was still asleep. She'd stuck to my side after our shower the night before, and I'd loved every second of it.

I sat up slowly and placed my bare feet on the carpeted floor. Pierce would be calling soon with an update on Brandon. We'd planned to all meet at his house that morning, then once we confirmed Brandon hadn't left his last location, we would board Pierce's plane and fly down. Pierce had taken care of the logistics, and all I had to do was figure out what to tell Gemma. It wasn't as though I could tell her I was on a manhunt. It would scare the shit out of her, and that wasn't my goal. I wanted to end Brandon Montgomery's reign of terror once and for all.

I grabbed my cell off the nightstand and checked for messages, but there weren't any yet. I collected a clean shirt and slipped it on before I snuck out of the bedroom. Gemma hadn't slept well since she'd been home, so I didn't want to wake her. She was mentally and physically exhausted.

My phone vibrated with a text as I descended the stairs and

headed toward the coffeepot. I tapped the screen, and a message from Pierce popped up: *See you at ten a.m.*

I had an hour and a half. A cold sweat rippled over me and my heart hammered. I was plotting murder, but that wasn't what bothered me. The fact that I had no regrets was what shook me up the most.

GEMMA HAD KISSED me goodbye and practically shoved me out the front door when I told her I was going to hang out with Pierce and the guys for the day. If she hadn't been smiling, I would have thought she was trying to get rid of me. Thoughts of the night before calmed any concerns, though. Not only had we had a great evening, but Gem had initiated the exercise Dr. Bernstein had suggested to us as well. It finally felt as though we were in a good place again.

Zayne drove Cade and I to Pierce's house, and I used the time to schedule an individual appointment with Dr. Bernstein the next week. I would see if Gemma wanted to go back as well. I hoped like hell she would. With one session, we'd already moved forward. There was no doubt in my mind that Gemma and I could make it through anything, but some guidance and support would move things along faster. Besides, I wasn't interested in bumbling around in the dark, trying to help Gemma and Dad. My fuckups had the potential to set them back, and I didn't want that on my conscience.

Zayne was pumped up about our mission, and I couldn't help but wonder what had happened to make him that way. Regardless, I trusted him implicitly. He'd proved himself over and over again, as a friend and a bodyguard.

Vaughn greeted us at the front of Pierce's house and motioned for us to come in. "Pierce is in the study. Sutton and Claire are in Portland with their parents for a few days, so it's just us."

"Does she know anything?" I asked, guilt gripping my chest for lying to the ladies. It wasn't by choice, but we weren't going to drag them into this either.

"Nope. If she suspects we're up to something, she hasn't said a word. Sutton has one hell of a sixth sense, though," Vaughn said.

"Even if Sutton were here, she would still stay out of it," Zayne added.

Gemma wouldn't. That was why I had to make sure she never found out about our plans. My biggest concern was that she would want to participate, and I couldn't let that happen. If we screwed up and landed in prison, I couldn't risk her future. It was enough that I was risking mine.

We each grabbed a cup of coffee, then Cade, Zayne, Vaughn, and I made our way to Pierce's office. My attention landed on the large window facing the back of the property. Trees lined the hills, the red and yellow leaves rustling gently in the breeze. Before long, dead leaves would be ripped away from the branches and carried off in the wind, replaced with a blanket of white. I couldn't wait for the snow.

"Hey, Hendrix." Pierce waved us in.

Cade and I plunked down in two of the three black leather chairs situated in front of his desk.

"How's it going?" I figured as a friend I shouldn't just ask him if he'd learned anything new without checking on him first.

"I'm geared up to end this motherfucker, if you want to know the truth." Pierce laced his hands behind his head and leaned back, the squeak of the office chair filling the room.

"What new information do you have?" I asked, ready to dive in. Maybe the guys could help me come up with a plausible story for Gemma. Vaughn would need one for Claire too.

"From my private intel, Brandon is still in New Mexico. There's been movement inside the house, and it appears there are four guards with him. Two are patrolling the property."

Zayne rubbed his hands together. "They're mine."

Pierce held up his hand. "I want Vaughn on those two. There's a hill that overlooks the home, and it will be perfect for Vaughn to shoot from."

Zayne's shoulders slumped, and he leaned back in his chair, disappointment in his expression.

"Hang on, Zayne. I'm not cutting you out of the fun. You possess stealth skills like no one else I've ever met. Once Vaughn takes down the two guards outside, you'll slip in and sneak up on the two armed men. With the satellite and infrared feed, we'll be able to see all of them. I'll be right behind you. Brandon is my target. I won't kill him, but I'll tranquilize him. This will buy us some time to move him easily. We need to be in and out in under three minutes. Quick and dirty."

I frowned. "Where am I in all of this?"

"I have the same question," Cade said, leaning forward in his seat.

Pierce stared at me and rubbed his chin. "Harrington, you're our getaway driver. If our plan goes well, we shouldn't have any surprises."

Seriously? I wanted in on the action.

"Don't worry, Harrington. Once we're situated in the abandoned warehouse a few hours away, you'll get first dibs at inflicting pain on the bastard."

Much better. "I can deal with that."

"Cade, you have a kid on the way, so you're staying home. If anything goes sideways, you'll need to let Jaxon and Grayson know, and they'll send us help."

Although Cade appeared crestfallen, he agreed. His baby took precedence over anyone else.

Over the next hour, we continued to chat and create a backup plan. We all agreed that we would tell the ladies we were having a much-needed guy's night out and would be home in the morning. Since they did the same on occasion, it shouldn't raise any suspicions. Gemma would be safe and sound with Mac, Dad, and Janice so that I could rest easy. Pierce had assured me that they would be well-guarded with Jaxon and Tad on duty, but I also felt better knowing Cade was home. He was our last defense.

Once we had our strategies in place, I excused myself. I needed to grab more coffee. Plus, I was having a tough time sitting still. I was ready to take this son of a bitch down. My adrenaline had kicked in, and I vibrated with excitement while I entertained thoughts of beating Brandon to a bloody pulp. Pierce's plane was already fueled up, and in my mind, the quicker we got this over with, the sooner we could all start to actually live again.

I removed my phone from my pocket as I entered the kitchen. I wanted to call Gemma and see how she was doing. I was curious to find out how her mental state was after the previous night as well. I hadn't had a lot of time to talk to her before I left, but she seemed like she was doing better. I certainly was. Maybe I was hypersensitive since so much shit had happened, but a nagging voice kept calling my name. Shoving the inner dialogue to the corner of my brain, I attempted to maintain my composure.

I filled my cup with more liquid caffeine, then raided Pierce's fridge for some milk. After adding a splash to a mug, I located a spoon and blended my drink.

My mind flashed back to my stay here while Gemma was gone. I'd been a damned mess. Inwardly, I groaned. I'd punched Pierce in the face. He should have knocked my ass out, but he didn't. Instead, he had helped me get my head on straight. At least I'd calmed down since then.

My phone buzzed and I flipped it over, staring at the screen. My body immediately grew rigid, tight with nerves. I hurried to the kitchen table and sat down before I answered the call.

"Hello, Hendrix." My mother's face filled the small rectangle.

"Hello, Allison." I wasn't pulling any punches with her. My job was to get her to open up to me, not to bond. I wasn't clear about her agenda, but I needed to find out. She obviously wanted to talk since she continued to contact me.

She offered me a lazy smile as though she didn't have a concern in the world. Her dark hair reached her shoulders, and her piercing blue gaze bored into mine. I'd always thought I'd gotten my eyes from Dad, but now I wasn't sure.

"Well, apparently you know who I am. You're a smart young man. I didn't figure it would take you long."

I leaned back in my seat, absorbing all of the details behind her. Pierce had instructed me to look for any brand names on soda cans or bills with a company name and logo on them. He was assuming she was sloppy enough to leave items out for me to see. Allison didn't come across as a person who would mess up like that, especially since she was aware that I knew who she was.

"I had some help." My hands fidgeted beneath the table.

Allison's long fingers toyed with the gold necklace around her neck. It accentuated her white blouse nicely. One thing I could say about her was that she was always impeccably dressed when she used FaceTime to connect with me.

"Why are you reaching out? I mean why now? It's been more than twenty-two years since you left, and you never reached out. I was three when you disappeared from my life, so what's so special about now?"

"Timing is everything. You're grown, successful, and about to get married. Plus, you needed my help. I'll cross lines no one else in your life will."

My forehead creased in confusion. "You helping me find Gemma … we would have found her later that evening on our own."

"Yes, but she died. If you'd shown up any later than you did … well, you would have had to plan a funeral instead of a welcome-home gathering."

My heart hammered against my rib cage. She was right. I hadn't wanted to entertain that idea because I couldn't handle thinking about Gemma's limp and lifeless body on the gurney anymore.

"True."

"Mom?" a male voice called from behind Allison.

I caught a glimpse of a guy as he entered the room. He appeared to be close to eighteen. He casually strolled over to Allison. His dark hair was short and wavy, and he seemed shorter than I was but thick and stocky.

"Come here, Draven. I want you to meet your brother, Hendrix."

I nearly fell off my fucking chair and onto the floor. *Brother?*

Draven bent over and waved at me. A movement caught the corner of my eye from another part of the room, but Allison moved the phone, blocking my view.

"Hey, man." Draven tipped his chin up, then placed his hand on Allison's shoulder.

"Hey." What else was I going to say?

"I'm sure you have a lot of questions, but I'll give you the short and sweet. I met a guy after I left you and Franklin and got pregnant. The life I lead isn't for a family, so Draven lived with my aunt and uncle until he turned eighteen. Two years ago, he moved in with me."

I nodded, shock coursing through my body. *A brother.*

"Love your music, man." Draven straightened up. "I've always known about you and Franklin. Mom's kept tabs on you for a while. When she would visit Aunt Martha and Uncle Chester, she would update me."

The hair rose on the back of my neck. *How long has she been watching me?* "I still don't understand why you've reached out now."

Allison shifted in her chair. "You need me, son."

"I fucking needed you when I was three," I spat. My words were harsh, but I was running out of patience. "I needed you to not dive into criminal activity and be a goddamned mother." My nostrils flared, my anger nearly reaching a boiling point.

"I understand your frustration." Allison's blue-eyed gaze penetrated my soul.

"I'd be pissed, too, bro." Draven ran his hand through his hair, his attention moving away from the screen.

"Regardless of what you've learned about me, I've always loved you, Hendrix. When I chose this life, it would have been wrong to drag you into my world. Franklin didn't deserve it either. His career was taking off, and he would have had to give up everything for me. As crazy as it sounds, I protected you both. I still love you and Franklin. There's not a day that goes by that I don't think about you and your father."

Dammit. Her insane logic was starting to make sense to me.

Allison angled the camera toward the movement I'd seen earlier.

Holy. Fucking. Shit. I stood and picked up my phone off the table, gaping at the bloody and beaten shell of a man bound to a chair in the corner of what appeared to be a log cabin.

"Is that …?" I pointed, but my words refused to cooperate.

"It is. What Brandon did … what he allowed his guard to do to Franklin was inexcusable. Once the videos of what he'd done to Gemma were sent to me …" She paused. "I hope Gemma never remembers what she lived through. You both deserve to have a wonderful wedding. She's beautiful, Hendrix. Inside and out. Gemma has a good heart, and it's obvious she's crazy about you."

I ran a trembling hand through my hair. "How did you learn all of this?" I continued to stare at Brandon Montgomery. His head lolled to the side, and he attempted to speak against the dirty gag in his mouth.

"One of my men has been working for Brandon. I have enough proof to put him away for the rest of his life, but I refuse to take a chance that the piece of shit will walk free again. He has a lot of powerful men on his payroll." She paused, a sinister smile easing across her pretty face. "But I have more."

I gulped. "What are you going to do with him?" My voice was deep and raspy.

"Well, Draven is in training to take over the business when I'm ready to retire. So he'll help me end the problem."

She was going to kill him. *My God. My family is even more fucked-up than Gemma's.*

I gripped the phone tighter. "How will I know when it's over? If he's gone, then Gemma and I can stop hiding. Dad too."

"There won't be any doubt in your mind," Allison assured me.

Draven strolled across the room and jerked Brandon out of the chair. He untied his feet, then tugged Brandon's jeans down. Brandon's eyes widened with panic. In a few quick moves, Draven turned Brandon around and bent him over. The lens remained on Draven he raped Brandon. I slammed my eyes closed, unwilling to witness anymore, but could still hear the muffled screams.

"You're allowing your son to rape Brandon?" This situation was beyond messed up. Allison was seeking revenge for Dad's assault by allowing her son to inflict the same physical and emotional pain. *Insane.* I gagged as bile burned my throat. I wasn't sure if I would be able to hold it down.

"An eye for an eye," Allison said calmly. "I'll apologize now. I don't have time to make Brandon suffer for what he did to Gemma."

Grunts came from the room, then a chair scraped across the hardwood floor. Draven joined his mother again, wearing a mischievous grin. He smoothed his shirt and buttoned his jeans as though what he'd done was just another normal day in his life. Maybe it was. I stared at them, speechless, as my brain struggled to make sense of this sick situation.

"It will take a while to process. I'll always have your back, son." Allison tapped a manicured finger on the table.

"What if I don't want you to? Have my back I mean," I asked, my voice cracking.

"Everyone needs their mother." She kissed her fingertips, then tapped her screen. "One last thing, darling."

I flinched at her term of endearment. "I wanted to congratulate you on your upcoming nuptials, since the original wedding was disrupted."

The glint of a gun caught the light, and Allison handed it to Draven. The camera followed Draven as he approached Brandon again. Tears streamed down Brandon's cheeks as he straightened in his chair, shaking his head. I heard more screams as Draven stopped and pointed the firearm at Brandon.

"Wait!" I yelled. "I need to tell Brandon something." My palms grew sweaty as I waited to see if Draven would back away.

"Go ahead," Allison said.

"Brandon ..." The lens zoomed in on his face. "I wanted to let you know that Gemma is alive. I lied to you. You really did kill her, but the EMTs brought her back to life. She's safe with me again."

Brandon's eyes nearly popped out of his skull, and his face flamed with anger.

"I can confirm Hendrix's story. What he said is true. The EMTs were able to revive her at your house in Montana. It sounds like you've lost all the way around."

The pop of the gun blared through my speaker and Brandon's body snapped backward so hard the chair teetered on two legs.

"Here's your wedding gift." Allison allowed the view to remain on a lifeless Brandon. His eyes were wide-open, and his forehead sported a bullet hole.

"You see, son, Brandon and I were also business competitors, and I needed him out of the way. The Dark Circle Society can't rise again. Ever."

"Jesus," I whispered. I'd just witnessed the murder of Brandon Montgomery from Pierce's house.

"I'll dump the body where the FBI can find him in a few days." Allison's expression softened. "Don't feel bad, Hendrix. This wasn't just a wedding gift. I had to eliminate the competition." She flashed me a kind smile. "I'll be in touch. Please give Franklin my best."

Her screen went blank, and my iPhone clattered to the floor. I sank to my knees. Only then did I spot a pair of black boots behind me. I whipped around, my heart pounding so hard I thought it would burst out of my body.

"Easy, Harrington." Zayne reached out for me, but I scrambled backward, avoiding him.

"What did you see?" My entire body shook as I struggled to understand what I'd seen. *Brandon Montgomery is dead.*

"Some fucked-up shit." Zayne pulled the kitchen chair out and sat at the table, motioning for me to do the same.

I scrubbed my face with my hands, then retrieved my cell off the floor. "I have a brother," I said as I wearily sank into the seat.

"Was that the dude I saw?" Zayne asked, concern flickering across his features.

I nodded while I tapped my finger against the corner of my phone case. Determined not to lose my shit over everything I'd just learned and witnessed. I took several deep breaths.

"Yeah." I rubbed my sweaty palm along my jeaned thigh, my mind replaying everything I'd seen. "Did you see Draven shoot Brandon?"

"Yup. And the way your mother was talking, there's no doubt that Brandon got what he deserved."

"She said it was my wedding present." I focused on the ceiling, then my attention landed on Zayne.

"Pretty good gift if you ask me." He paused. "Your mother is scary as shit, though." He glanced out the window that overlooked the patio.

"You were standing there for a while." I leaned back in my seat. "I guess when a body is recovered, I'll breathe easier."

"You need to breathe easier now. That fucker was as dead as they get. Not only did I see the bullet hole in his forehead, but the camera was trained on your brother and Brandon when the gun went off too. Allison flat-out said she needed to eliminate the competition and squash the Dark Circle Society from making a comeback. Plus, she saved all of us some time and effort." Zayne chuckled. "My time is valuable, so I appreciate it. Plus, if our mission had gone south … let's just say this kept you out of hot water."

"Harrington is in hot water?" Pierce asked, strolling into the kitchen, followed by Vaughn and Cade.

I stared at them blankly, my thoughts still whirling around like a goddamned tornado.

"I don't think I can even articulate what happened. Zayne can, though." I pointed at him.

Zayne stood from his chair. "Harrington needs a minute. His mom just FaceTimed him, then put a bullet right between Brandon Montgomery's eyes."

Pierce stopped in his tracks as Vaughn's brows shot up to his hairline. Cade gaped.

"Actually, my brother shot him," I added, still stunned from what I'd seen.

Pierce leaned up against the counter and folded his massive arms. "I was on my way to tell you that we'd lost track of Brandon. Over the last few hours, while we were talking, he disappeared. I have no idea how it happened, but someone knew what the hell they were doing. One minute he was there. The next, he wasn't. No one saw shit. All we know is that the house was full of gas, and the guards were knocked out. They dropped the canisters down the chimney, which makes me want to plug ours up now."

"It was Allison's men." I drummed my fingers on the table, my head clearing slowly. "She said the FBI will have a body in a few days."

"Son of a bitch is dead. I saw the whole thing." Zayne grinned like a Cheshire cat.

Vaughn clapped his hands together. "Man, this calls for a celebration. Once that bastard's body shows up, I'm telling Claire, and I say we all get together and celebrate. Goddamn, we've tried to get rid of this son of a bitch for a few years now. It's done. Maybe your mom will take out Dillon Montgomery next. Prison is too good for him. Plus, after what happened with Brandon's release, I'm not interested in that sick piece of shit getting out of prison too. But if he does, I'll be waiting. I'm not screwing around anymore. I'm tired of being the good guy in this situation."

"Same." Zayne slapped Vaughn on the back.

I stood slowly, focusing on Pierce. "Tell the FBI I'll tell them what I saw, but that's it. I won't continue to gather any information if Allison reaches out again. She's helped me twice. If it weren't for her, Gemma would be dead. Now she took care of Brandon. They can get pissed if they want to, but it's time for me to take my life back." I held his gaze while I waited for him to respond.

Pierce nodded. "They'll need to talk to you first, and you need to understand, they might have a tail on you if you won't help them. Although I understand exactly what you're saying and why, the FBI is going to view it differently."

It took me a few seconds to realize what Pierce was saying. "They'll think I'm helping her?" I barked out a half-crazed laugh. "Let them. I'm taking my wife, and we're getting the hell out of here anyway. I'm so fucking done."

Zayne, Pierce, Cade, and Vaughn stared at me. *Am I so messed up over what I just saw that I'm making the wrong decision?* My attention swept over the kitchen, then out the window to Pierce and Sutton's patio.

"Yup, I would do the same," Vaughn finally said. "When Dillon Montgomery was after Claire, we were ready to run. Once that shit show was over, we stayed. Our family is here, but after Brandon, we might be down for a change of scenery too."

"Sutton and I have already discussed it," Pierce said. "We'd love to take a long break. I have other men who can update me daily, and I can run the business from anywhere in the world. Franklin and Janice are in too."

"Mac and I will go," Cade said. "I haven't talked to her yet, but she won't want to be away from her family. We can visit mine at any time. I'm sick of constantly looking over my shoulder."

"So everyone is going to relocate and take over a new city together?" Zayne asked, his words laced with surprise.

"We've talked about it," Pierce replied.

"Well, you assholes are the only family I've got, so let me know when and where. I'll start packing what little shit I own," Zayne said.

My overworked nerves calmed a bit. We were all in this together. There wouldn't be any goodbyes. If everyone else was on board, Mac and Cade would join us. Now all I had to do was talk to Gemma. My fairy godmother must have wormed her way inside my thoughts and granted my wish to serve Brandon's head on a platter to Gemma as a wedding gift.

My gut churned, and fear snaked down my spine. Unfortunately, that fairy godmother was my biological parent, and she'd made it clear she planned to keep tabs on me. No matter what I told myself, I wasn't going to be able to move on from what I'd witnessed and who Allison and Draven really were: sick, fucked-up people.

I had a sneaking suspicion that she and Draven were now a part of my life. I wondered how Gemma would feel about it and if she would want to marry into a crime family. *Shit. What if she can't deal with the news and she leaves me?*

My hands trembled, and I clenched them into tight balls, forcing myself to swallow my anxiety. There was only one way to find out if Gem would stick around, and that was to talk to her. No secrets, just the truth.

2 8

The sound of the front door closing behind me sent my pulse into overdrive. I'd talked myself out of telling Gemma about my mother and brother a million times on the ride back to Dad's. Again, I bounced my thoughts off of Zayne. He told me the video of Gemma that Brandon had sent was real. My gut twisted into a million knots with the information.

Zayne said if he were in my shoes, he would sit her down and have full disclosure about Brandon, Allison, Draven, and the video. Zayne reminded me that keeping that kind of secret from her would eventually break me, and if she found out about it from someone else, she would never trust me again. I also had no idea how much she remembered, or whether she thought the memories were just dreams. Maybe some clarity would help her move forward. I'd already planned on telling her if the video turned out to be real, and Zayne's reminder just confirmed my decision.

My breath caught in my throat as I climbed the stairs to locate Gemma. Each step seemed like an eternity, my legs growing heavier and heavier. *How am I going to tell her all of this?* I'd thought her father was crazy, but my mother and brother had officially taken first place for craziness. I wondered again if it was fair to ask

Gemma to stay with me, under the circumstances, and marry into a crime family.

Gemma's and Mac's giggles floated down the hall. I peeked into the game room, where they were watching a comedy with Sandra Bullock. I forgot the name of the film the moment my attention landed on Gemma. She was so beautiful, and I was so proud of her. She'd been knocked down over and over again but continued to pull herself back up. The best thing I could give her ... I pressed my hand to my chest and massaged away the pain that had settled in. Regardless of what I wanted, I had to set her free. She deserved so much more than to be connected with Allison and Draven. *What if Gemma does something they don't like? Will they murder her too?*

Tears welled in my eyes, and I gripped the doorframe, my knuckles turning white and my pulse ringing in my ears. Before I told her, I needed one more evening. I needed to kiss and hold her for one more night. I walked toward the couch slowly, unwilling to let her go yet.

Gemma spun around, our gazes connecting and my heart lurching into my throat.

"Hi! I didn't think you'd be home until tomorrow." She flashed a smile at me that reduced me to putty. I wasn't sure I could live my life without her. Gem was the color in my black-and-white world. She gave me life. A reason to live. Someone to love.

"Plans changed. A work thing for the guys came up."

"Wanna watch some movies with us?" Mac asked. She had her legs stretched out in front of her and her feet propped up on pillows, abiding by her bed-rest orders.

"I'm actually going to steal my fiancée for a little while." I wondered if that would be the last time I said the word *fiancée*.

"Oh. Okay." Gemma stood. "Mac, do you want me to wake up Cade for you?"

"No, he needs to sleep. I've got my phone. If I need anything, I'll call Mom." Mac flashed us a toothy grin.

"Sorry to interrupt your girl time." I waved at Mac and took Gemma's hand. Guiding us down the stairs, I led her through the kitchen and outside. The wind blew my hair into my face.

"The guesthouse?" Gemma asked, her expression growing serious. "What's wrong, Hendrix?" She sounded afraid, and it nearly gutted me.

"I just want some time with you alone. The house is big, but it still feels crowded." I hadn't lied to her. It was the absolute truth.

I unlocked the front door and pocketed the key. I led Gemma into the living room, released her hand, and flipped the switch on the gas fireplace. "Stay put."

I kissed her forehead before I located the candles in the bedrooms and bathroom. When I returned, I placed them on the end tables and the mantel. After I lit them, I walked to the kitchen and spotted the bottle of red wine Zayne and I had picked up on the way home. Zayne had snuck it down here for me so Dad wouldn't be around it. I removed two wineglasses and popped the cork. Usually, I would pour an average amount, but that night called for a little extra.

I carried the drinks over to her, then placed them on the coasters. Gem's gaze followed my every move. She gave me a sweet smile as I dimmed the lights. I pulled my phone out of my back pocket and opened my Spotify app. Once I'd connected to the Bluetooth speakers in the house, I played "Moved" by Laces.

I set my iPhone on the sofa and extended my hand to Gemma. "Dance with me."

Her shoulders visibly relaxed as she realized I wasn't going to shatter her world. Not yet, anyway. I needed one last evening before I told her and she left me a broken man. There was no way she would want to stay, and I didn't blame her. I could no longer offer her the life she longed for, or that I longed to give her.

I took her hands and placed them around my neck, bringing her body flush against mine. "I love you so fucking much, Gemma Thompson." I pressed a kiss to her beautiful lips, burning this moment into my mind forever.

We swayed to the music, our eyes locking. Her expression contained so much love I couldn't breathe. She was my world, the beat of my heart, and I wasn't sure I could live without her.

"I love you too." She ran her fingers through my hair as we closed our eyes and lost ourselves in each other.

I ran my hand up her back, then gently cupped her neck. She was so warm and soft. My pulse kicked up as the images of Brandon's dead body broke through my thoughts. I gave them a swift kick in the ass. I'd deal with that shit later. "Running" by Abi Ocia reverberated through the speakers. I'd listened to that song on repeat when Gemma was gone.

I tilted her chin up. "Everything I do is for you. Don't ever doubt how much I love you."

"Hendrix, I've never second-guessed you." She slid her hands down my back, and my erection pressed into her stomach.

"I need you," I whispered. "I need you nice and slow, baby."

She nodded and slipped her hand beneath my shirt and across my skin. I sucked in a breath at her light touch.

My fingers bunched up her hair, and I kissed the curve of her neck. There was nobody but us. The rest of the world disappeared as I lowered Gemma to the living room floor. The flames flickered in the fireplace, casting her in a delicate light.

She continued to make eye contact with me as I flipped open the buttons on her shirt, revealing a royal blue lace bra. I gently moved the material away from her right breast and cupped her swell gently. Every touch, every taste, every moan, and every *I love you* would be tucked away in my heart forever.

Over the next half hour, I made love to her. This time, she connected with me on every level. Our souls found each other with every thrust and caress. She claimed me all over again.

After we finished, she curled up next to me and placed her head on my chest. I smoothed her hair, and within a few minutes, she fell asleep. I reached up on the couch and grabbed the blanket. Although I could have woken her, I didn't want to. I would suffer a sore back to have her in my arms for the rest of the night, because when the morning came, my world would forever be changed.

The most beautiful blue eyes peered up at me the next morning. I'd gotten up and blown the candles out during the night, but Gem had slept through it. We hadn't even touched the wine, but after I talked to her and shattered both of us, I wouldn't be opposed to morning drinking.

"Hi." I smiled at her and pressed a kiss to her mouth.

"Last night was amazing. Thank you. It was so nice to feel as though I was fully present with you. Like, emotionally. I don't know if I'm explaining it well." She sat up and stretched, the blanket falling to her waist.

I gave her breast a gentle squeeze. "I've missed you." I cupped her cheek in the palm of my hand. "Are you hungry?"

"Yeah." She scrunched up that adorable nose of hers. "But I don't want to go back to Franklin's yet."

"Me either." I climbed off the floor and gathered our clothes. Since I'd left the fireplace on, the room was a comfortable temperature. "I figure someone will come looking for us, so we should at least put our clothes on." I gave her a lopsided grin. "I'm fine if you want to run around naked, though."

Gemma laughed while we dressed. I started some fresh coffee, then brought her a cup. She settled on the couch and tucked her leg beneath her, staring at me. "Hendrix?"

"Yeah, babe?" I asked, playing it cool.

"I know that we needed to reconnect last night, but I also feel like there's more to it. Why don't you tell me what's going on?" She reached over and held my hand.

She was right. I'd had my last evening with her. It was time to be honest with her and put all the secrets out in the open. I was just afraid I wouldn't be left standing after it was all said and done.

I blew on my coffee and took a drink, the hot liquid burning my throat as it traveled down my esophagus. "I don't know where to start, Gemma." I hung my head, my hair covering my face. In one final attempt to locate my courage, I glanced back up at her. "There's nothing I won't do for you, Gemma. Nothing."

She stroked the back of my hand with her thumb. "Baby, I understand that. Whatever it is, it's going to be all right."

"You might not say that when I'm finished." Fear and anxiety drowned my words.

Deciding I should start with the worst news, I told Gemma about the video. Horror twisted her beautiful features as I explained the contents Brandon had sent me. An unbearable ache spread through me as Gemma's sobs wracked her body. She collapsed to the floor and released a wail that I would never forget. Gem wrapped her arms around herself, releasing cries that wrecked me. "Oh God. Oh God." She rocked back and forth.

I knelt next to her and moved her hair away from her face. "Babe, he's dead. Brandon Montgomery is dead. He can't hurt you anymore."

Her head snapped up, and she looked at me. "Dead?" she croaked.

"Yeah. I saw his body. He can't ever hurt you again."

"Did you ...?" She searched my face.

"I was going to, but someone beat me to it. For now, please understand that it's over. Brandon won't ever hurt you again."

Gem remained on the floor and leaned her back against the couch, still trembling. "Does Mac know he's dead?"

"Not yet. I wanted to talk to you first."

She bit her bottom lip, tears in her eyes. Finally, she said, "But how could you want to stay with me after what happened? You saw it all …" She hiccupped. "At least I finally know what's wrong with me."

I sat on the floor across from her, my heart in my throat. "Nothing is wrong with you. It's the lingering effects of the drug. I'm pretty sure you're coming out of it. I think Dr. Bernstein can help you too."

My hand shook, but I didn't try to hide it this time. I swallowed the fear and grief, then sucked it up and explained about my mother and brother.

Gemma stared at me, speechless. It was a lot to take in. I wasn't sure how the hell she'd be able to process it all.

"Your mother?" Gemma grimaced as though the pain was too much for her to handle. "We'll never be free from her. She killed Brandon, and now …" Gem choked on her words, her hand flying over her mouth. Tears streamed down her cheeks again.

Everything inside me screamed to gather her in my arms, but I couldn't. "I'm so sorry, Gemma. All I've ever wanted to do was love you and keep you safe and protect you, but I can't even offer that to you now." My words sounded defeated even to my ears.

A heavy silence hung in the room. Then she sprang off the floor, and her eyes narrowed. "I can't …"

30

My heart splintered into a million pieces with her words. Although I'd tried to prepare myself for her breaking off our engagement, hearing her say she couldn't do this anymore fucking killed me.

"I can't live my life in fear anymore. I'm so glad I can't remember what Brandon did to me, but I'm even more grateful that the son of a bitch is rotting in hell." Gemma tucked her hair behind her ears and pursed her lips. The same lips I would never be able to kiss again. She knelt next to me. "Hendrix Harrington, what are we going to do about our future?"

I blanched. *Did I hear her correctly?* "What? You're not leaving me?"

A gentle smile slipped into place, and she rolled her eyes, laughing. "I love you with every fiber of my being, and nothing you could ever say will make me change my mind. Brandon couldn't ruin us, that video couldn't ruin us, and your mother and brother can't ruin us. You're mine, god dammit, and I'll go kicking and screaming like a lunatic before I ever let you go."

Tears clouded my vision while I grabbed her cheeks and pressed my mouth against hers as though my life depended on it. It did. I'd thought she was going to tell me she couldn't marry into a crime family. Thank God I was wrong. My fierce and protective fiancée was still that. *My* fiancée.

Unable to control my emotions, I pulled her into my lap, then kissed her over and over again as our tears mingled. "I thought you would leave me," I whispered against her ear.

Gemma sniffled. "That was stupid."

We laughed, and I clung to her, swearing with everything inside of me that I would cherish each moment I had with this amazing woman. "Sounds like it's an opportunity for a new beginning."

Gem smoothed the hair from my face. "As long as it's with you, I'm all in, Mr. Harrington."

"I love you so damned much, Gem."

A loud knock interrupted us.

"I realize that we have some more things to talk through, but please understand that I have no intention of going anywhere." She stood and held her hand out to me.

"Gemma!" Zayne called.

"Come on in!" she called.

Zayne flung open the door, his attention landing on us. "Is everything good?"

I wiped the tears from my eyelashes. "Yeah, it's all good." I flashed him a silly grin. Zayne understood precisely what I was saying.

"Mac sent me down, Gemma. Your wedding dress arrived."

Gem's face lit up like a kid on Christmas morning. "Oh my God." She put her hands on my shoulders and kissed me. "Oh my God." She ran toward Zayne, spun around, then back to me. "I'll see you in a little while." She kissed me again and waved goodbye before she disappeared.

"I'll make sure she gets to the house safely." Zayne followed her, leaving me alone with my thoughts.

I collapsed on the couch and allowed the tension to ease away. The worst part was over, but I still needed to tell the rest of the family. I wanted to wait until Brandon's body was found, though. Maybe Pierce had some additional information by now, but I suspected Allison wanted to get a few days ahead of the FBI before they located

Brandon. If she were as careful as she'd been in the past, there wouldn't be anything to tie her or Draven to Brandon's death.

My phone vibrated on the table, and I snatched it up, hoping it was Allison with the location of where she'd deposited Brandon. A live feed notice flashed on my screen, and I opened it. The sound of men yelling and dogs barking shook my speakers, and I turned the volume down. The FBI was running through a heavily wooded area. I held my breath as I continued to watch. Five minutes later, Brandon Montgomery's body was recovered. The camera zoomed in on him. His body had stiffened up, and his eyes were still blank and lifeless. The footage ended, and a *turn on your tv* message appeared.

I scrambled to my feet and sprinted out of the guesthouse and up the hill. Dad, Mac, Cade, Janice, and Gem needed to see this. Bursting through the door, I scared the shit out of poor Ruby.

"Sorry, Ruby!" I rounded the corner to the entryway, panting from my sprint. "Dad! Dad!" I ran to the living room and turned on the 4K flatscreen over the fireplace.

"Son?" Dad hurried down the hall, nearly frantic, with Janice on his heels.

"This is good, Dad." I rushed over to him and gave him a huge hug. "Sit and watch. I'm going to find Cade and the girls. I'll carry Mac down if I have to." I shoved the remote into his hand.

Janice grabbed his arm, and they sat down, glued to the television.

I darted up the stairs two at a time. "Gemma! Baby, I'm coming in." I stopped at Mac's bedroom. "You guys need to come downstairs right now. Where's Cade?"

"Dude, I'm right here. What the hell?" Cade stepped into the hallway from the game room.

I grinned at him. "Go to the living room. I'll get the girls. Hurry up."

Gemma flung open Mac's door. "What's wrong?" she said, her voice climbing in pitch.

I kissed her so hard I was afraid I might have hurt her. "They found the body."

Gemma's eyes widened. "It's official?"

"Yeah. Come on." I burst into Mac's bedroom and hurried over to her. I backed up to the mattress and sat on the bed. "Hop on."

"Hendrix, I weigh a little more these days. I can walk."

"Nope. You're on bedrest. Hop on. Come on, slowpoke."

She smacked me upside the head and Gemma giggled. I winked at her, then I carefully took Mac downstairs and placed her on the couch, where she immediately propped her legs on Cade's lap.

Gemma joined me in the entryway. Zayne stood behind us, a big-ass smile on his face.

"The body of Brandon Montgomery has just been discovered," the spokesperson started.

Mac let out a cry. "What?"

I nodded. "Yeah. It's over, Mac. You and the baby can go to sleep knowing you're safe."

Although Gemma and I hadn't discussed it, we were in sync enough to know it wasn't the right time to tell Mac about my mom. I wanted to talk to Dad about it first anyway.

Cries and whoops filled the room as the headline continued to scroll across the bottom of the television. Dad broke down as Janice held him. It had been a fucked-up few weeks. With this news, we could pick up the pieces and start our lives again.

Mac climbed off the couch and threw her arms around Gemma. They held each other while more tears flowed. All the pain and harm that Brandon had inflicted on us was over. We could finally start to heal. And it was all because of Allison and Draven. I mentally thanked them for setting us free. *At least for now.*

3 1

The next few days flew by as we finalized the wedding preparations. I'd talked to Dad and Pierce about Allison and Draven, but we'd decided not to tell anyone else for the moment. I wasn't sure Mac could deal with the stress anyway. Our primary focus was to figure out where we would all relocate and to help Mac with her pregnancy.

Gemma and I had moved back to our house. Pierce gave Zayne a week off, and Jaxon was assigned as our new security. Now that Brandon was dead, Jaxon didn't have to be in our space all the time.

With Gemma's blessing, I'd scheduled another appointment with Dr. Bernstein for couples' therapy, as well as one for myself. Since we were flying to the UK for our honeymoon, we decided we would start the sessions when we returned.

Pierce and Sutton were busy scouting out a new city for all of us, but we hadn't made any decisions yet. With emotions running high, it wasn't the right time. We were out of immediate danger, and I desperately wanted to take some time to relax.

And before I knew it, I was about to marry the love of my life in a small, intimate ceremony. I grinned at Cade, tugging the cuffs of my shirtsleeves. I reached for my black tux jacket and slipped it on.

"You ready to do this?" Cade asked, straightening my bowtie.

"Hell yeah." I blew out a sigh and smiled.

"I'm pretty sure everyone in this house is ready for you and Gemma to finally tie the knot as well," Asa added.

Once Brandon was dead, I'd reached out to Asa and invited him to the wedding. I hadn't known him as long as Cade, but he was a part of the band and a good friend. Although we'd kept in touch through texts, Asa understood how important it was for him to keep his distance. I couldn't risk putting him in anymore danger.

"When are you going to settle down?" I asked Asa, flipping him shit.

Asa adjusted his tie and cleared his throat. "I … uh. I wanted to talk to Gemma actually."

Cade and I quirked an eyebrow at our friend. "About?" I asked.

"Lydia." Asa couldn't contain his grin. "I wanted to ask Gemma if Lydia had ever mentioned me."

I folded my arms, analyzing him. "You're sleeping with her, aren't you?"

Asa scratched his chin. "I care about her … a lot. I'm just not sure if this is a casual thing for her or not."

I punched him in the shoulder, threw my head back, and laughed. "Asa, I never thought I'd say this to you. Ever since we met, you've partied and played hard, which I have no problem with, but dude, are you in love with her?"

Sutton, Claire, Gemma, and Mac's giggles floated down the hallway from upstairs, interrupting our conversation. The ladies had arrived early and spent the day helping Gemma prepare. Pierce, Zayne, Dad, Vaughn, Asa, and Cade had kept me busy with honeymoon plans.

"I'm sure Gemma will be happy to talk to you, Asa." I chuckled. "All I'll say is that there is no better feeling than when you find the one."

"Truth," Cade added.

"She's ready!" Sutton called while the girls filed down the stairs. Even though we'd chosen not to have bridesmaids, they all wore matching blue dresses. I was so grateful Gem had her group of friends.

I patted my tux pocket, relieved that the box holding our rings was safely tucked away.

Mac strolled toward me, sporting a baby bump. I hadn't noticed it since she'd been wearing oversized shirts, but with the dress, it was obvious that she was pregnant. She looked adorable with her round belly.

Mac placed her hands on my shoulders and beamed at me. "Love ya, bro." She kissed my cheek, and I pulled her into a gentle hug.

"Love you, too, sis."

She released me, then took Cade's hand.

"See ya there." Cade slapped my back and hurried to the formal living room that had been decorated with hydrangeas. Claire had located an archway for us, and red and white roses were delicately woven through the top and sides. Two angel fountains rested on either side of the platform. Gem and I wanted to honor John and thought the angels were appropriate. The shooting at the outdoor coliseum still weighed on me. John should have been with us on our wedding day. But the best part of the day was that Pierce had obtained his license, and he was officiating the wedding.

"Always" by Francois Klark began to play, and I turned my attention to the staircase.

Gemma stood at the top and stared down at me. My hand flew to my chest. Her new gown was formfitting with sapphires beaded through the bodice and a flared skirt. Her veil covered her face, but I could still see the smile that had stolen my heart the first time we sang together.

She descended the stairs slowly, then stood in front of me. "Hi," she said softly.

"Hi." I winked and extended my arm out to her. "Are you ready to spend the rest of your life with me?"

She peered up at me, her eyes flashing with excitement. "I was ready the first day you bugged me at the library."

I chuckled. She'd told me straight up to leave her alone that day, but I hadn't. The pull to her had been so strong that I couldn't ignore it.

Our family and friends were waiting for us as Gem and I walked down the aisle. Pierce beamed at us from the front of the room while Vaughn, Zayne, and Jaxon stood in the corners, all smiles. Vaughn had offered to take pictures of the ceremony for us. Claire had jumped on board as well, in case his didn't turn out.

We approached Pierce, then everyone sat down. "Let's do this," he said quietly.

I turned toward Gemma, and tears welled in my eyes. I hadn't anticipated that I would be this overwhelmed with emotions. Love. Excitement. Gratitude. I took her hands in mine and held her warm gaze.

"Gemma, you're always in my mind and heart. Even when you're gone, I feel you by my side. If I'm the tide, then you're my moon, always pulling me back to you. Our souls are tethered together for eternity."

Gemma looked at me, her lower lip trembling. "Hendrix, in my dreams you're the one that always waits for me. You're the sun that lights my path. You're the reason I sing and the air I breathe. Words will never be able to describe how much I love you. Your love has saved me time and time again."

I resisted the urge to flip up her veil and kiss her. Gem glanced at Pierce, and he grinned. "Do you have the rings?" he asked me.

I reached in my pocket, removed the box, then flipped it open. Gemma's engagement and wedding band rested in the box. The light glinted off the stones. She covered her mouth. This was the first time she'd seen them. "They're so beautiful."

I carefully pulled the rings out of the placeholders and slipped them on her finger. "I take you, Gemma Thompson, as my wife. With these rings, I also give you my heart and the rest of my earthly days. Even after I'm gone, I will belong to you for all eternity."

Gemma's chin trembled and she bit her lip. She sucked in a deep breath, then looked at Sutton, who handed her the little white pillow with my band on top of it.

Gemma removed the ring, took my hand in hers, then slid it on my finger. "I take you, Hendrix Harrington, as my husband. With this ring, I give you my heart and the rest of my earthly days. Even after I'm gone, I will belong to you for all eternity."

I took her hands in mine and waited for Pierce to make it official.

"By the power vested in me by the state of Washington, I pronounce you husband and wife." Pierce's voice boomed through the lower part of the house.

I gently pulled her veil back and tilted her chin up, pressing a long, sweet kiss to her lips—our first as husband and wife. I released her, and a silly grin spread across my face. "Hello, Gemma Harrington."

"Hi, Mr. Harrington," she said softly, grinning at me. She pressed her mouth to mine, a giggle erupting from her.

Whistles sliced through the air as I slid my arm around her waist and dipped her backward, deepening the kiss. I stood her up and peered into her eyes. "I love you."

"Oh, baby, I love you too."

Pierce's voice reverberated through the room again. "I would like to officially present to you Mr. and Mrs. Harrington!"

With the noise level from the claps and cheers, it sounded as though we had a hundred people in the house. Everyone tossed rose petals as Gemma and I walked hand in hand through the room and into the hallway.

I spun her around and pressed my mouth to hers again. "Are you packed?"

"The girls packed my bag, so I'm not sure what's in the suitcase. I have a feeling it's all lingerie." Gem giggled against her hand.

"Fifteen minutes," Zayne said, clapping from behind us. He grinned broadly and tapped his watch.

Gemma hurried up the stairs with me as fast as she could in her heels and dress, then we shed the gown and tux and changed into jeans and sweatshirts. It was a long-ass flight to the UK.

IF ZAYNE HADN'T BEEN with us on Dad's airplane, I would have made love to Gemma in the bedroom, but I didn't want her to feel awkward. Instead, she snuggled up to me and slept.

"She's looks happy," Zayne said, nodding at her.

"She does. It's good to see her like that again." I placed a gentle kiss on the top of her head.

"Congrats, man. I'm thrilled for both of you." Sadness flickered through Zayne's expression.

I adjusted my arm around Gemma, careful not to wake my sleeping bride. "The night in the van, when we were on the way to find Gemma, you said there was someone you were interested in. Or was I hallucinating under all the stress?" I shifted in my seat, attempting to get more comfortable.

Zayne cracked a grin. "It's complicated."

"Well, if she makes you smile like that, she's gotta be worth it. Where did you meet her?"

Zayne leaned forward and propped his elbows on his knees. He smoothed his eyebrow with his thumb, then looked at me. "I haven't officially met her, but a few months ago … she dropped dead at a party, and I gave her mouth-to-mouth and revived her."

"Are you fucking with me?" My voice came out louder than I'd intended.

"Nope. I've done my research on her, background check, even hired someone to find out who she was."

"And?" This was way better than I could have ever imagined.

"She's married." He sounded defeated.

"Dude, that sucks." I paused. "So, are you going to have some fun with Vicki while we're in the UK and blow off some steam?"

"That's the plan, as long as she understands exactly what's happening."

I respected his honesty. More than that, I appreciated his friendship. "Have a good time, man. You deserve it."

He stretched his legs in front of him and chuckled. "Even if Vicki isn't down with a few fun weeks, I'm sure I'll find some kind of trouble to get into." He leaned back and stared out the window.

I grinned. There was no doubt in my mind Zayne would definitely find something to occupy his time. I reclined the leather seat and pulled Gemma closer to me. She mumbled in her sleep, but she was smiling, so I knew it wasn't a bad dream. Finally, I closed my eyes, allowing myself to relax with my wife in my arms.

The next four months flew by as Gemma and I enjoyed every minute of our married life. After we'd sold the house in Maine, we designed our log home and chose fifteen acres to build on in Ontario, Canada. We'd visited several times and had fallen in love with the scenery. The home would sit on a hill, overlooking a lake. It would be the perfect place to write more music and decide our next steps.

The drug Brandon had used on Gemma slowly faded over time. On occasion, I would see the switch flip in her eyes, and she would crave something more than our normal sex life. I'd sat her down and discussed where I had to draw the line, and she agreed. *No choking* was first on my list. After that, we were more comfortable exploring new scenarios in the bedroom.

Dad, Janice, Cade, and Mac had also purchased homes. If we ended up moving back to the States, we would still have vacation houses in Canada. I wasn't sure I would miss Washington, though.

Mac's pregnancy had leveled out, and she was ready to pop any day. The preeclampsia had been an emotional roller coaster for her, but after Brandon died, her stress was greatly reduced, which helped her condition. Now we were waiting to meet the new member of the family. Even though we'd learned the gender of the baby months before, it would be great to hold the little one in my arms finally.

Sutton, Pierce, Claire, Vaughn, and Zayne were all relocating with us. It was funny how I'd grown up feeling lost and alone. Even after Janice and Mac opened their home to me, I had still felt like an outsider. Until Gemma. The first day I laid eyes on her was when she had fallen apart behind the college library. In those few quick seconds, I knew beyond a shadow of a doubt she was mine.

I glanced around our bedroom at Dad's place. All of the boxes were packed and ready for the movers. Dad and Janice had purchased another ten-thousand-square-foot home, and we would all be under one roof again while Gemma's and my house was being finished. I wasn't on board until Dad explained there was a guesthouse that Gemma and I could live in. Our alone time was important to us, and I refused to budge on it.

Allison hadn't contacted me in months, and I hoped it would stay that way. Maybe she was content with whatever updates she was receiving about our lives.

"Fucking hell!" Mac screamed.

Gemma stopped packing our bedroom, and we looked at each other.

"Oh! Oh!" Gemma's hands waved around as she searched the room for her purse.

"Good God! Get this baby out of me!" Mac yelled.

Gem ran past me and into the hall.

"Can you grab the bag?" Cade asked.

I hurried behind Gemma. If my sister packed like she normally did, there was no way in hell Gem would be able to pick up the duffel bag, much less take it downstairs. Mac's moans and pants continued as Cade helped her to the living room. She was too big for him to carry.

"Mom!" Mac yelled.

I checked my pocket for my wallet and phone, then heaved the duffel bag over my shoulder.

"You ready to become an uncle?" Gemma asked, her words laced with excitement.

"Yeah. Are you ready to become an aunt?" I was ready to have a baby with Gemma, too, but we needed more time to heal without danger lurking over us every minute.

Dad was impatiently standing by the door. When he spotted me with the huge-ass duffel bag, he hurried to relieve me of it and tossed it into the car. Mac and Cade would ride with Dad and Janice, and Zayne would drive us. Cade and Janice would be in the delivery room with Mac, and the rest of us would hang out in the waiting area.

I MASSAGED my forehead and stared at the big clock on the wall of the hospital. The last several hours had crept by as we waited to hear that Mac and the baby were okay. Dad paced the floor and made small talk, but his shoulders were tense. Stress rolled off him in waves, and I silently pleaded with anyone who would listen that we would have some good news soon. No matter how positive I attempted to be, I realized we were all thinking the same thing: *With Mac's preeclampsia, are she and the baby going to be all right?* The doctors had planned on a C-section, but then Mac started having contractions on her own.

Finally, Janice appeared. She was exhausted. Her hair stuck out of her ponytail, and her mascara was smeared. Gemma pulled on my hand, her wedding rings catching my eye. I loved seeing them on her finger. I loved that she was mine.

Dad rushed over to Janice, his face full of anticipation. "Mom and baby are fine," she said. "Come on back and meet Mac and Cade's baby girl."

Gemma jumped up and down and nearly squealed with excitement. "I'm so glad she's finally here!"

I hopped up and hugged her. I'd never seen her this excited about a baby before, and my chest filled with hope that one day we'd be celebrating the birth of our son or daughter.

Dad picked up Janice and spun her around. "I'm a grandpa!"

Janice laughed as he set her down. "You're a grandpa." She kissed him gently and patted his cheek.

From outward appearances, you would never know that Dad had lived through a kidnapping and sexual assault. He'd continued with counseling twice a week and had started wrapping up work with some of his long-term clients. With each day that passed, he seemed happier and more alive.

Janice waved us through the doors, and Gemma grabbed my hand, nearly pulling me down the hall. I couldn't contain my chuckle. Although becoming an uncle for the first time was exciting, Gemma's reaction was more than I'd ever hoped for.

We came to a halt at Mac's room, then quietly filed in. Mac was tired but happy as she cradled a little bundle wrapped in a pink blanket. Dark hair peeked out of the tiny hat, and the tiniest hand I'd ever seen waved in the air.

Gemma's hands flew to her mouth. "Oh, Mac, she's beautiful." She ran over to Cade and embraced him. "Congrats, Daddy. You're going to be amazing."

Cade wrapped his arms around her and flashed me a huge smile.

"Congrats, man." I hugged him next and slapped him on the back.

Cade stepped back, allowing Gem and me a closer peek. Dad and Janice were on the other side of the bed, staring into the sweetest little face I'd ever seen.

"Meet Hollister Richardson."

Tears filled Gemma's eyes. "I love her name." She looked at me briefly, then back at Mac. "Can I hold her?"

Mac smiled at Gemma. "I wanted you to hold her first—other than Cade and me, I mean."

"Why?" Gemma asked, surprised.

"Because I wanted to give you what you lost—a chance to fall in love with a brand-new baby." Mac leaned up and grimaced.

"Wait." Gem bent close to her, and Mac handed Hollister to my wife. A squeak escaped Gemma's lips, then she placed a gentle kiss on Hollister's forehead. "Hi, sweet girl. I'm Aunt Gemma."

Words couldn't explain what I was witnessing. Hollister held her little hand up and placed it on Gem's cheek. Emotions clogged my throat. This would be yet another memory I'd file away forever.

Hollister opened one eye and stared at my wife. *If I didn't know better, I'd say that little girl just healed my wife's soul.* All the pain of Gem's past slipped away from her features as she quietly bonded with her best friend's baby.

"You have to give her back," Mac joked.

Gemma laughed as she handed her over with mixture of regret and happiness on her face. She waited a minute, her expression changing rapidly as Franklin moved forward to hold Hollister. Then Gem stepped away and quietly left the room.

"Babe?" I asked, following right behind her.

Gem spun on her heel and threw her arms around my neck. Her shoulders shook with her tears. "She's so beautiful."

She sniffled, and I rubbed her back, allowing her to cry against my chest. "She is. The two of you together stole my heart."

She peeked up at me, droplets clinging to her eyelashes. "I don't know when, but I want to have your baby, Hendrix. Maybe even two."

My pulse skipped a beat.

"We can talk about it later. This has been a really emotional day for both of us." I smoothed a few loose strands of hair away from her face.

She shook her head. "I've been thinking about it since Mac announced that she was pregnant. I need some more time, but I want a family with you."

There were three times in my life that I would remember intimately. They were more than memories. They were so well-defined that I could remember the dates, the weather, the smells, and even what I was wearing the days they happened. The first was when I laid eyes on Gemma Thompson behind the college library. The second was the day she said, "I do," and became my wife. And the third was that day, seeing her with Hollister in her arms. I wasn't sure what the next day would bring, but as long as she was by my side, I could make it through anything.

"Are you sure?" I asked, hope rising inside me.

"Yes. I'm absolutely sure."

I kissed her gently, then more aggressively. I was oblivious to the people in the hospital hallway or the babies' cries that hung in the air. The only thing that I was aware of was this strong and beautiful woman in front of me. My wife. Gemma Harrington.

Breaking our kiss, I looked into her gorgeous blue eyes. "I can't wait to start the rest of our lives together. You're my forever."

"And you're my always."

DON'T MISS the Wicked Intentions Series. If you love romance, angst, and murder, then you'll love these standalones with an HEA. Click here.

Enjoy exclusive Love & Ruin bonus scenes, giveaways, and new release updates! Sign up today at https://www. authorjaowenby.com/newsletter

LET'S GET IN TOUCH! Connect with me here:
Author J.A. Owenby Website
Join my Newsletter
Follow me on Facebook
Join my Facebook Group
Follow me on Amazon
Join me on Goodreads
Follow me on BookBub
Follow me on Twitter
Follow me on Instagram
Join me on Pinterest

Where I'll Find You

J.A. OWENBY'S READER'S GROUP

I appreciate your help in spreading the word online as well as telling a friend. Reviews help readers find books they love, so please leave a review on your favorite book site.

You can also join my Facebook group, J.A. Owenby's One Page At A Time, for exclusive giveaways and sneak peeks of future books.

Dear Readers,

If you have experienced sexual assault or physical abuse, there is free confidential help. Please visit:

Website: https://www.rainn.org/
Phone: 800-656-4673

ABOUT THE AUTHOR

International bestselling author J.A. Owenby grew up in a small backwoods town in Arkansas where she learned how to swear like a sailor and spot water moccasins skimming across the lake.

She finally ditched the south and headed to Oregon. The first winter there, she was literally blown away a few times by ninety mile an hour winds and storms that rolled in off the ocean.

Eventually, she longed for quiet and headed up to snowier pastures. She now resides in Washington state with her hot nerdy husband and cat, Chloe (who frequently encourages her to drink). She spends her days coming up with ways to torture characters in a way that either makes you want to throw your book down a flight of stairs or sob hysterically into a pillow.

J.A. Owenby writes new adult and romantic thriller novels. Her books ooze with emotion, angst, and twists that will leave you breathless. Having battled her own demons, she's not afraid to tackle the secrets women are forced to hide. After all, the road to love is paved in the dark.

Her friends describe her as delightfully twisted. She loves fan mail and wine. Please send her all the wine.

You can follow the progress of her upcoming novel on Facebook at Author J.A. Owenby and on Twitter @jaowenby.

Sign up for J.A. Owenby's Newsletter:
  BookHip.com/CTZMWZ

Like J.A. Owenby's Facebook:
  https://www.facebook.com/JAOwenby

J.A. Owenby's One Page At A Time reader group:
  https://www.facebook.com/groups/JAOwenby